The
Girl
Who
Survived

BOOKS BY ELLIE MIDWOOD

The Violinist of Auschwitz
The Girl Who Escaped from Auschwitz
The Girl in the Striped Dress

ELLIE MIDWOOD

The Girl Who Survived

bookouture

Published by Bookouture in 2021

An imprint of Storyfire Ltd.
Carmelite House
50 Victoria Embankment
London EC4Y 0DZ

www.bookouture.com

ISBN: 978-1-80019-879-1
eBook ISBN: 978-1-80019-878-4

To my two muses, Pupper and Joannie

Prologue

"We live together, or we die together."

How simple he made it sound. It was all the same to him now; he had confessed to me not two days ago when he had typed his own name into the stolen blank of an official permit – our ticket to a free life, or a communal death sentence; one could never tell these days which one it would be.

I nodded out of habit – in a place like this, you learn to accept, without any reservation, anything that a man in a uniform tells you, if you know what's good for you – and smiled, in spite of myself, as he held my face in his warm palms.

"I will get us out of here," he repeated once again, with a sidelong glance toward the window. He didn't see the city which lay right in front of his eyes any longer; he peered much further, into the vague dream of a forest and the partisan brigades. "I will get us both to freedom. You believe me, don't you?"

I nodded again, feeling miserable and powerless yet smiling brightly, just like my mother was as she was being led to the gas van. While being marched to her certain death, she was smiling at me, courageous and reassuring, just so I would stay strong, just so I wouldn't succumb to the mass hysteria.

"Why the tears?" He tilted his head to one side, as though pitying me with those kind eyes of his.

How desperately he had tried to dig out of me that habit of instinctive submission to any word spoken by a *Herr Offizier* whoever that *Herr Offizier* might be. But, someone before him had driven the point across far too many times, accentuating it with rubber baton blows, riding crop whips, and a few backhanded slaps for good measure. *So, forgive me, Herr Hauptmann, but habits instilled by blunt, savage force will never be so easily eradicated by your soft voice and promises in which I don't fully believe.*

You'll change your mind. Surely, you will. There's nothing in it for you except for court-martial and death if your own people seize, or capture you and death if the Soviet partisans do. And all for what? A couple of dozen or so Jews who still cling to life despite all, and a girl, whose face you're holding in your hands now? You will change your mind at the last moment, Herr Hauptmann. You'll see how fast you will. You'll remember your recent promotion, your wife waiting for you at home, your comrades, and your country and you'll invent some suitable excuse for us to swallow before you send us to our deaths. But I'll still nod and pretend that I believe you just not to disappoint you with my truth.

"Happy tears," I lied for his sake, determined to keep my reservations to myself. But then something caught in my chest. Another barricade, which I'd so thoroughly erected, crumbled and fell, and together with it, the tears began falling, glistening between his warm fingers that always wiped them away with infinite tenderness. *Stupid, stupid girl, reaching for him and clawing at his stiff uniform, scratching at the eagle on his chest into which I wished to turn, on so many occasions, to fly away from all this misery and death and the land of the hope lost. Gullible fool, pressing your head into his shoulder and weeping in his embrace as he's promising something to you, which was denied to your kin by his masters, to which he still bows – your miserable, silly life.* And yet, my fingers coiled around his belt, my eyes found his again and I whispered his own words back to him before he'd take them back, "We live together, or we die together. You promised. Do not forget that."

Chapter 1

Somewhere in the west, the war was in progress, yet Frankfurt appeared to be entirely oblivious to it. Apart from a few subtle changes – our factory moving its production from civilian textile to the Luftwaffe parachutes, women donning the uniforms of the tram conductors and post personnel, official Wehrmacht vehicles honking impatiently at the civilians, and more crimson banners cascading down the buildings than usual, the city remained stubbornly un-military.

May was exceptionally warm that year. The sweet smell of the trees in bloom made one drunk with spring as soon as one stepped out of the buzzing beehive of the factory. The days grew longer; the sun now lingered in the reddening vastness of the sky for a while after the end of the shift and welcomed us back onto the street with a gentle kiss on our pale cheeks, before rolling reluctantly westward. As was my habit, I paused near the gate to soak in the last rays of the setting sun. Next to me, a group of women lit up their cigarettes in peace, away from the stern shift superintendent. Some of them had already removed their factory-issued uniforms and the navy-clad mass that had poured onto the street just minutes ago, transformed into women again, in their fancy, though somewhat wrinkled, Friday dresses.

Lily, my sister, who was only two years older than me and yet had the most profound conviction that she had all the right to act as, if not my mother then my legal guardian, to be sure, was already tugging my sleeve urging me away from the crowd. I remained rooted to the spot, stubborn and deaf to all her pleas and threats, my nostrils twitching when slight remnants of the tobacco hit them. The women were chatting about the new motion picture. I wanted to stay and listen at least; fat chance I'd be able to see it with my own eyes.

It promised to be good, judging by the dramatic posters that lined the newsstands, right next to the war bulletins and local news. *The Eternal Spring* – an undying historical romance set in the era of Ireland's fight for independence attracted more ogling bystanders than the *Frankfurter Zeitung*'s headline, *France's Fall is Imminent,* to its right. Apparently, France's fight for independence didn't inspire much interest or sympathy in the crowd as of yet; maybe later, some *years* later, when they make a motion picture about it and make the French speak German much as they did with their fictional Irish, then it would.

"Ilse, we have to hurry. The curfew." Lily pinched her lips into a stern line and took a resolute step forward, most definitely expecting me to follow her.

With a faraway look in my eyes, I barely heard her. I was more interested in the fictional Gloria's story, which was being re-told by one of my fellow seamstresses.

"And then what?"

It wasn't just me who held her breath as the plot developed.

"She leaves her British husband – that big shot in the magistrate – for that Irish freedom fighter," the lucky girl, who saw it together with her date, replied, her eyes flashing with excitement.

"Does she really?"

"Yes. It was so romantic!" the girl confirmed, rolling her eyes with enthusiasm.

"They say, Eugen Klöpfer was amazing!"

"He did a marvelous job! Lina Carstens was an absolute delight too!"

"Ilse, let's go!" Lily's hushed voice, the voice of reality, broke into the faraway world of my girlish dreams. "The curfew, mind you!"

The curfew. Amid that lively, chattering crowd I had almost forgotten that I didn't belong to it. A sudden wave of rebellion and some inexplicable longing for an act of revolt, no matter how small and insignificant, filled me that instant, overpowering and demanding belief that I act upon it.

"You go without me." I decided something for myself that evening. My hand, with my passport in it, dipped into Lily's handbag and, before she could break into her panicked protesting, I looked her square in the eye. "I'm going to see that motion picture."

"Are you quite mad?!"

I ignored her hissing above my ear, only hastened my steps away from her, from that factory, from my own passport that she was trying, in vain, to slip back into my hands.

A criminal case, if caught, but sometimes we all need to feel alive, or we'll go insane from the lack of air; that's why prisoners risk further sentencing and break out of prisons and that's why Jewish girls leave their passports in their sisters' hands – to gulp freedom just once more, before another wave would come and drown them all for good.

We still could get away with such mischief, the German Jews, that is. The *Frankfurter Zeitung,* for one, reported that the Polish Jews had to wear armbands with a blue Star of David on them, the failure to display which was punishable by severe measures, according to the newspaper. We were still indistinguishable, unmarked, forbidden from entering public places and parks, but spared at least this final humiliation. There was a talk about it right after the Kristallnacht, during which Papa's grocery store in our native Nidda was raided and destroyed but for some reason, it remained just that, talk. Frankfurt offered much more anonymity than our native town; no one knew us here and we could still blend in with the locals as long as we smiled at the police and didn't betray ourselves with that frightened look that instantly gave away the bearers of the cursed red "J" in their passports.

Even the spring in Frankfurt was different than in Nidda – dustier and louder. Nidda was more of a big village with the only difference that we had cobbled streets and street lamps but even with all these features, characteristic of a small town, the river encased in stone (which had given the name to our town) resembled a murky, weed-ridden stream much more than an actual river and the town's main attraction was a fountain built in the market square sometime in the seventeenth century. The life in Nidda, as I remember it, used to be lethargically peaceful. It moved slowly and stagnantly, much like the opaque waters of the Nidda river, into which my classmates used to jump in summer for a good splash, risking just as good of a hiding from their parents – but children don't think about such things when fun is in sight.

Our school used to be a long, narrow two-story building – a co-ed; the town was far too small for separate schools for girls and boys. The first time I realized that we – my sisters and I – were different from the rest of the children was when the new headmaster arrived from Frankfurt and, during his very first "roll call," pointed at me with his wooden rod.

"Stein, collect your books and go sit over there, in the back. Rosenblatt." The rod of doom was now aiming at another class-mate of mine, Hanne. "You, too." The new headmaster regarded the teacher, Fräulein Jung, wrathfully with his watery, bloodshot eyes. The collar of his shirt was so stiff with starch, it must have caused him great discomfort but his desire to impress transcended such trifles as personal convenience. "Have you received the new directives from the Ministry of Education?"

Fräulein Jung acknowledged him with a shameful nod.

"Why aren't you implementing those directives then? Jewish students must sit at the back."

I was already at my new desk by the back wall and so, I didn't hear what she replied to him; apparently, something to do with Hanne's short stature and bad eyes. I saw that Hanne was already squinting at the blackboard in her seat next to me. Thankfully, I was a full head taller than the tallest boy in my class and had perfect vision. Tough luck for Hanne though – the new headmaster didn't deem her eye problems and lack of height worthy of his attention.

What started with a crack, soon grew into a rupture which was impossible to ignore. The class was now divided into boys in new brown uniforms, girls in white blouses and navy skirts, and *the rest,* looked down upon by the uniformed crowd with the arrogant disdain of superiors. It was strange, really, what one headmaster could do to a class that used to be so united. Apart from that though, our life didn't change a bit, remaining positively boring and monotone for the next few years. Then, in November, the SA came with torches and trashed our shop along with a few others. While we were hard at work cleaning up the street early the following morning, they were busy gluing posters to our walls: *Deutsche! Wehrt Euch! Kauft nicht bei Juden! – Germans! Defend yourselves! Do not buy from Jews!* It was then that our parents decided it was time to leave Nidda. Not because of the posters, or the SA – or indeed the familiar faces of my schoolmates in their new uniforms – but solely because they didn't have enough money to start it all anew, the shop, that is.

Ever since the Kristallnacht had happened, Papa ceaselessly grumbled that those Germans from Nidda who had taken the Russian Empress Katherine the Great up on her promise of free land and left for farmlands in Russia some two hundred years ago were the smart fellows. Just his misfortune, his forefathers weren't among them. Lily and I couldn't quite tell if he was saying this in grim jest or not but we sometimes caught ourselves wondering the same. At least, no one had returned back to Nidda so far.

Consumed by my musings, I hadn't noticed I had reached the booth of the ticket seller. I slowed my steps down a bit, glimpsed the usual announcement near the entrance of the cinema – *Juden sind nicht erwünscht* – and wondered if I should just walk past it and head home as I should have. That's what Lily would have done. But I was not Lily.

"One, please," I demanded boldly, handing the seller the money and acting as though I belonged there, the Aryan girl.

The bored-looking man assessed me with his glance.

He'll ask me for my identification now and I'll have to tell him that I've forgotten it at home, he'll whistle for a policeman – there he is standing on the corner – and it'll be over for you, Ilse.

I smiled brightly at him. Sometimes I could easily pass for an Aryan. I was very tall, had fair skin, an oval face, blue eyes; only the hair was dark and lay around my shoulders in natural waves. However, half of the population of Germany was dark-haired. Sometimes, they asked for my papers when I would worm my way into a store in which I had no business being. No one arrested or even fined me so far. Some chased me off, grumbling something under their breath; some shook their heads with a knowing grin and pretended they didn't see a red J in my passport, so that I could buy goods meant only for the Aryans. It was the Frankfurt policemen's leniency that spoiled me, emboldened me to the point where I found myself where I was now, in front of the cinema, with its *Jews not wanted* sign.

"Just one?" The bored-looking ticket seller appeared suspicious.

"My date is running late," I lied, without batting an eye.

"Aren't you too young for dates?" He gave me one more critical once-over. "How old are you?"

"Eighteen," I lied once again.

I was sixteen. Schools in Frankfurt didn't welcome Jews, but a textile factory producing the parachutes for the Luftwaffe wasn't as picky. It was better this way, working, that is. At least I could bring some money to the family table instead of moping about our tiny apartment, with its scarce, mismatched furniture, all day long, like our youngest sister, Lore.

"Let me see your passport."

After a moment's hesitation, I fumbled with my handbag, thoroughly pretending to be deep in search of the needed item. After my search failed to produce any results and I had already braced myself for the sound of his whistle, he suddenly swept the money that I'd laid out for him before and presented a ticket, accompanied with a disapproving shake of the head.

"Take care one of your BDM leaders on duty doesn't catch you watching what you're not supposed to be watching. All of you want romance nowadays," I heard him grumble after I'd promptly snatched the ticket from him. "My daughter got in trouble with hers just two days ago. For the same thing, mind you. They check the theaters, your leaders. And you won't con them with not wearing your uniform, either."

So, today was a pass-for-an-Aryan day. I beamed my acknowledgment at him and dived into the safety of the dimmed lights and plush chairs. Sinking into the luxurious, eternal softness of my seat, I wept along with Lina Carstens, whose acting was indeed, a delight. One thing the ticket seller was wrong about, I didn't want romance. I didn't cry because they had what I didn't; I cried because the film had ended and it was anyone's guess if I'd ever get a chance to sneak into a theater again. I didn't want romance. I only wanted a normal life.

Chapter 2

Frankfurt. November 1941

Mutti sat near the window, nearly touching the windowpane with her temple to make out careful stitches in the last rays of the dying sun. Electricity was a luxury once again. We had long grown used to burning candles instead of using electric light but sewing by candlelight, with *Mutti's* bad eyes, was entirely out of the question. As I was polishing our mismatched, chipped furniture – a generous donation of the very first family in Frankfurt that Lily and I worked for as maids – I watched *Mutti's* creased forehead, her bloodless, pinched lips that used to smile ceaselessly at her three daughters and husband and almost choked with the most profound pity for her. I knew precisely which things she was desperately trying to work out in her mind. *Where else to get more orders, when dealing with a Jew had just been proclaimed to be a criminal case? Will Lore be able to deliver Frau Kästner's order without anyone noticing? Should Lore go after the curfew? She's a blonde little girl, took after her mother; perhaps, they won't stop her? What to do with Ilse and Lily? Ilse has grown even more and suddenly decided to develop a chest as though overnight! That's also my genes, curse them! Where to get the cloth to expand her dresses? Or should I give her mine? I can make do with two blouses and a skirt; she can have the rest. Take it all, my darling girls – my clothes, my food, my needlework, the blood from my fingers, my soul – just live, girls, just… survive.*

I missed the textile factory. I missed "pass-for-an-Aryan" days. On the left breast of my painfully tight dress, a yellow star with a single word *Jude* was now sitting. We had to purchase it from an office in the center of Frankfurt. I still couldn't comprehend how they could handle it with such ease, as though it was a simple merchandise transaction. *Here's your new Star, Fräulein Stein. Here are your instructions on how to put it on your dress or coat so it would be visible for everyone. Thank you for your purchase. We hope to see you again soon!* It was such a cruel mockery of human dignity, such an insolent display of inhumanity wrapped in typical bureaucracy. I was still puzzling over it long after, while still holding the sign of humiliation *for which I actually had to pay,* in my hands. The line of people was moving slowly past me – they, too, came to the wonderful German store today. *Thank you for doing business with us. Please, come again!*

The last of our rights had been taken away just two months ago, the last shreds of our dignity swept away by the wind of the war – this time in the East. Our kin was now hardly seen in the streets, in those few hours during which we were still allowed to buy our food while carefully maneuvering through the dark backstreets in order not to get anywhere near "Aryan" parts of the city. The first ones who'd caught a whiff of smoke and death – still invisible yet hovering imperceptibly with its scythe above our heads – disappeared among the waves of German intelligentsia and freethinkers some three years ago, after dutifully paying off the Nazis for the damage caused by the same Nazis during the Kristallnacht. The others, who still held onto some chimeric hope of things returning to normal, picked up and left in September, as soon as the Yellow Star Law officially went into effect. Now, it was only us left, the ones who could barely afford an electricity bill, let alone paying off the government tax and a foreign visa. Marked, shunned, forbidden to work, to walk, to breathe – I was almost certain they'd pass some sort of law concerning those last two notions I mentioned.

Upon hearing the loud knocking on the door, mother and I exchanged uncomprehending glances. After the Weinstein family, who used to live above us, had left in September, we had no visitors and didn't expect any. The fall swept through the city and along with it, the Gestapo, combing, raking through what remained of the Jewish community, sweeping the last of us, along with the fallen leaves. The Frankfurters were oblivious to it all. They went about their business, while we hid behind the curtained windows and bolted doors. Nothing was certain anymore. Each day became a gamble. Life itself grew unsettled; the air around us was charged with constant tension and the feeling of imminent danger from which there was no escape. We were trapped and already sentenced; sentenced for the crime we hadn't the faintest idea we'd committed.

Vati, pale and still clutching a newspaper in his hand, emerged from the bedroom. His gaze passed over us, almost not seeing and fastened itself, with an awed expression, on the dark hallway, from which the persistent knocking echoed, shuddering, reverberating with fear, through our very bones. The visitors didn't announce themselves yet but we all knew, on some instinctual level, who stood on the other side of the door. Lore's little palm, sweaty and cold, found mine, in the dusk of our unlit apartment; I gave it a reassuring press.

Vati stepped forward, hesitated for a moment and then suddenly gave a harsh, high-pitched laugh. "I suppose I should get that. Unlikely they'll go away if I don't."

Mutti slowly rose from her chair, oblivious to her sewing that slid off her lap and landed softly on the floor.

Lily never left the sanctuary of the bedroom. Without seeing her, I knew that she was staring obstinately at the book she was pretending to read, just to ignore the reality around her. She had given up on it by now. She wished nothing to do with it any longer.

After a moment's hesitation, *Vati* unlocked the door. Bright light coming from the staircase flooded the shadowy world of our cobwebbed apartment; basking in it, two plain-clothed men stood. I didn't catch the names, only the organization they worked for. They strode in, silently counted all of us including Lily in the bedroom and her book, behind which she was hiding her pale, terrified face, no doubt; handed *Vati* some papers and headed to the exit without any further explanations.

"Do we all have to appear in the Office?" *Vati* mumbled, trailing after them.

"Yes, everyone without exception," one of them replied without turning around.

The sun was almost set but we could still make out the words on the printed three-page summons bearing the stamp of the *Reichzentralstelle für jüdische Auswanderung* – Reich Central Office for Jewish Resettlement. With meticulous German pedantry, it announced the precise day and hour we were all to report to a train station for a medical examination, supervised by official physicians of the Office. We were allowed to take a suitcase and food for five days – a travel ration.

"One pair of boots; for women – one pair of stockings," *Vati* was reading out from the summons, his voice betraying his anguished state with a slight tremor, "two pieces of underwear, one work outfit, one sweater, two blankets, two sheets, one plate, one drinking cup, one spoon." He dabbed his forehead with the handkerchief. "One towel and some soap."

"Is that all?" my mother asked, her voice eerily extinguished.

"We are also to hand over whatever ration coupons we have left. Pets are not allowed."

"We don't have any."

"Yes, that's good, I suppose… It says here, they will all be destroyed."

For whatever inexplicable reason, that last remark of his stuck with me and stunned me into astonishment with its cruelty. I could understand their hatred for us but I could never comprehend their desire to destroy animals, whose only fault was that they used to belong to the Jews. What madness was it now? Admittedly, animals could have been spared at least.

The train would be provided by the Reich Bahn; no need to pay for the tickets. It didn't say where exactly we'd be heading, though.

"To Minsk," a bespectacled official from the Office for the Resettlement announced to us the following day before handing us more instructions and already shouting, "Next!"

Each of us, even Lore, had just signed the declaration, which the same official had put before us. I reread mine before he pulled it out of my hands impatiently. Its words would forever be emblazoned into my memory as something unbearably heartbreaking and unnecessarily cruel. *"I, the undersigned Jew, Ilse Stein, confirm that I am an enemy of the German government and therefore I have no right to the property I leave behind – furniture, valuables, money. My German nationality lapses and from November 8, 1941, I'll be a stateless person."*

Three years ago, almost to the date we'd had to leave our native Nidda. Now, to celebrate the anniversary of the Kristallnacht, they decided to rid themselves of the last Jews. Frankfurt lay just behind the tall, arched window of the Office but was already obscured from my view, already dissolving into a thick mist of the past, already some past-life destination, a mere memory.

"Where is Minsk?" Lore whispered, pulling on my sleeve.

"In Byelorussia. The Byelorussian SSR, to be exact."

"What's SSR?"

"Soviet Socialistic Republic."

"We're going to live with the Bolsheviks?" She sounded almost horrified.

My poor little sister, I thought with an ironic smirk. *You've been listening too much to the German radio and its constant propaganda.*

"Should be a welcome change. Can't possibly be worse than this," I responded instead through gritted teeth and immediately received a harsh, reproachful look from my mother.

"They'll provide us with lodgings in Minsk," *Vati* said to no one in particular as we headed to the exit, lost particles of sand amid the cruel sea.

The following morning each of us packed a suitcase, marked each with our names, dates of birth, and one single word, *Frankfurt*. Then, we packed a separate bag as we had been instructed. Papa's was thick with papers: his scholarship papers, bank accounts, and bankbooks – now nulled and voided yet required for some incomprehensible reason; stocks and bonds which he had purchased a few years ago and to which he hadn't any rights any longer. In *Mutti's*, was her life insurance and funeral funds with the location of the plots. In mine, I only had my birth certificate, a passport, and a small savings account book which *Vati* had opened in my name when I had just turned twelve. It, too, was now useless. The list went on, demanding to pack the keys and provide the numbers of safe deposit boxes; inheritances, rights of patents or real estate, art of any kind, collector's items, jewelry, diamonds, gold and silver objects, medals, gifts, compensations from insurance companies, mortgages, accurate descriptions of partnerships with names, addresses and telephone numbers of the partners…

"We're not coming back," Papa suddenly uttered, his voice thick with emotion. "We're never coming back here…"

Now that he stood in front of the window, I have just noticed how stooped his frame had become, how he had suddenly aged, shrunk into himself, how his face had taken on a waxy, cadaverous tint. Abruptly, he turned on his heel and appeared almost cross, defiant as his fingers clutched the star on his chest.

"I'm not ashamed of it. I'll wear it with pride, here or there – it's all the same to me! They won't break me. I'm stronger than…" He stumbled upon the right word, moved his lips as though searching for it, receded and lowered himself slowly into a chair, from the seat of which the stuffing had been bursting through like poisonous mushrooms through the roots of a tree.

Vati died two days later, on the train, after clutching his star for the last time. His body traveled with us for eight hours, his stiffening head perched on my shoulder, until the stop somewhere in Poland. Only then the SS hurled his corpse away, together with four other people from our car. Through an opened door, I could see the side of the tracks littered with bodies. Somewhere in the distance, strange men in striped uniforms were digging into the frozen ground.

"Who are they?" Lore's hand found mine again.

"Gravediggers. They will bury our *Vati*."

The young blonde girl was studying them with mistrust, working things out in her child's mind. "What is it they're wearing? Aren't they cold?"

I stared at my father's corpse – *Leopold Stein, the Jew* – until the door to our car was slammed with force and the lock turned by the gloved hand of the SS man. My eyes were full of tears, which, unlike *Mutti's*, never spilled over. A shudder of anguish ran through me without reflecting on my face. I could feel it turning into a mask, hard as granite, cold and unmoving. My heart barely turned inside my chest, heavy as a stone.

Mutti, with her tear-stained face, would not cease smiling at me with such painful tenderness about her. As soon as her husband died, she knew it was all over for her as well. *If her Leo couldn't endure this, if his strong, steady heart shattered inside his chest, she wouldn't survive this either. But what of her daughters, her darling, beloved daughters?* The smile jerked, wavered, almost contorted her face back into a painful grimace but with some inhuman willpower, *Mutti* forced it back into place, peering into my eyes and mine only. *I know why; there's steadiness in them which she couldn't find in Lily's or little Lore's. There's a promise to survive.* She wanted to believe that even when she has perished, at least one of her children would make it. I smiled back at her and nodded my silent reassurance. *I'll survive, Mutti. Whatever it takes, I'll survive.*

"Gravediggers," I repeated out loud, like an accusation. A woman, who had a place by the small caged window, turned to face me, startled from some sudden revelation.

"That, they are," someone remarked next to me, a bespectacled man with an ironic grin on his face. He, too, was looking at the SS man's hand, still clutching the iron bars of the window.

Chapter 3

We arrived at the break of dawn. It was a particularly dreary, dismal morning caught between the autumn and winter when the weather itself can't decide between the mist and wet snow and when the ground smells of rotting leaves, mud, and despair. The sun was lost somewhere between torn shreds of clouds, gray and heavy like everything in this alien, Eastern land. The city of Minsk was crumbling under their weight, or what was left of it, that is. Through a small, barred window, I watched the wet flag with a swastika on it slap against the flagpole of the train station.

The door to our cattle car opened with a groan, as though it, too, was dreadfully tired from our interminable journey. Rushed by the familiar *"Raus, raus, raus"* and the occasional blow of the whip, we spilled into the fog-shrouded outside, *the coveted outside,* of which we'd been dreaming for days with no end, crammed tightly together until a quarter of our cattle car had died and we breathed out in relief, for now, we could take turns to sit and even sleep.

Wisps of fog, sticky and foul-smelling, obscured everything from sight apart from the SS and their wolfhounds, looking ready to pounce. I clutched Lore's hand tighter. Minsk smelled of rotten earth and swamps, of something vaguely hostile and sinister. The stench, drifting from the field on the other side of the tracks was clinging to me, penetrating my nose and mouth, slipping down my throat. I saw Lily pick up a handful of dirty water from the puddle to satisfy her thirst; she managed to slurp it from her palm before I slapped her wrist in helpless fury. Her lips quivered in an apologetic smile. She didn't care any longer if she got sick and died.

The SS filed us with the help of their truncheons, poking and prodding us in our aching backs until they had us standing in the usual orderly and thorough manner. We were waiting for something or someone. In the icy mist of the Minsk morning, that *someone* rose above us, the dirty horde, from his podium and introduced himself as Oberscharführer Scheidel. He was the kind of a man I'd seen countless times in Frankfurt and never in Nidda; immaculate overcoat, clean-shaven cheeks, hands in leather gloves, and a look of utter contempt for anyone who stood below him. A perfect product of the Party.

"Welcome to Minsk, *Frauen und Herren*." His entire manner betrayed the narcissistic attitude of someone who takes pleasure in the sound of his own voice. "You may thank me now; I made room for you by getting rid of thirty-five thousand Russian Jews just ten days ago."

Malicious triumph stole over his face as, one by one, our heads instinctively turned in the direction of the field across the train station. The wind had picked up; the wind, blowing above the remnants of the recently unearthed soil and raising the shadows that now stood looming before us, invisible yet brutally real. We suddenly realized what the foul smell was. Next to me, a young woman began crying softly. Lore looked at her, confused and suddenly indifferent.

"Why is she crying?" she muttered, as though annoyed by such an unseemly display of emotion. "Surely she should know by now that the Nazis kill people."

I pressed my finger to my lips, giving a sign to her to be silent. *I should mind myself and my tongue when I'm around her from now on. She's picking up too many of my poisonous remarks.*

Scheidel's short speech was soon over; some sort of selection began instead. Rough, gloved hands were pulling us apart, separating families into mortified, shrieking entities, wide-eyed and trembling with a new sort of animalistic fear. The fog rolled in waves now, hiding us from each other. I lost the frail hand of my *Mutti* in the ashen air and was feeling around with my hand searching for her coat, in vain. I called for her in anguish but my voice drowned in the ocean of others. In a rare moment of clarity, as the wind tore at the mist and succeeded at parting it for a few merciful seconds, I glimpsed a row of vans waiting in the distance – metal beasts swallowing people one after another. I charged toward them, to where my mother was being led along with the others but someone gripped me by the collar of my coat much as one would do with a dog. The clean-shaven face of a very young soldier stared right into mine. He couldn't have been older than me. He said quietly, "If you want to live, go with the others," and he pushed me right into Lily's trembling, awaiting arms. Lore clutched at my coat with the desperation of a drowning person clutching at a lifesaver.

"How old is the girl?" A hand appeared out of the mist, threatening to take my youngest sister as well. Oberscharführer Scheidel himself.

"Fifteen, Herr Oberscharführer!" Lore shouted back coura-geously, despite the fact that her entire body was trembling.

"You don't look older than twelve to me." He regarded her with suspicion.

My back was wet with sweat. I tore a knitted hat off her head, revealing her blonde locks like some sort of magical protection from an evil omen. "She's our half-sister, Herr Oberscharführer! A *mischling*. Her father is Aryan."

He gave her a half-hearted, passing look; appeared satisfied with his inspection and shoved her back to us.

They kept herding us like sheep towards the trucks covered with tarpaulin but I kept looking back and screaming for my mother until I could see her no longer. I wished for her so desperately to turn around and wave goodbye. I knew it was the last time I would see her.

"Other people are with her. She's not alone," Lily said, as though this was supposed to appease me.

I tore my hand out of hers. I kept peering greedily at the vans, which soldiers were now locking. Suddenly, I couldn't get my breath. I smelled death in the air and one thought only beat its brutish tattoo in my mind. What a damnable business it was, not to be able to say goodbye to one's own mother. *Mutti, Mama, Ma, Mutter, my dear, dear mother!* I wished to scream but not a sound tore from my tightly sealed lips. In little Lore's face, I saw a reflection of my own – expressionless, gray, tearless. My shoulders suddenly felt as heavy as lead as though the weight of the entire world lay on them.

"They must be taking them to a different place," I spoke as though through a dream.

"I know, Ilse." Lore smiled bravely at me and gave my hand a reassuring press. She *knew,* but she would go along with my version just so we wouldn't fall apart, the sudden orphans.

Next to us, a couple was congratulating each other with "making it through". Someone shouted at them to shut up.

"The SA beat our parents to death back in '38," the young man explained with a guilty, quivering smile, as though apologizing for the fact that they didn't have to mourn anyone, again, the second time around.

It was a blessing of some sort, I suppose. After life takes everything from you, there's nothing else to fear, not even death.

*

The setting sun was sinking behind Kolektornaya Street, burying itself on the Jewish Cemetery. We were still building the wall. The SS hardly allowed us any time to put our belongings in our new lodgings and forced us out into the street at once. Soon, rolls of barbed wire found their way into our hesitant hands. Rushed by the shouts, several men were hurriedly digging pits for wooden rods, also provided by the SS. From the other side of the ghetto, guarded faces observed our actions with suspicion. From time to time, they exchanged knowing glances and murmurs until one of the SS men shot in their general direction without bothering to aim and thus dispersed the gathering crowd which, in his eyes, had no business watching us work.

"Your new neighbors," the same SS man remarked with a disdainful smirk. "You should be thanking us for allowing you to separate yourselves from them as quickly as possible. Soviet vermin." He spat on the ground as though the words tasted vile in his mouth.

So, that's why the wire in the middle of the ghetto, in addition to the one around it. In the course of a few days, we had become a ghetto within the ghetto, the German section, *the Hamburgs,* as the Soviet Jews mockingly addressed us. Their resentment, whenever we came into contact with them, was almost palpable; they had mistakenly assumed that the wall was our idea. They thought us to be the same as the SS who'd brought us all there – after all, we did speak the same language. We also had the audacity to try and organize the miserable semblance of vegetable gardens outside our houses in the ground which wasn't yet frozen solid – *such a German, bourgeois thing to do.*

The first couple of weeks were the most confusing. The Soviet Jews regarded us with infinite suspicion and positively refused to have anything to do with us; Gentile Byelorussians, who worked for the Germans, weren't quite sure what to make of us and what kind of a tone to adopt with us. Even Germans themselves, including the SS, suddenly stumbled upon their own superiority and issued orders that contradicted each other, confusing everyone even more. And so it happened that when Obersturmbannführer Strauch, the local SS authority, would line us up outside, to perform street cleaning duty, General-Kommissar Kube – the civil authority – who happened to be inspecting the ghetto that morning, would cancel it in horror and chase us off to clean the German Cinema House instead, for "cleaning the streets was surely for the Soviet vermin and not the people of noble German blood." Someone from Strauch's entourage duly reminded him that we weren't of *noble German blood* but of the Jewish type. Kube screamed, "Eastern Front!" at the unlucky SS perpetrator who'd actually listened during his racial purity classes – the threat, which promptly ended the discussion.

The matters complicated themselves even more after our *Juden-Altester* – the *Judenrat* Elder – Dr. Frank reported to Herr General-Kommissar that among the Jews, deported from Germany to Minsk, were people whose brothers currently fought for Germany at the front and that the *Ordnungsdienst* – ghetto's police service – consisted of men who had served in the German Army during the Great War, some of them of quite a high rank and some still having their medals of distinction on them. General-Kommissar Kube was thoroughly mortified and promised to bring the matter to the attention of the Führer himself. Obersturmbannführer Strauch rolled his eyes behind his back and in the same manner – behind his back – shot a few of those very such people, *of noble German blood,* that very evening. Kube was incensed, departed in a huff and soon returned from Hitler's headquarters with an order that *no skilled worker was to be harmed, as they were essential for the war effort.* Strauch sardonically remarked that most of the German Jews wouldn't fall under this definition for they were ordinary middle-class people and hardly knew any useful trade at all. Kube responded by setting up a special factory for the production of wagons since the German Army needed horse-drawn carriages more than cars. For the time, Kube's civil authority had won out, over the SS one.

And so, we lived, between heaven and earth, between "good Germans" and "Soviet vermin Jews," suspended in a sort of purgatory, for no one could decide what we were anymore.

The ghetto was an odd sort of place if a purgatory could be called "odd." At our squat little hut, there was a number on the door, twenty-three. When our newly appointed Elder, Dr. Frank, had just directed us to it, we'd mistakenly assumed that it was the hut's number, like in some Bavarian Inn, the civilized people that we were. The Soviet Jews burst out laughing as we marched next to them to work as someone mentioned that they lived in the hut number twenty-three.

"Try to make it hut number twenty-two one morning during the roll call and the SS will see to it that it'll be hut number zero by midday," one of the women guffawed, speaking to us in Yiddish. We understood most of it, just like they, the Yiddish-speaking ones, understood us, the Hamburgs.

That particular morning, we failed to comprehend the meaning of her words, were too proud to ask for clarification and therefore dismissed it as a pitiful attempt at jesting. A week later, when, in the hut across the street, the local ghetto police discovered a runaway, the coin dropped at last. It dropped, when every single inhabitant of the unfortunate hut was taken outside and shot, including teenaged children.

Before, I had only seen death on the screen. It was always either noble and beautiful in a hero's case, or well-deserved and approved by the audience in the villain's. Who were the executed men and women that day? I suddenly didn't know. It dawned on me that I'd never seen anyone getting shot in real life. I realized that I'd never seen so many people getting shot one by one, in front of my eyes, to such an extent where I lost count of them marching toward the pockmarked wall and adding their body count to the ever-growing heap. We were forced to line-up outside our huts and watch the execution. The entire dreadful affair was beyond any comprehension.

I remember very well that it was Monday. I remember how violently my body trembled – from the cold, not the terror (I convinced myself of that to stay strong, just not to faint) as my own countrymen slaughtered my own countrymen in cold blood, in this madness of a morning, in this foreign, broken skeleton of a city, ravaged by the bombs in the war of annihilation. Against them, against us; I couldn't tell anymore. A film of tears washed everything away before my eyes, mixing together the snow, the blood, the corpses we had to drag away as soon as the SS finally had their correct body count for the hut with the number twenty-seven. Twenty-six corpses lay in front of it, minus one – the runaway, their unwitting executor. I remember clutching an SS man's sleeve – I still don't know how I dared to do it; perhaps, I still believed that they were my fellow Germans, who spoke my language – to take pity on my little sister and at least spare her this grisly task. *I'd take all of them to the cemetery myself. I'd drag them all with my own hands, just don't let my Lore touch them. She's far too young. She's still a child. You took her childhood from her already; don't make her into a corpse-carrier, to top it off.*

He did take pity on the little girl. He allowed her to carry the dead teenagers.

The Soviet Jews looked at us with sympathy that day, for the first time. We had ceased to be the same, as the SS, to them. We became fellow sufferers, the victims who had the misfortune to speak the language of the enemy and therefore, it was all right to barter with us through the barbed-wire wall.

Chapter 4

January 1942

A pair of black, shining boots tracked muddy, melted snow across the freshly mopped hardwood floor. Heaving a sigh (but only after the owner of the boots was out of hearing range), I dunked the rag back into the aluminum bucket, with *"Dom Kino"* – Cinema House – written on one side in red letters and threw the rag onto the floor in helpless anger.

"One way to put it, they do it on purpose," Rivka sniggered from her corner where she was polishing the legs of the chairs with something smelling strongly of citrus. "Another way to put it, they don't give a brass tack. They don't even notice that we're here. It's all the same to them, as long as the floors and the furniture remains clean. Who cleans them, who starches their shirts, who washes their dirty undergarments, it's of no interest to them. It is as if we have already ceased to exist. As if they have already succeeded in killing us all."

She was a chatty one, Rivka. And beautiful, too, with wide, bottomless eyes and fine, sharp features. She spoke to me in Yiddish; I replied in German. It would have amused the SS, such an unorthodox form of new communication now widely adopted in both ghettos, had they paid any heed to us.

The muddy tracks were slowly fading before my eyes. After a moment of wrathful impotence, I began scrubbing the floor angrily, imagining that I was erasing those black-boot footsteps from this earth, forever. I've never been so obsessed with such a fierce, all-consuming hatred directed at a uniform – any sort of uniform – as I was now. It had a million faces and yet no face at all. All of them – blond, dark-haired, blue-eyed, dark-eyed, handsome, ugly, cruel, smiling, German, Austrian, Lithuanian, conscripted, volunteers, SS, Wehrmacht – they all morphed into a vague faceless bearer of death and torment and I refused to see them for anything else.

"Those are beautiful hair clips you have. The SS didn't take them, did they?" Her voice betrayed an emotion which I couldn't quite decipher. *Surprise? Envy?* "They took everything from us as soon as they admitted us here, last summer. And then after that, every other week, they conducted raids until there was nothing else for them to take from us except for the skin off our backs. So, they began shooting us when we 'failed to produce the required quota.' That's all that Herr Kommandant knows, the quotas. *This much silver by tomorrow. This much gold in two days.* For the failure to comply – you know what. Familiar business."

"They didn't take anything from us yet. Only our mother, as soon as we arrived." I stared at my hands that were red and raw from the cold, dirty water and that ceaseless, useless scrubbing.

"Are you here with your husband?"

"No. My two sisters. I have no husband. None of us are married. The youngest one is only twelve."

"How old are you?"

"It feels like seventy."

"My father made it out of the city just before the Germans surrounded it. I couldn't go. My son was in kindergarten and there was bombing, so I couldn't get to him. No, no; he survived, my little Yasha. But it was too late to run afterward. Mama stayed with us too but then there was the *Oktyabrskaya Revolution* parade. You must have heard by now what they invented, the SS. Such creative minds, you Germans are! So very cultured, true playwrights and directors, I tell you!" Her voice was suddenly harsh, snappy. "I was taken to the woods early that morning, to chop wood with the rest of our brigade, so I learned about what happened from a friend who watched the whole spectacle unravel from her window. The SS surrounded a certain area with police and the dogs, lined people up as if for roll call, and handed the ones in the front row a huge banner with *Long Live the 24th Anniversary of the Great Socialist October Revolution! Long Live Comrade Stalin! Long Live the USSR* on it. Then, they gave the rest of the people small red flags as well and ordered them to march along Komsomolskaya Street and out of the gates, all the while filming and photographing the entire procession. I don't know how far they told them to march but I do know in which ravine they threw the bodies later. You must have seen it from the train when you arrived. I was assigned to the burying brigade. I buried my own mother – at least that I got out of it. She'd like that, the fact that it was her daughter who was throwing soil on top of her grave, even though she lay there along with thousands of the others." She paused and then added softly, "That was right before you arrived, the first transport from Hamburg. Then from Frankfurt. Then from Vienna. There was so many of you and no place to put you. But they're inventive, your compatriots. They figured this little mathematical problem out."

"What are you telling me this for?" I was suddenly furious. "My mother is also dead! I didn't kill yours!"

Rivka regarded me in surprise. "I wasn't accusing you of anything. Just making conversation."

"Well, make it about something else or don't make it at all!"

I almost expected her to call me a German bitch or some such. I sounded like one but I'd rather her despise me and not talk to me at all than talk to me about that. An inexplicable sense of guilt burned my cheeks in spite of the absurdity of it.

She was quiet for some time. Then, she spoke again, as though nothing had happened. "Those really are very nice hair clips."

"A whole lot of good they do when one has almost nothing to eat."

"You could trade them for food," Rivka remarked nonchalantly.

I stopped my scrubbing for a moment to look at her. She was looking at my head instead, assessing the value, it appeared.

"Yes, those are worthy of at least ten potatoes and some canned preserves. Perhaps, even some *speck,* if you're lucky."

"They're my father's gift." I touched my hair self-consciously. "I can't trade them for a piece of smoked fat."

They're all I have left of him.

Rivka shrugged and resumed her polishing. The grand piano, on which she was working, stood by the window. Absentmindedly I wondered why my compatriots didn't bother removing the tape from the glass; did they expect the Soviet planes to come back with a vengeance? Hardly. Our troops stood near Moscow from what I last heard. No one was coming back to reclaim the city. We were all stuck here for the time being.

I chewed on my bloodless, chopped lip, working things out in my mind.

"Where would I get *speck* anyway? Or potatoes, for that matter? Surely not from *your* side?"

Yes, we were stuck here, utterly and irreversibly at *the uniforms'* mercy. Curiosity, or hunger, got the better of me. I surrendered. I began considering, calculating; ten potatoes equaled a whole month of potato soup. Canned preserves meant some meat that Lore could put on her bones. A piece of smoked fat – my mouth began to water at the mere thought of it. I could almost smell its heavenly aroma. That was the stuff; it would see us through January at any rate. How cold it was outside! All outhouses had been long chopped for wood. Whoever was caught doing their business in the open, was shot, just where they squatted, in the pile of their own excrement. The SS thought it befitting.

"Not *from* my side, but *through* my side," Rivka supplied with a grin. "We live worse than dogs, worse than you, the Hamburgs, even, but don't forget, we're from around here. We were born here, we grew up here, and we still have friends on the other side – in the city, in the forest where half of the Soviet troops disappeared last summer. You have only your SS. You choose who you want to deal with."

I pondered her words for a few infinitely long moments. At last, my red, stiff fingers found their way under my clothes and pulled a golden chain from under the layers of two sweaters, a blouse, and two undershirts.

"What about gold? Would they take gold?" Our very first Frankfurt employer, Frau Novak, gave it to me 'for good luck,' together with furniture for our new, bare apartment. It was a little easier to part with it than with *Vati's* hair clips.

Rivka gestured for me to hide it at once. Another pair of black boots hurried past us. Her precaution was undoubtedly timely, however, completely unnecessary; he almost stumbled into my bucket and cursed it instead of me, who'd put it in his way. Rivka was right. They positively refused to see us.

"Gold is even better," her assurances came from under the piano, in a hushed whisper; *the Boots* had left the door to the hallway open. "It'll fetch you some king-worthy rations; trust me on this one." With that, she was back to polishing the brass wheels on the piano's legs.

Rivka needed a few days to "organize things," she said. She didn't brag when she implied that they, the local Jews, knew their way around here. Some of them grew up in the fenced-off area where the ghetto now stood; the rest had long mixed with the local population, intermarried, wore their cosmopolitan attitude with pride, and therefore had more than enough willing Gentile allies on the other side of the fence. They were much more resourceful than us, much more cunning, and certainly far bolder than us.

"Boris will meet you tonight, on the corner where Respublikan-skaya Street crosses Shpalernaya Street, right by the fence of your Sonderghetto," Rivka instructed me in a whisper a few days later as we marched out of the gates to our assigned working place – the German Cinema House. "Do you know where it is? Good. You'll recognize him by his *Judenrat* armband. Yes, he's a member; don't look at me in such surprise. How do you think he has access to all those goods? He can leave, together with Mushkin, twice a week to the city on a special pass, that's how." Ilya Mushkin was to the Soviet Jews what Dr. Frank was to us, their *Judenrat* Elder; that much I'd learned by now. Rivka paused, allowing the file of SS men to pass by us on the street and only then continued, "On your way to the fence you'll see a little girl in a red hat sitting on the stairs of the house on our side; if she waves at you, walk to the fence and wait for Boris. He'll appear within minutes. If the girl runs inside the house, turn around and leave – it means the patrol is nearby and we'll have to try the next day."

To my luck, the patrol didn't happen to upset our carefully organized plans that evening. That evening, we ate potatoes with *speck,* the entire hut, the whole twenty-three of us.

"That was very unpractical of you." Rivka expressed her disapproval by shaking her head the following day, quickly concealing a piece of smoked fat in her pocket – her share for putting me in contact with Boris. "You could have fed your sisters for weeks with that ration."

"I thought about it," I admitted reluctantly. "But then just couldn't do it. Those girls in my hut are somebody's sisters too."

She regarded me for a very long moment, then extracted a deliciously-smelling wrap from her pocket and silently lowered it into mine. "Don't start protesting now. I have a husband in Minsk, a Gentile. He brings me food almost every day; made himself his own entrance near Dmitrova Street. I won't go hungry. Go feed your lot. You Hamburgs need it more than we do."

Chapter 5

January 1942

In Jubilee Square, the January sun, dull and distant, stared at our frost-bitten faces as they assembled us, in columns, in front of the Labor Exchange. Despite the big name, the house itself was a small affair, wooden and painted green, with wood carvings around the windows intricately cut in a typically Slavic fashion. The routine was familiar by now; listen to your name and assignment, join your respective brigade, and march down Respublikanskaya Street and out of the ghetto. Past the shells of bombed-out buildings, past bomb craters still visible under the cotton of snow, past stiff, frozen corpses of Soviet prisoners of war lining one of the streets.

The daredevils had been plotting a revolt in one of the POW camps; even managed to steal weapons and ammunition from one of the German factories producing them right here, in Minsk. But, as always happens, someone got caught, someone got acquainted with the local Gestapo, and the result was now lining the road that we took to work, as a preventative measure, *so that the Jews wouldn't get any ideas into their cunning heads.*

"It's not even that," Rivka explained, carefully searching for a familiar face among the dead. Her brother was in the Red Army, she'd told me; just called up when the war broke out. She'd had no news from him since. "The ground is frozen through and through; they can't dig a pit to bury them all. We'll have to wait till it thaws out a bit. Then, they'll give us shovels and put us to work."

"Good thing, too," a stocky woman to my right added, "there won't be any pogroms for now."

No, there weren't any organized pogroms but the SS still came in the middle of the night, drunk and savage and terrorized both ghettos, the *Ostjuden* and the *Hamburg* one, without any discrimination.

Roused from their beds and the floor (whoever was fortunate to occupy which), barefoot and trembling, we stood at attention before them, hoping to guess what they came for tonight. *Was it gold? Quickly, Lisl, give them your gold earrings so that they leave us alone. They want us to undress and dance for them again? Inge, you sing, you have a beautiful voice. We'll dance. We'll do anything just so they don't take us outside and shoot us as they did a week ago with four girls from the house next to us.*

Dr. Frank tried reporting it to the ghetto Kommandant Redder when Redder summoned the Sonderghetto Elder to his office, but Herr Kommandant's facial expression spoke for itself upon hearing the report; the incident with four dead Jewish girls was the last thing he would investigate. *As for that silver,* he tapped his paper with his pencil, *he needed Dr. Frank to collect by next Monday this exact number...*

Which song would our SS guests like to hear? We'll sing whatever you like and we'll dance for you and give gold to send to your girlfriends at home. Just leave as you always do afterward so we can catch another couple of hours of sleep before it's time for us to gather in Jubilee Square again.

This morning we were assigned to laundry duty. Inside the laundry room, the steam obscured the walls from view. Today, Rivka and I would wash the officers' dirty undergarments while Byelorussian women next door cleaned and starched their uniforms. We, the Jews, were not deemed worthy to touch those, only the socks, underwear, and sweat-stained undershirts piled in baskets next to the tubs with scrubbing boards in them. It would have been inconceivable for them to learn that women were ready to fight for the chance to be assigned laundry duty; we could spend the entire day in a hot, steamy room! It was considered almost a holiday.

For the first two hours, I scrubbed army garments against iron washboards as hard as I could but then, after Rivka's expressively arched brow and ironic smirk, didn't bother anymore.

"As long as it smells fresh, they won't know the difference," my Soviet friend remarked knowingly. "Why grind your hands into mincemeat for them?"

I suppose, no reason.

"Amazing how your perspective changes under certain circumstances, isn't it?" Another washed pair of underpants landed in a tub where we rinsed them before hanging them to dry. Rivka wiped her forehead and nodded a few times as though to emphasize her point. "Three years ago, my husband and I went to the Cinema House and saw a newsreel about Germans now being our friends and allies. Now, I scrub the floors at the same Cinema House where the Germans watch their newsreels, in which their compatriots keep murdering their former allies. Not even a year ago I was Raisa Belinskaya, an engineer and a citizen of the Soviet Union. Now, I'm Rivka Belinskaya, a washerwoman and a Jew. Not even a year ago, my co-worker Pasha Serebryankin was a good lad who knew many a good story and didn't work for the German police and didn't beat up my friends for trying to smuggle food back into the ghetto to feed their families. Not even a year ago, my husband thought that we were all Byelorussians and could never have imagined, in his worst nightmare, that he'd have to occasionally hide his own wife and son in his own apartment so that they didn't get killed during the pogrom."

"Not even a year ago I worked in a factory and made parachutes for the Luftwaffe together with other, Aryan Germans," I continued, forgetting the sock in my hands for a moment. "Not even a year ago, there wasn't a star on my clothes with the word *Jude* on it and my parents were still alive. Not even a year ago, I'd never think that my own countrymen would kill them."

"Don't make a new song about it now. It's all water under the bridge. Now, it's *to rescue ourselves and to fight for us.*"

"What?" I looked at her. From Rivka, the oddest glance this time, apprehensive, considering.

"Time to change the water, I'm saying."

Holding her rolled-up sleeve with one hand, she searched in the soapy tub and pulled the rubber plug out of the water. I followed her example. I was slowly learning everything from her, my only connection with the outside world the language of which I didn't even comprehend. She knew how to survive and she'd teach me how, so I could teach my *Hamburgs* in return. Having drawn a new tub, she was now busy stuffing hers and my pockets with aromatic soap which was stacked in the laundry room in abundance.

"Take it, take it, don't be daft! You'll trade it for potatoes at the market tonight. Do you want your sisters to eat or no?"

"If the police find it—"

"If the police find it, you give them four pieces from your left pocket, and keep the four from your right to yourself."

"You're giving me too much…"

"These you will tie to your thighs with your garters. And these two you will put in your bra." She tapped her temple with her finger in a universal gesture of accusation of someone not using their head and suddenly laughed. "You Germans may be highly intelligent but God forgive me, you're not too savvy when it comes to the simplest things."

"We're not used to stealing things, I suppose." Almost apologetically, I grinned back at her.

"You'd never survive in the Soviet Union then. Everyone steals everything here. That's just how things work. Factories have quotas for stealing."

"You're joking."

"Oh no."

Suddenly, she was stripping bare. To my mortified look, she pointed at the clock on the wall. "Lunchtime. Your compatriots will not show their faces here for the next thirty minutes. Bath time."

With those words, my ingenious friend discarded the last items of her clothing and immersed herself into a hot bath, heaving a sigh of blissful relief. So, that was the main reason why Soviet women were ready to fight for the laundry assignment. They washed right here, scrubbing themselves off with fine German soap before throwing the Germans' undergarments in the same dirty water. Suddenly, such an insolent and courageous, tiny act of resistance ignited the most profound sense of admiration in me. I began tearing off my clothes too. She was right, after all, my cunning Rivka; my regimented compatriots would only interrupt their lunch in case of an armed revolt breaking out under their window, no less.

She regarded me approvingly as I immersed myself in the water and nodded to some thoughts of hers.

"There are partisans in the forests."

I barely heard her words. The chatter of the Byelorussian women in the room next to us drowned her soft murmuring. They wouldn't bother or denounce us either, Rivka assured me. Half of them were her friends. They would even share their lunch with us later after the Germans have theirs and allow us to eat.

"So, I've heard," I replied carefully, wondering what it was she'd been tip-toeing around lately.

"A lot of ours escaped the ghetto to join them."

"Yours."

"Yes, ours. The Soviet Jews that is."

"All right."

Rivka began soaping her finely-shaped, white arms. "Would yours... be interested in cooperating with us? We can assist in many things. We can smuggle out some of you as well."

I considered carefully. "We would never survive there, even if the partisans take us, which I doubt."

"They will," she assured me quickly. Something told me that she'd already had this conversation with *someone* and that *someone* had promised her *something*. "They're not the Red Army; they're freedom fighters, independent ones. They welcome everyone, who wants to fight against the Hitlerites. Their only condition is that each fighter must bring something useful."

"Like what?"

"Something they can use; a radio transmitter, a typewriter, medical supplies... weapons."

I met her pointed look. For a few moments, I didn't know what to make of it.

"Where would I get weapons?" I asked with a cautious grin. I suddenly didn't know her. She was as foreign and treacherous as the land to which we were now confined.

"I bribed someone to get you assigned to this kosher duty, didn't I? So, I can bribe someone just as well to get you assigned to a munitions factory. Some of your compatriots as well. Whoever is interested."

I didn't trust her. She caught on that. "You're wondering why we're not getting our own people into those gun factories, aren't you? Don't look at me like I work for the Gestapo now; I promise, I'm something quite the contrary. You see, after what happened with the uncovered revolt in the POW camp, the Germans banned us from the munitions factories. But only us, the *Ostjuden*. Someone from our *Judenrat* learned that you, the German Jews, aren't on that list. Some of you work there. They trust you. They don't expect treason from you. They know that you're just as good at following rules as they are; that *you would never steal anything...*"

In the meaningful silence that followed, I finally realized what she was saying. Rivka's grin grew wider, culminating in a veritable Cheshire Cat's toothy smile. "Have no illusions, Ilse. They won't stop until they slaughter us all. I don't know about your obedient compatriots, who mistakenly assume that it's only our heads the

SS are after, but we are planning on getting out of here and in as big a numbers as possible. I picked you because you seem like a sensible enough girl. You know how to adapt, to survive; you learn quickly and you're not afraid."

"No, I'm not. But I need time to think it all over. Don't worry, I won't tell anyone about what you proposed, not even my sisters."

"See?" She slapped the water in apparent delight. "You do know what's good for you. Think about it and let me know when you're ready. But don't take too much time. Spring is coming. The earth will thaw out. You know what will come next."

Chapter 6

February 1942

"You're not afraid," Rivka had said. I wonder what else she would say had she seen me now.

I splashed some more water, tinted with rust, onto my burning face and lifted it to a cracked, rust-stained mirror that graced the wall of a women's bathroom – the only one in the entire armament factory. It used to produce Mosin-Nagant for the Red Army; now, it produced Škoda guns and Mauser rifles for the Wehrmacht under a civilian German engineer's supervision. He often invited distinguished guests from the German headquarters, strode down assembly lines with the proud face of an over-achiever, talked insufferable statistics and numbers while the distinguished guests nodded solemnly and the workers stood with their hats in their hands, heads bowed low.

I regarded my reflection in the glass – a pale girl with wary, shining eyes, dark hair covered by the kerchief; a small bruise on the right cheekbone, still visible but already healing, from two days ago when a Lithuanian guard from the Black Police had hit me – twice. The first time because I happened to be walking by him as we were being readmitted into the ghetto after a day's work and second because I looked at him in astonishment after he'd hit me for nothing the first time. He must have felt better after that second slap – at least it was justified.

Lousy underground material I was, at any rate. Lousy, through and through. All morning I spent with every sense of mine strained to its utmost, with eyes darting from one supervisor to another, with hands so wet with fear that clips with bullets kept sliding out of them. And yet, when the moment was right, when every supervisor just happened to have his back to me, I lost my resolve at the last moment and dropped the clip into the box where it belonged instead of my pocket where it should have gone according to Rivka's plans. And now, look at me, hiding here with *"thief"* written all over my face when in fact I didn't even have the guts to go through with the whole enterprise.

Them, the Soviets, were made of much harder stuff than us, the tender children of the great German civilization. They came from a country of workers and peasants after slaughtering their masters in cold blood and argued with each other as to whose district's commissar hanged more enemies of the state during *Ezhovshina*. We still changed into "proper attire" for the evening after work, had a Sonderghetto book club and a small string quartet which played Mozart on Sundays. Lousy underground material, if I say so myself. They were the anarchists; we cherished our order, even when it was the order in which the SS lined us up for execution. They killed, bribed, stole, lied, and schemed to stay alive; we regarded them in horror and called them Slavic savages.

But at the end of the day, who had the *speck* and who slowly starved to death? Who managed to make people "disappear" to the other side of the barbed-wire fence and make everything legal according to the papers that they submitted to Kommandant Redder? Who had the connection with the Gentile, "Russian" side as they called it? Who knew how to make it to the partisans, swelling in numbers around Minsk? There was no going back to German civility, not for someone who wished to survive – I suddenly realized it that day. Not in this place. I would just have to teach myself how to be *a savage* like them. Savages had a chance. My cultured kin already had one leg in their communal grave.

Empty-handed and empty-minded, I trudged back to my work station to produce more bullets so that the SS would have enough to shoot us all later. Unlike most of my compatriots from the Sonderghetto, I had no illusions on that account. The pogroms were not only for the Slavs, as many stated with a knowing look about them; for the SS, it was all the same. We weren't divided into Germans and non-Germans any longer. We were divided into the ones wearing the uniform and the ones whom they shot, regardless of their nationality.

Amid the mechanical noise of the death factory, my fingers coiled around a clip with five long, hard-nosed bullets for the Mauser Karabiner 98K rifle, caliber 57mm, on their own accord. For a few interminable moments, two possibilities struggled for power inside of my frantic mind. *Into the box or into the pocket?*

Soviet *Judenrat's* Elder, Ilya Mushkin, had just been arrested, tortured, and executed for aiding a German officer who had wished to abandon the whole SS business and join the partisans. Certainly, Mushkin was no hard-boiled agent-provocateur from a spy novel and yet he risked his life to stand up for what he felt was right, to aid not just a fellow Jew but *a former enemy* who had had enough of that senseless killing as well, who was sickened by what his own fellow SS men did daily, to the point where the prospect of shooting at his own former comrades was easier to conceive than going along with their atrocities for one more day. Rivka said the Gestapo treated him no better than Mushkin.

The pocket.

The hard noses of the bullets were stubbornly digging into the seam of its lining guided by my cold, now resolute fingers. If Mushkin martyred himself for a German, what was one stolen clip? *Yes, they'll shoot me if they find it. Surely, Mushkin considered them shooting him for that German as well.*

"I stole one Karabiner clip," my lips hardly moved as I whispered my confession to Rivka later that day.

Trembling from cold and shifting from one foot to another, we stood in a column in front of the gates of the ghetto, waiting to be readmitted inside. I half-expected her to burst out laughing.

"That's good," she whispered back instead, looking straight ahead of her. Hirsh was performing the search today – a good thing. The cunning fellow from the Soviet *Ordnungsdienst* always went out of his way to make a good impression of a most thorough search, before his German supervisors; in fact, he hardly ever "found" anything despite feeling the items rolling through the cloth under his fingers. "That's five bullets to kill five Germans. Now, we just need a gun to go with it."

"They go with the rifle. I can't steal a rifle."

"The armaments factory produces handguns as well. You can risk stealing one of those, can't you?"

Slowly, I nodded. The line moved unhurriedly forward, an endless parade of shuffling feet and rags – a sorry sight good only for rested nerves. The routine was familiar by now. Hirsh would undoubtedly whack a couple of the strongest, sturdiest men from the column – a prearranged business, no doubt – and demonstratively wave confiscated items in the air. But so many ignored, "non-kosher" goods went back into the ghetto that the "whacked" men marched back inside with smiles on their faces. Their comrades would smuggle enough to trade on the small market set up on the Krymskaya Street and feed their families for a few days. The ever-present chief of the German police Gattenbach would raid and shoot up a makeshift market with monotonous regularity but mere hours after his departure, people would trickle back quietly to proceed with their barter, obstinate and resolved to survive just to spite him and his troops. Hirsh positively refused to take his "share," Rivka also noted, with unconcealed pride in her voice, on her compatriot's accord, no doubt. *"Bring whatever you may to the hospital,"* he would say. *"Or to the orphanage. They need it more than I do." They did practice what they preached, those communists,* I thought to myself for the millionth time. We only lied to our own people and pretended that we were better than them.

In the course of the next few days, I managed to smuggle enough parts out of the munitions factory to assemble an entire handgun out of them. I snatched them from different assembly lines on my way to the canteen or bathroom right under my unsuspecting fellow Germans' eyes. The biggest parts I dropped into my boots; the bullets went into the double bottom of my mess tin; the smaller pieces – under the lining of my pockets. The meeting with Rivka and her friends was set for Sunday, not due to it being our day off but more due to it being the SS's day off and therefore they wouldn't bother with searches, the disciplined, punctual compatriots of mine. I could have brought them the parts but what could beat the official, solid look of an assembled weapon?

I emptied my pockets before the man who I hoped would help me put it all together. With reluctance, he agreed to admit me to his small apartment when I insisted that I had something of utmost importance to discuss with him. *Some unofficial Judenrat business, if he could spare ten minutes of his time; I know it's dinner time and you have already changed into your proper evening attire to have your potato-peel soup, but I had seen the Cross for War Merits on your lapel before the SS took it and I know that you've been to the war...*

"I won't be joining you for dinner, don't worry," I called out to his wife, who was setting the table in a tiny kitchenette and thoroughly pretending to be unbothered by an unwelcome guest. I completely pretended not to notice her relieved look. Her husband, Herr Weiss, rearranged the parts I laid out before him with a guarded look. I sniffled quietly. My nose kept running as the damn cold wouldn't leave me alone. "Can you put it together?"

"No."

"It's not for me. It's for someone—"

"Who wants to go to the forest and join the partisans," he finished calmly. He didn't have the face of a soldier but rather, of an intellectual, whose eyes had been dulled by far too many books he'd read and forehead creased by far too many thoughts those books brought up. He didn't belong here. He belonged in a study wainscoted in mahogany, making notes on the theory of something. He didn't belong to the first war either, but it claimed him just like the ghetto did now. He seemed to know what was going on. "I can't assemble it because you're missing two parts. There should be two return springs on either side of the frame."

Catching a blank stare from me, he sighed, walked over to the window, hunted for something in the semi-darkness of the corner, behind the heating element which didn't produce any heat; fished out something, wrapped in a rag, at last.

"Just take this. I'll arrange more parts for myself tomorrow." Shielding himself from his wife's eyes with his back, he quickly pressed a pistol into my hands and only stepped back into the light once it disappeared into my pocket. I didn't ask any questions. I knew he worked at the same munitions factory, just had no idea that he was stealing parts as well and had even assembled them into something that could actually shoot and then concealed it carefully, prepared for a fight like the soldier that he was. Perhaps, I was mistaken about him. Perhaps, I was mistaken about the rest of my proud, truth-rejecting *Hamburgs*.

"Thank you."

"Don't mention it."

I hesitated. His wife cleared her throat in the kitchenette. Herr Weiss told her to begin without him but her wifely duty triumphed and she remained rigid and stiff-backed, with her spoon clenched in her hand as she pretended that the aroma of the potato-peel soup didn't have any power over her whatsoever.

"I'm leaving," I announced to no one in particular and started for the door. Then, already in the threshold, I took hold of his sleeve again. "Would you be interested in the meeting—"

"No," he stopped me abruptly. "No meetings. This," his eyes fell on my pocket in which his gun sat, warm and snug, "is for personal use. For when they come… surely, you understand. And if I were you, I wouldn't go there either. The Gestapo have just executed the head of their *Judenrat*. What do you think they will do when they catch the rest of their underground?"

With a solemn nod, I turned on my heel to leave him to his dinner. I was mistaken, after all, it turned out. It wasn't for resistance, it was for his stubborn German pride. He simply didn't want to go their way; he wanted to go on his own terms.

"As though the SS would care," I muttered under my breath, running out in the street. To them, a dead Jew was a dead Jew, whether they shot him or he shot himself. They'd strike his name from the list and go on about their business.

I had less than fifteen minutes to make it home before the 7 p.m. curfew. The streets were already deserted, wiped out by fear and darkness. Anyone caught outside after the curfew would be shot and all that business. Tonight, I wasn't afraid, for the first time. Tonight, I had the means to defend myself. I suddenly understood the ghetto underground and the risks they took. It wasn't just out of righteousness and principles and everything that had long lost its value on the black market. It was out of a craving to feel strong again, powerful; not some defenseless sheep that are led to the slaughter but a force to be reckoned with. A tiny drop that will eventually crack the stone in two.

I gave them the gun that Sunday. To part with it was more difficult than I imagined it would be, but Leib, a young man with bright expressive eyes, was thanking me so profusely as the weapon traded hands, that I felt that he'd have much better use for it than I. He bowed his head and promised, in his accented Yiddish, to kill as many Germans as he could, as soon as he joined the partisans; suddenly realized that he was speaking to a German, confused himself even more, apologized, reddened to the roots of his hair when I assured him that I didn't take any offense and only regained his composure once I offered him my hand to shake and wished him the best of luck with the partisans.

"First soap, then bullets and guns." Rivka was in the best mood as she saw me off at the barbed wire, which separated our two ghettos and in which an exit had been made by the already familiar Boris. She held it up for me and carefully rearranged the line as soon as I was safely on the other side. "Soon, we'll be smuggling people every week."

I smiled and waved at the figure, obscured by the darkness, before setting off on my way home. Perhaps, I was mistaken about myself also. Perhaps, I could do it after all.

Chapter 7

March 2, 1942

The day of Purim started out as usual – Jubilee Square, filing into work brigades, the march with an escort. Some civilians still stared as we were led outside the ghetto and along the streets; most had long ceased to bother. They had their own affairs to attend to, their own working quotas to worry about. Only children still waited in ambush along the streets and never missed a chance to throw a few "rocks" into the column. We smiled and waved in gratitude when the SS got distracted; the rocks were, in fact, potatoes. Children waved back and smiled, also behind the SS men's backs.

Yes, the day started out without any change. It was the evening that met us with charged silence, forbidding faces in front of the closed gates and muzzles of the submachine guns staring ominously at our peaceful columns.

The SS didn't say a word yet, except for their usual *"Halt,"* but people had already sensed something, felt something deep in the pits of their hungry stomachs, now so well-trained on both food and danger. We started emptying our pockets, discreetly, in silence; burying scraps of whatever we could steal that day, in the snow, with the tips of our boots. No one inquired as to why they weren't readmitting us back, only listened to the evening air, pricking our ears like the animals we had become, cagy and alert. *No gunshots so far. No cries of children torn out of their mothers' arms. No pleas from the elderly. Silence.*

Glances were exchanged, the very first ones, anguished and hopeful at the same time. *Perhaps, a Purim's miracle? Perhaps, just*

a check-up of some sort? Perhaps, General-Kommissar Kube is visiting?
Perhaps, we won't have to die today?

A *Judenrat* member stepped cautiously forward, began inquiring something in his correct, polite German and got shot by an enraged squad commander before anyone could comprehend what had happened.

"Were you not told to wait, you brainless swine?!"

The crowd swayed and shied to the side as his muzzle turned on us.

"Back into line!" Another wrathful shout followed; immediately after, to emphasize the point, a short warning burst of submachine gun fire that strafed the ground to our right, herding us back into our place. "Face down! If you can't wait like normal people, while standing, you'll be waiting like the rats that you are, with your noses to the ground!" We instantly dropped to the snow, covering our heads with our hands – sheer survival instinct. "The ones who move will be shot on the spot if shooting is the only language that you understand!"

All illusion was lost, shot along with the *Judenrat* man and left for dead in the middle of the holy day. No God was stronger than the SS. The SS killed God in front of our eyes. Soon, we would follow; everyone was sure of it.

The dusk hid in the west, replaced by the night, as black as our killers' boots. They lurked among us, the predators; buried in the snow, we froze from paralyzing fear and waited for the merciful death. Anything was better than this agonizing terror, the anguished uncertainty, the SS-imposed wait.

The snow slowly melted around and under me; it would quickly turn into ice as soon as the temperatures plummeted, as they always did in this God-forsaken place at night. It stung my bare cheek and made my teeth ache on the side on which I lay. I dared not move. Shots were fired from time to time at those unfortunates who couldn't stand the torture with the snow any longer and shifted their position to alleviate the pain.

A lone searchlight brushed our heads leisurely and, as far as my eye could see, traveling after its morbid path, lay one big mass grave with bodies scattered about like torn dolls. Numbness replaced the intolerable ache in my legs, covered only by thin woolen stockings. As another pair of black boots stopped near me, I wondered if that was how people lost their limbs to frostbite. One of the boots now stood on my back; after a few minutes, the soldier changed the position and put his other foot in between my shoulder blades – not hard and heavy, just to keep it off the snow. The SS man was cold too. At the last moment, I prohibited myself from stirring and making him shoot me for it. My sisters were in the column also. I couldn't die because I hadn't taught them how to steal yet.

A well-dressed man came running by, *the director of something* – I didn't quite catch the title with which he began threatening the SS commander. Apparently, his factory workers were among the half-frozen almost-corpses in the snow and he demanded their immediate release. The SS commander mentioned some high orders, got thrown off track by the man's authoritative bearing and his fur-lined coat, muttered something about fetching his commanding officer and disappeared for the next fifteen minutes.

"Sarin?" Another voice soon joined the factory director's in his indignation. "Is Sarin here?"

"Minsk prison warden," someone to my left recognized the voice, announcing the title with a hushed measure of respect.

The SS men, left without their commander and his *high orders,* reluctantly allowed Sarin to identify himself and get up. It seemed that the prison warden had managed to obtain some sort of release form for Brigadier Sarin, but Sarin, whose face I couldn't see, positively refused to go anywhere unless the entire brigade was released. That the SS, without their commander, could not authorize.

The commander reappeared with two other men in tow; I recognized the first one at once. So, General-Kommissar Kube was here after all. His face was waxy and stone-like, a posthumous mask, in the ghastly shade of the searchlight. The other one I had never seen before. Round spectacles on the hooked nose, unimpressive stature, a typical bureaucrat, a far cry from a virile SS soldier – it seemed for a moment as though someone thought it to be an excellent joke to dress one of our kin in the SS uniform.

"Obersturmbannführer Eichmann," he introduced himself to the factory director.

"Are you in charge here?"

"Jawohl."

"I demand an immediate release of the men who, as you can see according to this list, all fall under the category of skilled workers. Without them, the production of the factory under my management will virtually stop. You can't even begin to comprehend the consequences this will have on the Wehrmacht and—"

"We have already filled our quota for today," the officer, who called himself Eichmann, interrupted him calmly. "All of these people are free to go."

Only the following morning we learned that the SS under his command had executed over five thousand people.

*

In the morning, the sun reluctantly spilled its light over the ghetto. A collective moan reverberated through the crowd as the Labor Exchange officials started filing us, *the Hamburgs,* into a separate column judged solely on the body count and not our "skilled worker" life ticket. We began shouting and waving our skilled worker cards even more frantically when we noticed that it was only women they wanted, just like the SS the day before. The SS demanded five thousand people; the Labor Exchange officials, only a handful.

"It's for work," they tried to calm us. "No one will shoot you!"

Wasn't that what the SS was telling the ones, who were left inside the ghetto, the day before? *No one will shoot you; we only need to fill our quota.* They sounded so official, so reassuring, too. The only mistake they made was to say in reply to the Housing Department official's Dolsky's question as to what kind of Jews the SS wanted to report for work, *"Ganz egal"* – *it's all the same. Women, and children, and the infirm ones – just give us five thousand.* He instantly knew what they were up to; how helpless he must have felt with no time even to warn anyone.

They marched us toward the Government Building, the grandest surviving structure in all of Minsk. Past the statue of Lenin, torn off his pedestal yet still lying, forgotten and no longer threatening, half-buried in the snow. They lined us up in the square, facing the entrance, with staff cars and trucks parked in front of it. In most windows of the Government Building the glass, shattered during the battle of Minsk, had been replaced and glinted brand-new and clear in the rays of the rising sun. Only a few windows were still boarded with plywood sheets, shards of glass still baring their teeth around it. Much like the occupants didn't bother with Lenin, they spared themselves the pains of prying off the wreath, with hammer and sickle, mounted at the very top; merely covering it with a black banner with two SS letters on it – a suitable, mourning color for the occasion. Women around me glimpsed the banner too and quickly averted their eyes.

Rivka was not with me today – it was only the German Jews that someone had requested. I had waved her goodbye and shouted my thanks and my sisters' names at her as we were being led out. Who knew if I'd be coming back?

"Attention!" We straightened out at the command, shouted by an SS Rottenführer, a thin, ruddy-faced fellow with watery blue eyes that kept tearing from the cold. It was almost amusing what good, disciplined soldiers they had managed to make out of us by now.

I stared at the ground in front of me as an officer stepped out of the building and approached the Rottenführer to exchange salutes with him.

"As you requested, Herr Leutnant. Two hundred and fifty German Jews. All females," the Rottenführer reported and slammed his heels together.

"Thank you very much. Most obliging of you, after you shot nearly all of my workers yesterday and left the entire building without heat," the officer commented sardonically.

"I apologize, Herr Leutnant. There must have been a mix-up in the papers."

The officer released an irritated sigh and inspected the line in front of him.

"You all speak German?" He addressed us directly for the first time.

"*Jawohl,* Herr Leutnant."

We even responded in their fashion now. A little trained army indeed.

"Are you all healthy?"

"*Jawohl*, Herr Leutnant."

"Anyone has lice?" After a few moments of silence, he went into pains of explaining, "You'll be working near and in the Government Building, so it's important that you're perfectly healthy and don't carry anything that can transmit such dangerous diseases as typhus. You'll all be checked by medical personnel later today and they will immediately discover deceit. So, I would really appreciate it if you didn't waste my time and told me right away if you don't fit the criteria. If you don't, you'll return to your usual workplace tomorrow. Count today as your day off."

Subtle glances were exchanged along the line. No one wanted the day off. The day off meant no worker's ration. Women silently deliberated if they should risk it. Out of the corner of my eye, I noticed the officer's wrist jerk impatiently as he clasped his hand behind his back. He was growing annoyed with the silence, no doubt and the memory of yesterday was far too fresh to risk any uniformed man's wrath.

"They will tell you if they have lice if you allow them to return to work today and not tomorrow." I don't know what prompted me to address him and not even properly at that. Our SS escort glared at me; the officer, however, turned to me, inclined his head, suddenly interested. "They won't receive any food rations if they miss a day at work," I went on to explain. "They can't afford a day off, lice or not."

He walked up to me and stopped. I kept my head down as they had taught us, looking at the hem of his long, blue-gray overcoat and the tips of his boots, polished to mirror perfection.

"What is your name?" His tone changed from harsh and abrupt to polite, reminiscent of the manner one would adopt when talking to a woman, not a sexless working force as most of them took us for.

"Ilse Stein, Herr Leutnant."

"Willy Schultz. A pleasure to make your acquaintance, Fräulein Stein."

A hand, encased in a warm, fur-lined glove, appeared in front of my downcast eyes. I glanced up in confusion. He was smiling, apparently amused by my reaction.

He was older than most of the rosy-faced SS around us, in his late thirties perhaps. I guessed his age not so much by the lines around his eyes, the color of which oddly matched the color of his coat but by a certain measure of weariness in them, as though it wasn't the first war he'd seen and now was infinitely disappointed by the manner in which humanity was progressing.

"You can shake it. I don't bite."

Under the Rottenführer's mystified glare – *why would anyone want to shake hands with a Jew?* – I carefully placed my bare palm into the Leutnant's and gave it a tentative press.

"You should wear gloves in this weather, Fräulein Stein. It's not Germany; you'll freeze your fingers off without noticing."

He sounded as though he were genuinely concerned. I shot him another mistrustful, probing glance wondering if his sense of humor matched the SS one. Mostly, it was they who amused themselves in such a manner at our expense.

"Today is my sister's day," I replied in an even tone.

"I beg your pardon?"

He was still holding my hand in his, only now he covered it with the other. I contemplated yanking my palm out of his but decided against it at the last moment.

"We have only one pair of gloves among the three of us. So, we switch days."

Now, I was outright staring at him, waiting for perhaps one more "witty" remark. He only blinked a few times, blankly, before dropping my hand. Suddenly, he was pushing a pair of his own gloves into my hands, repeating, "Take them, don't be silly now," until I finally clasped them in my frozen fingers, unsure as to what to do next.

"Aren't you going to put them on?" Back to smiling from *Herr Offizier*.

I did as he ordered me, growing annoyed with his games. No one showed us kindness here. They were all out for our blood and that's how things stood between us. Every act of goodwill was a ploy of some sort. I mumbled a quiet *thank you*, yet felt my nerves being ready to snap. I didn't trust any of them, *the uniforms*. This artificially-created sense of normality unnerved me even further; I didn't like the sudden change of the habitual state of things.

Herr Offizier, meanwhile, hid his hands in his pockets, waiting for me to say something. I stood before him, silent, like a statue.

He must have realized that I wouldn't talk without being addressed first. Must have recalled how it was with women from his first brigade, now all dead. "Where are you from, Fräulein Stein?"

"Originally Nidda in Hesse. Deported from Frankfurt."

He encouraged me with a nod. His pale, clean-shaven cheeks were growing rosy in the frost. He must have been cold; not cold like us, frozen stiff in our thin coats but not as comfortable in his warm overcoat with its fur collar as he was when he'd just stepped outside to inspect us. I wondered why he wasn't going back inside. It must have been warmer there, than here, even though the central heating wasn't on. They would have had some sort of heating lamps, most likely.

I avoided looking at him. There was something different in him, something different from the others which I couldn't quite put my finger on and that confused me even further. I was afraid of him more than I was of the SS because I failed to understand his motivation.

He shifted his weight from one foot to another. He couldn't bear this Russian winter, I could see it.

"What did you do in Frankfurt? Any qualifications?"

"I worked in the factory that produced parachutes for the Luftwaffe, Herr Leutnant."

He broke into a beaming smile and pointed at the insignia on his uniform cap.

"The Luftwaffe," he announced cheerfully.

Only now I realized that he didn't belong to some special commando unit. *The Luftwaffe*. Proud knights of the sky who nearly leveled the entire Minsk to the ground. I wondered if he flew a bomber or a fighter.

"Perhaps, it was one of your parachutes I was wearing during the Polish campaign."

"Perhaps," I conceded politely.

"I had to bail over Holland a few times. Perhaps, it saved my life once."

"Perhaps."

He appeared to be waiting for me to say something else, to continue with this oddest sort of conversation but I stood before him like a Carmelite monk on leave. We were all freezing and wondering if we would get a chance to eat today and he wished to exchange pleasantries.

"How would you like to be in charge of my new brigade, Fräulein Stein?"

I looked up at him once again, searching for a hint of some intended malice on his face. But he appeared suspiciously well-meaning, with blue, honest eyes and lips that would not stop smiling at me.

"As you wish, Herr Leutnant."

"Splendid. Please, count one hundred and ninety-seven women for me, the ones who don't have lice. I only need two hundred for the heating brigade and these two ladies are all that's left of it." He motioned at two young women clinging to each other not too far from him. I didn't even notice them before. "You will be number two hundred."

"Can the rest return to their usual assignments?" I asked him before he'd turn around to take his leave and forget all about us.

"Of course."

"They'll need an official paper explaining why they're late."

"Yes, yes, *he'll* sign whatever needs to be signed for you."

The SS Rottenführer straightened a bit under yet another glare shot in his direction. It seemed, his kin were in some sort of hot water with the Luftwaffe now, even though I had little idea how the two branches were even related and even less concerning who had the authority over whom.

"And one more thing; after Fräulein Stein makes a list of workers, I want you to copy it and sign; if something happens to my new workers, I will hold *you* personally responsible for that. Do you understand?"

"*Jawohl*, Herr Leutnant!" A sharp click of the heels.

For some reason, I breathed out in relief when Leutnant Schultz had finally left.

Chapter 8

"How do you know him?"

The girl was about my age, perhaps a few years older, a black bundle covered with a gray shawl. Just like everyone around, she wore almost everything she owned under that coat. Just like the rest of the Byelorussian Jews, she addressed me in Yiddish.

"You don't beat around the bush here, do you?" I remarked ironically without taking my eyes off the list, ensuring that everything was in order. The SS Rottenführer was smoking and pacing with great impatience nearby, but I'd rather risk his annoyance than misplace someone's name and leave that person without their daily ration.

"Have you known each other before the war?" The girl looked at me askance. She barely reached my shoulder yet had the bearing of a right NKVD officer. Must have been one of those, fanatical Party kinds. I easily recognized the type by now – we had those in spades in Germany and they didn't differ much from the locals in their zeal. Same sect – different idols.

"No. First time I've seen him in my life."

Satisfied, at last, with the list, I ran up to the Rottenführer and handed it to him. To sweeten his sour mood, I diligently lowered my head and murmured a *"Bitte, Herr Offizier,"* emphasizing the title and putting just enough tremor in my voice. Two things they liked; feeling important and being feared; I'd learned it well by now. He straightened his shoulders a bit under his private's uniform, nodded curtly and started in the direction of Sovietskaya Street, waving the small column of "rejected" women after himself with a languid grace of a Feldmarschall, no less. *Good. Now, he won't beat any of them up on the way to their respective workplaces.*

"He gave you his gloves." My new acquaintance didn't give up on her interrogation. After I left the remark without comment, she moved to stand right in front of me, blocking my path. "Why was he so nice to you?" Her gaze zeroed on the yellow star sewn onto my coat. "You're not even a *mischling*. You're a full Jew."

"Thank you for establishing that fact." I swung round in the hope of giving her the hint to stop it, with her third degree.

She clasped my sleeve instead. "Tell me how you know him; that's all I'm asking!"

I wondered if she indeed belonged to the NKVD or some such. I began considering reporting her.

"Herrgott!" I yanked my arm out of her grip in annoyance. "He gave me the damned gloves – so what? Don't make a song and dance about it! He's *your* boss, *you've* known him longer than I have; *you* tell me why he did it!"

She regarded me in silence for a few moments.

"You really didn't know each other prior to this day?" she asked again, but this time more conciliatory.

"No. I promise we didn't know each other prior to this day." I softened my tone a little as well. "I'm pretty sure he's had a bit too much cognac in his coffee this morning to keep him warm and was feeling uncharacteristically nice and generous, that's all."

"Nice? Schultz?" She arched her dark brow. "No. Efficient and superficially polite, like the rest of them, yes; but nice? I wouldn't go that far."

"Then, I guess, he fancies me," I replied in jest. "Who knows, perhaps he'll send his adjutant with his calling card this very evening and invite me to the local Luftwaffe ball."

Judging by her thoroughly confused look and brows knitted tightly together, she took my words literally.

"I'm joking," I clarified, just in case and offered her my hand. "My name is Ilse, by the way."

"Liza." She grabbed my palm and gave it a good, firm, Soviet shake. "Are you from the Sonderghetto?"

"Yes. You'll have to tell me what it is exactly you did here with your brigade."

"The boiler house is over there." She gestured toward the steep slope that started across Sovietskaya Square. Along it, rail tracks ran. Liza pointed at the unloaded cars. "Trains with supplies – wood and coal – stop right in front. We unload the cars and slide the wood and sacks with coal down the slope. Part of the brigade, which works below, stacks it all there and another part brings it to the boiler house. A few people work inside. Stepan, our only man, shovels the coal into the furnace. Obviously, unloading cars is the hardest job while the boiler house is the most kosher duty – it's nice and warm inside. Make sure to rotate the shifts, will you? Sonya, our former brigadier, didn't. I told her it wasn't fair, not a communist thing to do but she preferred double rations that she collected from the ones who bribed her to get the best assignment. Her own father would have disowned her, had he known! To Siberia, with no further investigation! Stupid cow! Always thought only about herself!" She was suddenly furious.

All because of unfair assignment distribution? I sensed something deeper in her tone, thought about asking but then didn't.

I gestured my new brigade to follow me. We started in the direction of the slope. From the boiler house, faint smoke was rising.

"The Germans have been working it overnight," Liza explained. "Only a few soldiers and just so that the pipes wouldn't burst from the cold. It's freezing inside the complex. They all curse those muttonheads from the SS."

"I thought it was the SS headquarters." Over my shoulder, I checked the black banner. It was still there.

"Only a few floors. Field police or some such. The Luftwaffe occupies the rest, but since it was the SS that entered the building first last June, it was they who hoisted that black drape there. First come, first served, I suppose, even though the Luftwaffe made most of them move out already in July."

"Were you here, in Minsk, when they came?"

"Yes. Most of us are locals. The whole brigade was local; I've known many of them personally, even from before the war." Her voice was strangely detached, as cold as the air outside. "After yesterday, only Fanya and I are left. The rest of the brigade – gone."

"Yes, Schultz said that. Damned business."

She nodded. My eyes teared, in the cold; hers were dry. "We were waiting outside, in the snow."

"Us, too."

"Yes. There were probably a few thousand workers lying near the gates." Liza sniffled and pulled her woolen shawl onto her forehead. A few strands of dark hair framed her temples. She seemed preoccupied now, somewhat lost. "We were all skilled workers; they were not supposed to shoot us."

"They shot everyone who moved."

She was quiet for some time. Then spoke, her voice suddenly harsh and accusing. "It's all Sonya's fault. She said she had to use the bathroom. What bathroom, in the middle of all that?! I, for one, did my business under myself when I couldn't tolerate it anymore. So did the rest. But not Sonya, no. She, Sonya, is the commissar's daughter, she's better than that. She said they had no right to forbid us to use the facility and got up, the stupid cow."

I imagined very well what followed but didn't want to ask.

"They just mowed down everyone around her, just like that, without warning, for nothing." Liza spread her arms wide, moving them in a deliberate, deadly circle. "No one else moved. Their only fault was lying close to the one who dared to rise to her feet when it was clearly *verboten*. I should have reported her as a commissar's daughter, to the SS, when they came, in the beginning, to make those lists of theirs. I knew what she was in for and I kept quiet;

risked my own life not denouncing her. If I'd only known that because of her, all of those girls…" Her face was flushed with emotion. It was fierce and agonized and forbidding and sorrowful all at the same time. I averted my gaze, preferring to look at the train tracks instead. "The bullets missed only two of us, out of two hundred. Purim's miracle, eh?"

"Are you religious?" I asked out of the blue, not even sure why.

"I'm a communist." She finally shifted her eyes back to me, seemingly relieved with the change of the subject. "Are you?"

I shrugged with indifference. "I'm nothing, I suppose."

"You must be something." She offered me the first smile. It was warm and tender – a miracle on its own that this girl could still smile. I almost admired her strength at that moment.

"No. You know, I envy you, the *Ostjuden*. You at least have your ideology. You take your strength out of it. We have nothing. We *are* nothing. They took everything from us and gave us nothing back."

"What do you mean, gave you nothing back? You got the gloves out of the deal, didn't you?"

I stared at her straight face; caught the beginning of another smile, snorted after finally getting the joke through my thick skull and then outright burst out laughing, hysterically, until tears sprung to my eyes.

*

We stood in front of *the Yama* – the Pit – as it had already been baptized by the population of the ghetto, promptly reduced by a few thousand. Beside me, Liza was speaking, her voice breaking from time to time. Yet, her eyes were dry, almost as black and impenetrable as the night around us.

"After they readmitted us to the ghetto, you, *the Hamburgs*, went on your merry way but us, they made us bury the bodies. And after we finished the task, they told us, *'Well, Jewish filth, since we're letting you live, show us how grateful you are. Kneel'.*" She threw a rock into the pit. There was no gravestone to put it on. "So, we knelt in the snow till midnight."

"Your knees must be killing you," I said. Nothing else occurred to me to say in the face of this nameless horror.

"My soul is killing me," she murmured broodingly. "My knees are fine."

She threw another rock into the mass grave, still not covered with the fresh snow – a black scar on the face of pristine whiteness – and turned her back to it.

We started in the direction of the Obuvnaya Street where Rivka lived. It didn't take me long to learn that Liza was familiar not only with Rivka herself but with the entire underground business conducted in the Soviet part of the ghetto. Lily begged me to stop it with them, to mind my own affairs, to keep my head down – the usual *big sister Lily* mindset. I had long abandoned the idea of arguing with her and trying to open her eyes to the bitter truth; it was all the same to the SS. They shot equally often at the feeble and the strong, at the underground members and the quiet types, at the skilled workers and random sorts. The Pit was the proof of it; the snow in front of the ghetto gates, in which I lay yesterday, still stained with blood this morning, was the proof of it. And so, every evening I would crawl through my "exit" in the barbed wire again.

The truth was, I needed them like one needs air after being submerged under water for a very long time. It had long transcended from pure curiosity and desire to barter some food to something more meaningful, purposeful, organized; something that still instilled hope in people living in this rat trap. I knew I didn't belong with them. I didn't even understand their language once they would switch from Yiddish to Russian in the heat of a discussion, forgetting all about me; yet I craved those clandestine evenings and their company like a drunkard craving his schnapps.

In Rivka's apartment, the cigarette smoke whirled and crawled toward the ceiling, obscuring the familiar faces. Here was Boris with his dark, brooding gaze – an unofficial underground leader; here was Eli, a Polish Jew who'd known Boris from some prewar communist business; Klara and her blonde mop that had tricked more than one German in the Russian side – the underground's liaison with the Gentiles; here was Efim, who worked the printing press for the German *Minsker Zeitung* during the day and for the underground *Zvezda* at night; here was fox-faced Styopka-Kaznachey, who knew the local forests like the back of his hand and took people to the partisans, invariably returning for more, to this hell of a place, instead of joining the freedom fighters himself. *Not yet, not just now,* he would say, with his sly grin. *When we have enough people on the other side; only then. When the entire ghetto is empty.*

I extracted a can of sardines out of my pocket and put it on the communal table with more pride than I did with a gun, a few days earlier. It was a custom for everyone to bring whatever they could so that Rivka's elderly mother could make something out of the goods while we discussed the pressing matters. Among several potatoes, a few slices of bread, some grains, and dried apples my offering gleamed dully like an unexpected lump of gold in a starving miner's hands.

"Where did you get it from?" Boris was suddenly suspicious.

One couldn't blame him for his diligence. Rumors traveled fast while one hurls coal from wagons and Liza had plenty to say about several members of the *Judenrat* being shot during the massacre. In their places, collaborators now sat, according to the same rumors traveling the coal vine – the exact reason why she was so suspicious of Schultz suddenly being so kind to my modest persona. The Gestapo were planning to plant their people everywhere, now very much aware of the illegal underground meetings. The Gestapo were the only people around who ate German sardines, in olive oil no less.

"From the Air Supply unit," I replied, before someone shot me by accident. "Liza and I work there now."

"Yes, we know that much." He still wasn't convinced. "Did you steal it then?"

"No." I hesitated before explaining. "Leutnant Schultz gave it to me. He's our brigade's supervisor."

"He appointed Ilse as a brigadier," Liza supplied, much to my relief. "And me, as her substitute. We are to go into his office every morning to get ration cards for everyone."

"And your new ration cards include sardines?" Boris arched his brow skeptically.

"If that's the case, I want to work for the German Air Force too," Styopka-Kaznachey guffawed behind my back. "Rivka, can you organize something on that account?"

"Da zatknis ty," Rivka barked at the jokester in Russian; something to the effect of his needing to shut his trap, judging by her intonation and pulled forward at once. "He gave it to you himself?"

"Yes. For my sisters," I clarified. "But we have enough to eat. I gave them my day's ration. I figured I'd bring it to you instead."

"Thank you." Boris rose to his feet and shook my hand. Food items soon disappeared in the direction of the kitchen. "So, what kind of fellow is he, that new *nachalnik* of yours?"

I recognized the Russian word they used for a "boss".

"He's all right, I suppose." I was aware of all eyes still zeroing in on me, some still suspicious, some – already scheming something. "An odd sort of fellow, if I'm completely honest."

I still wasn't entirely sure what to make of him. Earlier that day I went up to his office to give him the list with his new workers' names and retrieve their ration cards for lunch and found myself even more confused. After ushering me inside, Schultz took my coat, pulled out a chair for me – *I hate eating alone, don't you?* – and treated me to freshly baked bread with butter and jam, eggs, and coffee. After quite a one-sided conversation during which he talked and I mostly sat there trying to eat as much as I could – one must take the good when it comes – he suddenly thrust a can of sardines into my hands. *"For Lore and Lily."* The announcement came in tandem with a beaming smile, which spelled, *See! I remembered the names of your sisters!* Then, he finally released me, almost forgetting about the ration cards for which I had come in the first place.

"I think he fancies her," Liza suddenly chimed out with a coy grin on her face. I felt the blood leaving my face at once. I wished to slap her for that big mouth of hers.

"He does not," I assured the assembly, which fixed their eyes on me with even greater interest than before. "He's just... the Luftwaffe. They're a little different from the SS. They're like General-Kommissar Kube – the sentimentalists."

"Sentimentalists, you say?" Efim narrowed his eyes.

"He gave her his gloves." Liza, again.

I closed my eyes and slowly opened them again. "As I said, sentimentalists. Same Germans, just an approach that is a bit different. They don't mind us dead but don't like seeing us suffering. That's all there is to it. He fed me, gave me the sardines for my sisters and now he'll sleep well at night; won't be ashamed to look at himself in the mirror in the morning. They do these things to separate themselves from the SS, to elevate themselves to a different position. But deep inside, they're all the same. He was only annoyed that his building wasn't heated that night, not because his workers got shot for nothing. It's all the same to him, who supplies his office with coal, as long as it's warm inside."

Boris exchanged glances with Rivka, considered something for a long time while sucking greedily on his makhorka. Someone next to me sniffed the air. My mouth, too, was salivating at the aroma of the *ukha* – fish soup made out of my canned sardines and their potatoes. Rivka's mother was singing something in the kitchen, a joyful song this time. On a small blanket, by the stove freshly fueled with wood and coal – the latter, mine and Liza's present – Rivka's son Yasha played with two wooden soldiers. Boris came to a decision.

"You must go up to him every morning, right?" he started. "Could you, perhaps, chat him up a bit while you're there? He's quartered with the SS in the same building, isn't he? Maybe, he has friends among them. They talk to each other, discuss their days, complain to each other about their superiors, moan about *operations scheduled in such cold.*" He gave me a pointed look. "Smile at him, ask him how his morning is going, what else is new, that sort of thing."

My laughter came out a bit too scornful for my liking but it was too late to take it back. "Do you actually believe he'll buy it?"

"Why, it's innocent enough. And you happen to be a girl who's easy on the eyes. He's all alone there, with his comrades. And here you come, a piece of civilian life. They all long for it, a little chat with a good-looking girl."

I was already shaking my head adamantly. "No. You're not German. You don't understand. We're not 'good-looking girls' to them. We're vermin. They're raised with that hatred in their hearts. They drink it from their mother's breast, together with milk. They will never see us as equals. Dirt under their feet is of more value for them than us. As much as I would love to help you, your plan just won't work; I'm telling you this right now."

"Yet, he gave you his own gloves," Rivka noted without looking up.

I thought I saw a hint of a smile on her face. Perhaps, it was just a shadow. Whatever the case, I had nothing to say to it.

"Why don't you try and see how it goes?" Boris suggested. "You have nothing to lose, really. If he tells you to leave off and not to stick your Jew-nose into his business, you'll do just that. But if not…"

It could be a mine of so much-needed information, it read in his eyes. I remembered that he'd lost many of his *Judenrat* comrades to the Pit and promised to try.

As she walked me to my "exit," Liza touched my sleeve. "Are you mad at me for telling them?"

"No."

"You are. I can tell."

"I'm not mad. I'm upset because you're putting false hope in their hearts. That whole gesture with the gloves… it was not what you thought it was."

"Because I'm not German?" She sounded almost amused.

I pursed my lips and didn't answer.

"I think it's you who's mistaken this time," she spoke again after a pause. "I think he does genuinely like you. No, don't start another argument with me now, will you? I need to believe in something good still existing in this world. Don't give me such dirty looks. I didn't tell you my story before, but maybe if I do, you'll understand. When they first took us all here, to the ghetto, they began sorting us at once into 'useful' people and the rest. I was an engineer before the war but I lied to the SS man with the list and told him that I was a tailor. I was put in the 'useful' category. My husband, who worked in a conservatory and was far too honest to know what's good for him, told the SS he was a musician. He got shot."

"I'm sorry."

"Me, too." She took a deep breath and raised her head towards the sky, dusted with stars. "You asked me if I was religious before. I am. My religion is a world, in which people coexist in peace and where musicians are very useful people and where German pilots can like Jewish girls from the ghetto. Sounds absurd, I know. But so do all other religions and therefore, I'll stick to mine if you don't mind."

I didn't.

Chapter 9

Overnight, the temperatures plummeted. The morning dawned even colder, with icy gusts of wind tearing at our exposed faces. Tears froze on my eyes; the scarf covering the lower part of my face, which was also embroidered with frozen vapor, grew stiff with cold. Even the planks of wood seemed frozen solid, stuck to the sides and the bottom of the freight train cars, weighing a ton, unyielding and mocking in our small, women's arms. We'd been unloading the supply train for a little over an hour only, yet it felt like an eternity. I don't know who had it worse, our part of the brigade or the one which handled the wood as we sent it down the steep, icy slope, braving the snow while they trudged toward the boiler house with their burden. It had never occurred to me that the walls of hell were made out of ice.

Along the train tracks, Liza was marching toward me purposefully with a young woman in tow. I shoved another piece of heavy lumber down the slope with my foot and watched them approach.

"Comrade Brigadier," Liza began, still a bit out of breath. "Tell this *Fräulein* that she can't be using the facilities every thirty minutes. She doesn't seem to understand that she's not the only one to be considered and that we have quotas to fill. It is the third time she's asked me to be excused since the beginning of the shift!"

The young woman's black eyes gleamed with wrathful disdain as she pointedly looked away from Liza as though refusing to acknowledge her very existence.

"It's my time of the month," she supplied instead. I recognized a Berliner's accent at once and an attitude to match.

"Stiff luck," Liza countered in the same abrupt tone. "Time of the month or not, it doesn't give you the excuse to disappear for fifteen to twenty minutes at a time, while the others have to pull double duty for you!"

"Quite an un-communistic spirit you're demonstrating, *comrade,*" the young woman drawled maliciously. "Wasn't it your dream to build a farmer and worker's paradise? Well, go ahead, work."

Liza began saying something in her logical manner, something universally reasonable and self-evident, that other women had to suffer through the same, that no one around had it better than her, that it would only be fair if the duties were shared equally among all – the Berliner only barely deigned to acknowledge Liza's arguments with a scornful smirk and an ice-laced cruel jab of, *Speak German to me if you want me to understand you. I can't comprehend your Bolshevik gibberish.*

Liza paled, stiffening next to her. My face had grown dark as well; suddenly, I was consumed by an inexplicable desire to strike her porcelain-white face under her expensively-made, department-store shawl.

"You sound like the SS that have put us here," I growled, through gritted teeth. "Apologize at once!"

The Berliner was not impressed. "The SS meant to separate us from those Bolshevik barbarians. I am not obeying her orders and I am sure as hell not apologizing to her." Another arrogant nod in Liza's direction.

I felt a vein bulging on my temple. I wished to slaughter the conceited cow properly at this point.

"You are still obeying *my* orders though." Her smile melted at once. I turned to Liza. "What is her current assignment?"

"Boiler house."

I arched my brows. "And she's shirking even that assignment? Comrade Gutkovich," I addressed Liza Bolshevik-style, even though ordinarily we addressed each other by first names only, "assign her to my part of the brigade permanently if you would be so kind."

The Berliner's face grew long. She blinked at me in apparent confusion. *Aren't you supposed to be on my side? You're from a Sonderghetto, just like me. We are different than them; we're better!*

You ignorant fathead, I wished to take her by the shoulders and give her a thorough shake. *That's precisely the mindset that has landed you and me here in the first place and yet, your skull is too thick to take it in and process it. No human being is better than any other.*

The Berliner regarded the mountains of unloaded lumber in horror, began to tremble; then, tears came, bitter and hysterical like those of a child who had just been unjustly punished.

"Are you a communist too, then? Is that why you're siding with her?"

"I'm not a communist and neither am I siding with anyone. I'm only doing what's right."

Liza gave me a warm look. She didn't appear triumphant, merely grateful.

"Get to work," I barked at the Berliner, pulled Liza's list with the names of the brigade's personnel and marked the one I had just reassigned, using a stub of a pencil. "Baumann. And if I catch you shirking again, I'll report you to Leutnant Schultz. See how fast he sends you back into the ghetto and takes away your worker's ration card."

I expected her to curse me out properly and stalk off; instead, she fell in a heap at my feet, sobbing uncontrollably. "I can't take it any longer! I'm not supposed to be here! It's all a horrible mistake! I'm from a good family! My father is a well-known physician who treated the elite of Berlin! I studied in Vienna myself! I was supposed to graduate and have my own practice! I had a fiancé, a Doctor of Law… We often joked that we were to be two doctors…"

The rest of the words dissolved in tears, in incomprehensible sobbing and pain that was surprisingly easy to understand. Suddenly, Liza was kneeling in the snow next to her.

"Stop it, stop it at once! You can't cry here; the SS will see and punish you! My husband got shot too. Was yours? I know… It's all right. It'll get better. It will but only if you think of the present and never about the past. If you keep going to the outhouse to cry all day long, you'll lose your head soon. Start working instead. Work yourself until you fall off your feet in the evening. Work yourself until you're so tired, you forget everything else; understand?"

I watched Liza lead *an almost Doctor* Maria Baumann away. I was suddenly overcome with a strange sense of melancholy. I almost envied them for their loss. They were a few years older and therefore had someone to remember; they had fragments of real, civilian life to which they could still cling. I had been born a bit too late and mine was cut short before it even had a chance to begin – no university, no dances, no stolen kisses in the dark, summer alleys. Maria Baumann lived in Vienna and Berlin; I only saw Frankfurt and Minsk. With strange clarity, I realized that this was where I was most likely to die.

No. No thinking this way. I won't let them break me before my time. I'm strong. I'm brave. I'll live. Somehow, I'll live.

I stood without motion much too long. The cold began seeping through my clothes. After prying the scarf off of my frozen face, I pulled the gloves off with my teeth to ensure that my fingers were still intact. I couldn't feel them any longer and one had to be diligent about the first signs of frostbite. The SS had their opinion on the *useless eaters;* the ones, who couldn't work any longer, invariably fell into this category. My hands were white as snow, with blueish veins and even bluer nails but still intact and working. I blew on them before working my way back into the gloves. They were still warm inside.

"Fine gloves. Are they keeping you warm?"

I turned on my heel swiftly, ready to burst into a torrent of apologies, ready to scramble back to my working place after being caught at procrastinating in such a shameless manner. Leutnant Schultz hesitated between an amused grin and a scowl after my startled reaction. I realized that my hand was still pressed to my chest and forced myself to lower it.

"You look as though you'd just seen the great sea serpent." He finally decided to turn it into a joke. "Am I really that terrifying?"

"No. No, you're not." I grinned in spite of myself. "I thought you were one of the SS men or the Black Police." I removed the glove once again and passed my hand over my forehead, collecting the beads of sweat that broke out on it. Quite the reaction we've developed to the Germans' voices startling us in such a manner. "Is everything all right with the heating? I know that the last few days have been quite cold and we're doing everything that we can to keep the entire complex thoroughly heated but if something is not—"

"Everything is fine with the heating; don't worry about that," he assured me at once. "I just had a few free moments and wanted to see how the work is going."

"The work is fine. I was just going back to it. I only wanted to see if—" *If I froze any of my fingers off. But I can't quite tell you that, can I?* "I thought I had a splinter."

Not a much better version but it would just have to do.

"Allow me?"

I hesitated before removing my gloves once again and offering him my numb hands for inspection. I almost wished I had at least one scratch on me. *He'll slap me silly after he doesn't find anything and that'll be the end of the fish soup for you, Ilse.*

Schultz pulled his gloves off and took my hands in his. "They seem fine to me. Just very cold." He cupped his hands around mine and pressed them together. "The gloves aren't helping you," he proclaimed with a shade of disappointment in his voice.

"They are. It's just today and yesterday. This winter is nothing like I've ever seen and it doesn't want to go away." I finally sensed some warmth in the ends of my fingertips, the faintest echo of a sensation.

"No, it doesn't." He lowered his head and blew on our hands, started rubbing mine in his.

I held my breath for some time then finally found the courage to pull them carefully away.

"It's hurting my bones," I explained with a smile, not wishing to offend him. "The warmth."

"*Ach,* yes. I should have thought of that. I'm sorry."

In silence, we both pulled our gloves back on. I threw a longing glance at the train car, on top of which women were regarding us with interest, lumber forgotten in their hands.

"If you don't have any complaints, Herr Leutnant, I won't hold you any longer. Most certainly you have more important things to do than watch a brigade unload a wagon with firewood."

I made a tentative step towards the train. He followed me, in the same hesitant manner.

"Is it all right for you? The work, I mean. They look heavy." He motioned his head at the wood planks.

Why did you request an all-women brigade then? To be surrounded by skirts, whatever it is that those skirts do? Are you all really so lonely here, on the Eastern Front, that now even Jewesses will do? I almost asked. Then, didn't.

"They are heavy," I replied instead, in a very even tone.

Schultz lowered his eyes, nodded a few times silently. Then, almost apologetically, he said, "I know they are. I'm sorry for making you hurl all these tree trunks. But it's the women who they shoot at the first chance, you see; not the men. And now, you're all 'skilled workers,' with a good ration and an exemption from execution."

All two hundred of us. I was suddenly mute. Mute and thoroughly ashamed of everything I said about him to Liza, to Boris, to Rivka. He waved at the women from my brigade amicably and they waved back at him, reluctantly and unsure but they did.

"Well, I won't bother you any longer." He bowed at me slightly, looked at my hand but decided against offering his to me for a parting shake this time. Probably sensed the hostility I tried so thoroughly to keep away from my voice, from the manner in which

I had worked my way out of his warm palms. "Report to me please once you're finished with your shift, will you?"

"Of course, Herr Leutnant. Thank you."

"For what?" He smiled at me one last time.

I shrugged awkwardly and said nothing, just smiled back. *For keeping us alive.*

*

Inside the Government Building, it was not just warm; it was hot. The heat rose in waves from the radiators, causing the windows to quiver against the glowing sunset. Amber light soaked the corridors. Amber light gleamed on Leutnant Schultz's NSDAP pin, right in the middle of his right breast pocket. I somehow failed to notice it before and now I suddenly couldn't look away from it.

So, you are one of them, after all.

"Can I help you with something, Ilse?"

I looked up at him sharply, cringing inwardly at the familiarity.

"You told me to report to you after the shift was over, Herr Leutnant."

"Yes, I know. I meant to say, is there anything I can do for you? You know what I mean."

His voice was soft, much like his whole demeanor. He sat at his desk, littered with papers, almost without moving, as though not wishing to frighten the wild, skittish animal in front of him. Near his hand, with a pencil in it, a can of sardines stood, along with a loaf of bread – the good bread, the ones that the locals baked for the Germans. He saw me staring at it and slowly pushed both items in my direction.

"For you and your sisters."

"Thank you, Herr Leutnant." I took the can but only brushed the top of the loaf before hiding my hand in my pocket. Away from temptation. "I can't take the bread."

"Why on earth not?"

"They search us at the gates. I can hide the can well enough but there's not a chance in the world I'll be able to conceal an entire loaf of bread. As soon as they find it, it's a beating or perhaps a bullet for me, depending on who's on sentry duty. Not worth the risk. But thank you all the same."

He pondered something for a few moments. "What if we cut it into pieces? You can risk hiding a few pieces, can't you?"

"I suppose, Herr Leutnant."

"You can call me Willy when it's just the two of us."

My smile dropped of its own volition, a guarded expression replacing it once again. He sighed, annoyed – with himself – and rubbed his forehead in a defeated manner. "You must forgive me. The blasted war has been dragging on for a few years and I'm a bit out of practice with civilian talk and particularly around ladies. Though, it should be noted that I've never had a reputation as a ladies' man, so that explains me acting like a complete and utter muttonhead. I hope you will excuse me and my lack of manners. It is unintentional, I promise."

I thoroughly tried to keep a straight face but then felt a smile faltering on the corners of my lips. Schultz was beaming too, half-embarrassed and half-delighted at finally making me drop my guard.

"Apparently, you had at least some success with the ladies; one of them married you after all." I nodded at his wedding ring.

He looked at the golden band as though he'd seen it for the first time, suddenly confused.

"*Ach*… yes. That. She took pity on me."

I didn't ask the name of the woman who stood next to him in the picture that he kept on his table. He chose to leave her nameless also. From where I stood, I saw that she had dark wavy hair and a coy smile. He was wearing a civilian suit. It must have been taken before the war.

He produced the knife from the cardboard that stood near the wall, helped me cut the bread, then gathered the crumbs into his palm and was about to drop them into the wastebasket when I grabbed his wrist, emptied his palm into mine and quickly devoured whatever was in it. He stared at me like *I* was the great sea serpent this time. I immediately apologized. *Instinct, Herr Leutnant. We had indeed been reduced to a miserable, animalistic lot and no one can help us any longer, not you, not God himself.*

He hunted for something in his pockets with sudden urgency, produced a stack of bills – *he didn't know I was so hungry; could I perhaps buy something on the black market?* I shook my head at once, vehemently. Money was worse than bread. For bread, I'd only get beaten; for money – occupation money available only to the troops and civilians – I'd be making an acquaintance with the Gestapo and that option did not sit well with me. *It's really all right and Herr Leutnant shouldn't worry himself over it. The bread will do just fine. Could he perhaps turn away just for a few moments to allow me some privacy? I need to stuff the slices where the cursory search wouldn't reveal them, that is the stockings and the bra.*

"You can use my bedroom." He pointed at the door at the end of the room. I, for some reason, thought it was only a closet. "And take all the time you need."

He helped me open the door. With my hands full of bread, I stepped inside and stood in astonishment for a while, the reminder of a half-forgotten, past life hitting me like a steamroller with the sheer force of the normality of it. It was a former adjoining office, no doubt, but so very cozy and pleasant now, after it had been remodeled into a bedroom, with a narrow brass bed by the wall, neatly made; a round table in the middle, framed by two chairs, a desk facing the other wall, with a lamp and a typewriter on it, and flowers everywhere. They were artificial, the Soviet type, waxy and somewhat discolored by the sun yet at that moment I thought I'd never seen anything quite so beautiful. Flowers… I thought I'd forgotten what they looked like. Of all the places, to find them here, to be reminded that even out of the blood-soaked ground the multicolored cloud of flowers will blossom once the spring comes again, for it was the way of nature, to conceive life out of death itself.

The room swam before my eyes. I wiped the tears but they kept flowing, round, like pearls from a torn necklace. I ripped both sweaters off and two undershirts under them, just to occupy my trembling hands with something. The bread was breaking in my hands, it was so fresh. I began sobbing. I suddenly felt infinitely close to Maria Baumann, *an almost doctor,* in our common grief. I didn't belong here either. None of us did. It was all one big mistake, a miscarriage of humanity – that much she was right about.

"Ilse?" A tentative knock on the door. "Are you all right there?"

I took a deep breath, but it was all too much for me. I wept harder. *I have bread in my bra, and I'll get beaten or shot if they find it. And you have flowers in your room. How is it fair?*

"I'm fine," I finally gathered myself into a semblance of a human being who could at least talk. "It was a difficult day. A few days."

"A few months?" He supplied from the other side of the door.

"Yes. A few months. They killed my mother in a gas van. I didn't know what those vans were when they just herded them there… The *Ostjuden* told me later. I wished they hadn't. At least I had hope." The words poured out of me in a ceaseless torrent, a savaged artery spurting blood right out of the bleeding heart. "My father died on the train. I traveled with his dead body for several hours. His head was still warm when they threw him out in the snow, along with the others. Not even a coffin. Not even a grave for us to visit. What am I saying though? Who's going to visit him? They'll off us all during the next pogrom and throw us into something they'll name Pit Number Two on their official papers. All of us will perish. You'll see how fast they see to it."

From the other side, silence. I wondered if he was there at all or had gone to fetch a Gestapo agent to arrest me. I felt better now, empty. Didn't *Mutti* always say that a good cry heals all? My head felt lighter, that's for sure but perhaps that was due to the hunger. I didn't touch any bread apart from the crumbs I stole from Schultz's hand.

I began putting my clothes back in order.

"You don't have to go back to the ghetto tonight."

So, he was still there after all, also sitting on the floor, separated from me by a thin lacquered door. I pressed my head against it.

"You can stay here; I'll write a paper for you tomorrow. I'll make something up for them. Too much paperwork, needed a typist – that sort of stuff. They'll eat it up, as long as it has an official stamp."

I rose to my feet and pulled the door open. He stood up swiftly as well, adjusting his uniform. "Don't look at me like that. I only think of your well-being. I want you to have a proper night's rest, not among twenty other people but… You'll sleep in my bed, and I'll sleep in my office, on the sofa. You can even lock the door if you like; I'll give you the key."

I looked at him for a very long time, then smiled and gently shook my head. "It's very kind of you but I can't. I have to feed my sisters."

"Of course." He looked down.

I suddenly wished to reach out and press his hand but took the coward's way out and settled on brushing his sleeve with my fingers in a gesture of gratitude before quickly pulling away. I wasn't afraid of him any longer and neither did I resent him solely for wearing that hateful uniform. For the first time, I saw a man behind it; a man, who was genuinely trying to help and had not the faintest idea how. That tiny sliver of humanity, the madly exhilarating feeling of being treated like a person and not something worthless and temporary that would soon be disposed of, filled my soul better than any bread would fill my stomach. "I'm really grateful for the bread and sardines and your generous offer. I just—"

"It's all right; I really do understand. I have three sisters too. I would do anything for them."

This time, it was him who picked my hand and brought it to his lips to plant a gentle kiss on my knuckles. This time, I didn't pull it away as I did in front of the brigade. He still released it almost at once and stepped away to keep a respectful distance as I passed him on my way out.

"My offer will always stand," he said by means of goodbye.

I thanked him quietly and slipped out of the room. In the hallway, I slowly brought my fingers to my mouth, where he kissed them. My face was burning as though lit from the inside by some savage, invisible fire.

Liza looked me over with suspicion as we lined up to be marched back to the ghetto. "What is it with you? You're practically glowing."

"It's the frost," I mumbled in self-defense.

As the SS were busy counting us, I suddenly felt a mad longing to turn around and look at the window from which I could see the entire square not five minutes ago. I started, when I caught sight of Schultz standing at the window. I couldn't make out his face but I did see his hand clear enough when he lifted it in a friendly salute and waved at me. Quickly ensuring that the SS escort was looking the other way, I waved him back.

Liza was smiles all over her wry face when I turned back.

"What?" I grumbled.

"Nothing. The frost."

I gave her a dig in the ribs. She was laughing soundlessly.

Chapter 10

"Happy Birthday, Lore."

I kissed both of my little sister's cheeks – not so little anymore, a whole thirteen-years-of-age – and presented her with a package, wrapped in a local newspaper. She tore into the paper, gasped in excitement but then paled at once, looking at me sternly, almost with reproach.

"A dress! And a fancy one on top of it! Where did you get that, Ilse?"

"I didn't steal it if that's what you mean." I evaded a direct answer, with a hint of a grin.

"I wouldn't think you did. I mean, how much did you pay for it?" She smoothed the woolen, plaited skirt of it over her knees; brushed the embroidered collar and cuffs with her thin, delicate fingers, her expression almost painful. "How many days did you not eat to save up enough ration coupons for it?"

"Don't worry your pretty little head about it." I passed my hand over her blonde braids, crowning her head. "I ate, I promise."

She only sighed, as *Mutti* used to when she'd catch me at some mischief, with loving resignation. How much she resembled her, my little Lore. And how savvy she'd become for her age! Not every girl of twelve would think to supply a confident "Fifteen" in response to an SS man's, "How old?"

She knew better to work in a sewing workshop inside the ghetto rather than loiter in the streets together with the rest of the children; it saved her life, too, during the massacre of March 2nd. A savvy girl, indeed.

"Lore," I began in a soft voice. We were alone in our corner, sitting on the narrow bed on which we slept all together, all feet and arms in each other's faces – still, a better alternative to the floor. Lily was busy preparing something special for the birthday girl in the small communal kitchen along with the other women. Good; no need for her to hear this conversation. She'd just start panicking again and ruin it all. "I got this dress with a purpose. Rivka said she can get you out of the ghetto. They do it and with young girls in particular, when there's little chance to send them to partisans, so they came up with this brilliant idea. With your looks, you'll easily pass for a Gentile—"

"I don't speak Russian, or Byelorussian, for that matter," she interrupted me at once. "I'll never last there, in Minsk."

"We took that into account, don't worry. We'll place you together with an ethnic German family; they work with the underground as well and already agreed to it. They all speak German among themselves. The accent is different but you'll just have to pick it up, practice a lot and try and speak like them. Back home, you used to mock Berliners so well; do you remember? I think you won't have any trouble with picking up the ethnic Germans' speech manner. As for your workshop, they'll take care of it as well. The usual routine; you fell ill, you died of typhus. Dr. Kulik will sign your death certificate. The Housing Department will remove your name from the list. They've done it many times before; the system works, fear not. They won't punish us because of you."

Lore considered for a very long time. "That's why the dress?"

"Yes. I'll get you good shoes, too, in a couple of days. Maybe stockings, if Rivka's connection comes through."

Lore only smiled and covered my hand with hers. "No need to bother, Ilse. I won't go."

I had just begun protesting but to all of my protests she just sat there and looked at me with those infinitely blue *Mutti's* eyes and smiled serenely until I finally realized that she wouldn't be persuaded or frightened or threatened into escaping.

"I'm not leaving you two here," she said; a young woman, not a child any longer. "We're all getting out of here, or we're all dying here. I don't see how I'd be able to live with myself if I survive and you two perish. No, Ilse, that just won't do. I'm sure you feel the same. Otherwise, you wouldn't have bought this dress."

That night, I went to tell Rivka not to worry about the documents for Lore and make them out for some small child instead, the one who couldn't talk yet. The orphanage was overflowing with them; certainly, she'd find a proper candidate with ease.

Liza met me at our usual "exit" and helped me pin their Soviet, empty yellow star to cover my German, with the word *"Jude"* in the middle, with it. Enough for patrols if they happen to cross our path.

"Let's hurry." She put her arm through the crook of mine, leading me hastily away from the Sonderghetto's side. "It looks like it's going to rain. You don't want to get caught in that nasty business; not in March, you don't."

"Lore's not going," I informed her, missing a step in the dark.

"Watch it." She pulled me closer. "Don't ruin your boots. If that sole comes off, you've had it. I don't know about Germany but here in Byelorussia, the snow lies throughout the entirety of April at times. I doubt Schultz has a suitable pair of boots for you."

I left her friendly jest without comment. I suddenly couldn't joke about him with the same ironic ease as before. It wasn't Rivka who helped me get that dress; it was his doing, wherever he got it from and what tales he told the maker, I didn't even ask him; I wouldn't dare do something of that sort. I merely mentioned that Lore's birthday was coming up and thanked him once again for the sardines he kept supplying us with daily and which we could trade for some flour and margarine and make a first-rate cake for her, thanks to his generosity. His eyes lit up; he was now asking me if she wore the same size as I did. I thought it odd but nodded my affirmation.

Most of us wore the same size now – size 42, half-starved, half-worked to death. A week later, he presented me with this plaid masterpiece, lace, and good quality wool and the hem with some extra material, since Lore was still growing. I lost all faculty of speech. Schultz only smiled a bit embarrassingly. *He knew all about what teenage girls liked for presents,* he explained; *he grew up with three of them.*

After that day, he had forever ceased to be a joking matter, *a sentimentalist.* He had become something entirely different but what precisely, that I was still yet to understand.

"Did you hear what I said about Lore?"

"Yes, I did. I thought she wouldn't go but didn't want to discourage you."

"Why did you think she wouldn't go?"

"Would you go?"

I didn't answer anything for a while. White clouds of vapor from our mouths shimmered against the yellow sickle of the moon. We crossed Komsomolskaya Street and strode resolutely towards Rivka's quarters. "No. I wouldn't go anywhere without them both."

"Rivka didn't go either. She could have run together with her father when the whole affair had just broken out and there was a chance to escape the city. But she refused to leave her little Yasha and mother."

"Yes, I know. She told me."

"She trusts you."

"I hope so."

"I trust you too. Even though you sound mighty like the SS when you start yelling at the brigade to move faster."

I nudged her with my elbow in mock offense. She laughed, her white teeth gleaming in the darkness.

Suddenly, as soon as we turned the familiar corner, the flood of light from the powerful flashlight – only the SS and the Gestapo had those – hit us in the face. Instantly blinded, I shielded my face with my hand, which was unceremoniously yanked down by someone with a submachine gun. Its muzzle was now prodding my stomach even through layers of a coat and two sweaters underneath. The flashlight lowered to my chest, in which my heart was beating itself with brutal force against my ribcage.

"You two live here? Which floor? Apartment number?"

I opened my mouth and slowly closed it again, feverishly trying to conjure up some Yiddish words. Nothing came to my mind with the best will in the world.

"We're further along the street, *Herr Offizier*." Thankfully, Liza was already shoving her papers under the light of his electric torch, jabbing her finger at the house number. "That house over there on the corner is ours. It's only six-thirty, *Herr Offizier;* we didn't break the curfew, did we?"

"Slow down with your jawing! I don't understand your gibberish!"

They understood everything all right, just never missed a chance to mock the locals' language. Liza diligently repeated everything as slowly as possible.

Someone pulled the front door open and the street was once again flooded in the light coming from the staircase. I instinctively shied away from two men in civilian clothes, who carried a body out, then – a second one, a child's lifeless form. I recognized Yasha's face. After that, Rivka's turn came. Next to me, Liza clasped my wrist; her hand was trembling as well. My flesh crept with the dreadful realization that had we come twenty minutes earlier, our bodies would be lying here in the snow as well, riddled with bullets.

They appeared to have forgotten all about us as they counted bodies laid out in the snow next to each other – nine overall. I didn't see Boris among them. Soon enough, we learned the reason for it.

"Do you know this man?" The same hand, which shone a torchlight in our faces, now held a picture to our eyes. Familiar, brooding features came into focus. It was him all right, Boris Makarsky, an unofficial leader of the Minsk ghetto underground.

I took enough time to look at it and then shook my head slowly, in obvious disappointment. Liza nodded hers though, with enthusiasm.

"He's from the *Judenrat*. I've seen him there a few times. Don't know the name though."

"Have you seen him around here? While you were walking here?"

"No, it was quiet, *Herr Offizier*. We didn't see anyone. It's almost curfew; everyone's at home by now…"

"As you should be."

"Allow us to go?"

"Yes, get lost."

In front of Liza's apartment's door, we held each other by the forearms, trembling like two rabbits surrounded by bloodhounds. A ceaseless torrent of frantic whispers followed; we didn't hear each other, muttered something incoherently until someone opened the door downstairs and she quickly pulled me inside her apartment and shut the door after herself.

It took us a while to calm down. It took even longer to process it all; dead Rivka, her mother, her son, Styopka-Kaznachey, Eli, Zyama, Abram… we couldn't make out who else was among them.

"Not Boris, though."

"No. Must have escaped. Ilse, stay with us tonight. You can't possibly risk going back."

I shook my head. I had to risk it. "What if the midnight check happens and I'm not there?"

We both knew all too well what it would mean for the rest, not just my sisters.

"I'll walk you back then. In a couple of hours. Even the Gestapo must go to sleep."

When, three hours later, she lifted the barbed wire at the place of my "exit," I caught her whisper, barely audible in the wind. "Who do you think betrayed us, Ilse?"

I looked at her, suddenly frozen in between two sides. "You don't think it was me, do you?"

Her remark about the SS was reverberating through my memory like some demented echo. I was the only outsider in their underground group. I was the only one who had enough sardines to spare; the German Jew and therefore, half-enemy, guilty by association.

"No," she answered at last. "I don't think you would risk it."

I scowled. She shrugged with a small smile. "You know what they do to the traitors. War-time justice and all. If you were alone, it would have been an entirely different matter. You wouldn't risk them going after your sisters though. Don't worry, I'll tell them that when Boris asks me about you. I know he will. Don't fret. He'll find the perpetrator eventually. And then, who knows? Maybe there wasn't any perpetrator in the first place."

"What do you mean by that?"

She gave a shrug. "I mean, it could have been one of Styopka's people who the Germans caught in the forest. They roughed him up, then promised to spare his life if he told them who brought him to the forest. He'd tell them all about Styopka and Rivka and Boris and what not, as long as they weren't kicking him about with steel-lined boots any longer. We all like to think that we're brave when it comes to such matters, but… have you ever been beaten? Really beaten?"

I shook my head slowly. A couple of whacks on the back didn't count as beating in this place. She meant the Gestapo and their beatings didn't come close to the half-hearted slaps the SS awarded us here from time to time.

"Neither have I. And to be completely honest with you, I don't know if I'd keep quiet."

"You would."

"I wish I had your conviction."

"You would," I repeated. "You have the requirements for it. You were raised to believe in a greater cause, in the sacrifice of one person for the sake of the others. When the time comes, you'll see for yourself what I mean."

She only smiled at me pensively.

*

Superintendent Richter stalked along the column, observing us from under the rim of his cap's visor. April was approaching and the sun stood high, casting a shadow on his face. I don't think anyone had ever seen him without that cap and therefore we only knew what the lower part of his face looked like; pale cheeks, sharp jawline, thin lips, either pinched tightly or shouting orders for yet another massacre. It could have been a massacre, today. A fine way to start a Sunday morning, in the SS men's eyes that is.

He stopped at last; lifted his gloved hand, calling for silence. Not that it wasn't silent before. He merely wished us to stop breathing, no less; some of us did hold their breaths, against their own will.

Superintendent began to speak.

"You must be wondering why I've gathered all of you here today, both German Jews and the *Ostjuden*." A long, meaningful pause. Except for the birds, screaming wildly overhead, the silence was perfect. We were awaiting our verdict. "The first announcement I'd like to make is the following; there will be no more pogroms, so you have nothing to fear. Except for individual types of *Aktionen*, during which we'll be weeding out criminal elements from your midst, the SS won't conduct any other kinds of operations."

Someone from the *Ordnungsdienst*, the ghetto police, began clapping enthusiastically – a habit from Soviet meetings, no doubt – but quickly ceased and pulled his head as far into his shoulders as he could. An SS man shifted a submachine gun on his shoulder and cast an inquisitive glance in his superior's direction. Superintendent Richter waved him off with languid grace. He was feeling generous with us today.

"As I said, there will be no more pogroms. However, in return, I expect something from you and that something is cooperation. You will cooperate not only with the new members of the *Judenrat,* yes, the ones appointed to the executed traitors' positions but you will also cooperate with the Gestapo agents in their search for the criminal elements, as well as your local ghetto police. We have beheaded your underground; soon, we'll finish off the lowest ranks. It would be in your interest to aid us in this task. Whoever makes an anonymous report and helps us uncover the remaining criminal elements, will be generously rewarded."

With a bullet in the head, I mentally finished for Richter. He was wrong on one account; they didn't "behead" anything. Yes, they executed a few members, a liaison with the Russian side, her son and elderly mother, but they still had neither Boris nor even Efim, the underground printer and they knew it. Yesterday, they issued an ultimatum that the residents of the ghetto must turn at least Boris in; otherwise, they'd execute the entire *Judenrat* (with the exception of their newly appointed people, of course). People hesitated, exchanged hushed remarks, but Boris was still missing, carefully concealed somewhere under the Gestapo's very noses.

"And do yourselves a favor and forget thinking about running off to your forest friends." Richter meant partisans, no doubt. His mouth twitched in disgust as he spat out the last two words. "All that agitprop from your so-called leaders is nothing but empty promises. They tell you what suits them. I'll tell you the truth, no one waits for you on the other side. No one wants you there. Are you aware of all the instances where your praised partisans scorned and laughed at your miserable lot that showed up in the forest? If they made it that far, that is. Sometimes, your Military Counsel, which used to work in the city – yes, *used to* as we have eliminated nearly all of them in the course of the past two weeks – used to purposely send your people in a false direction so that they'd fall into our hands, instead of making it safely to the forest. That much your underground leaders didn't tell you, I bet."

He snapped his fingers, and a disheveled man was instantly produced in front of us, framed by two SS men towering over him. He stood, stooped and trembling, twisting his cap in his hand. Faint yellowish bruises were still visible on his face, but apart from that, he appeared to be unharmed.

"Tell them what the people from the Military Counsel told you," Richter commanded.

The man cleared his throat, threw an anxious gaze at the crowd in front of him. "They told me that the partisans didn't want us among them. They said, Jews make miserable and cowardly fighters and are only a liability in a partisan war. They said they'd rather work on 'liberating' their own Red Army POWs from the camps for them to join the ranks than bother with the Jews."

The hard mouth curled upward in satisfaction. Richter seemed pleased with what he'd heard. "Well? Now that one of your own kind has told you the truth, do you finally believe it? We are not your enemy. We provide you with work, food, and shelter. Outside, you'll die. Cooperate with us and you'll live. You may join your people now." He motioned to the man with the cap. "So that next time anyone wants to open their mouth and accuse the SS of their violent behavior, you'll remind them how it was the SS that granted you your life, not the partisans and certainly not the communists."

Richter turned sharply on his heel. The music began blasting at once, "Blue Danube", almost offensive in its unsuitable sentimentality. The SS stayed and made sure we listened to it to the end.

Chapter 11

April 1942

"Do you think the partisans really don't wish to accept us?"

I had this conversation a day ago, with Liza. But Liza was Jewish, just like me. I wanted to ask for a German's opinion.

Schultz smeared a fat layer of butter on top of the bread and added an even fatter one of jam to it. It was dripping onto the plate as I accepted it into my hands. Our breakfasts had become a usual morning routine by now and he had all but persuaded me and quite chivalrously at that, that I was doing him a huge favor – *oh no, it was not charity at all; he really did detest eating alone.*

"No. I think the SS want you to stay put where you are, that's all," he replied calmly.

"Because they still need us as workers?"

"That and also because once a ghetto Jew escapes into the forest, he becomes a partisan. And they fear those worse than the plague."

"Do you think Superintendent Richter will go through with his threat concerning the *Judenrat?* Will he really shoot them all and all because of Boris?"

"They have just executed over five thousand people. What do you think?"

"What would you do if you knew where Boris was? Would you come forward? Just to save the others' lives?"

Schultz looked at me. "Do you know where Boris is hiding?"

I shook my head. A few weeks ago, I wouldn't even contemplate discussing anything of this sort with someone wearing a uniform. With Schultz, everything was somehow different. I trusted him, despite my better judgment but I did. It was my profound conviction that he wouldn't betray me even if I said that I knew where Boris was.

"Does Liza?" he asked again.

I said nothing. I didn't know myself. I thought that she did. As the time of the ultimatum was running out, she began to look more and more anguished, muttered something aloud about the sacrifice and posed questions as to what was more important, a life of an individual or the masses, quoted Marx and Lenin, lost track of her thoughts and ended up looking at me helplessly. I only stared blankly at her much like Schultz was staring at me now. He, too, didn't seem to have an answer to this question.

"I don't know, Ilse. That Boris must be very important for the others if Richter wants him so."

"He's the head of the entire underground. He's connected with the Minsk Military Counsel as well."

"They arrested most of the Counsel."

"Yes, I know," I sighed. "Shall I tell Liza to report Boris then? To save the others from execution, at least?"

Schultz was quiet for some time. He picked up a spoon and began lining up jam-covered raspberries across his plate. "I don't think I'm in a position to advise you of anything, Ilse. I'm not the one who will suffer if some Luftwaffe pencil-pusher makes a mistake giving the wrong advice to his brigadier." He offered me a soft smile. "I only know what Boris Makarsky means to *us*. I don't know how important he is to *you*."

"He is." I lifted my face to his. "He gives us hope."

"Don't report him then. Hope is perhaps the most important thing for you now."

I pondered his words, chewing slowly, then washed down the remnants of the sandwich with army-issued ersatz coffee. It tasted divine. I even closed my eyes, drinking in the aroma together with the hot caramel-colored liquid itself; he even had the cream for it.

When I opened my eyes again, Schultz was regarding me with the oddest expression on his face.

We looked at each other for a long time without speaking. A radio was playing softly in the background. Zarah Leander was singing about love. I suddenly recalled an anecdote that women used to discuss with such delight at the parachute factory in Frankfurt. Reportedly, Minister of Propaganda Dr. Goebbels once asked the Swedish actress if Zarah was a Jewish name, to which she wittily replied, *And what about Josef?* Dr. Josef Goebbels chuckled at the jest and signed her up with the UFA, a major German film company. She became an instant success.

I smiled dreamily at the memory. I was free then. Free to walk the streets and sneak inside the cinemas even. Free...

"What is it?" Schultz mirrored my grin.

He wanted to hear the story that made me smile. He wished to be a part of my world but that part was long gone and dead and there was nothing to tell any longer.

"Why do you want to kill us all?" I asked him instead.

He pulled back slowly, blinking at me in astonishment. "Why would you say that? I don't want to kill anyone."

I outstretched my hand. My index finger stopped within centimeters from his Party pin. I'd never touch it. Even the mere thought of it was repulsive. "This... *thing;* it says that you do."

"It's just a harmless pin."

"Yes, it is. It may be harmless on its own but every single person, who took every tiny bit of our rights, wore one. The new headmaster at my school, who made me sit in the back; SA troopers who trashed Papa's grocery in 1938; Gestapo agents, who came to our apartment and gave Papa an order for our resettlement; the office clerk who gave me the blank in which I had to sign that my German nationality lapses and I become a stateless person." I shrugged. "It takes a village to kill a Jew," I finished, purposely distorting the saying.

I half-expected for him to order me out and never to come back. To start protesting and defending his position perhaps, explain that *"certain things that a young girl like myself didn't understand,"* talk politics and what not. Instead, Schultz reached for the pin and slowly undid it, pulled it out of the cloth leaving a narrow hole in its place and lowered it onto the table.

"Better?"

When I didn't reply anything – I really didn't know what to say – he pulled the top-drawer open, swiped the pin into it and closed it again.

"Are you planning on taking it off and hiding it every time I come here?" I felt a ghost of a grin growing on my face again.

"No. I plan never to wear it again. It should make things easier, don't you think?"

"Won't you get in trouble?"

"I'd rather risk the wrath of my superiors than yours."

"I'm not in a position to threaten you with my wrath, as you call it."

"Perhaps not openly. But sometimes you give me one of those hateful looks, and I wish for the ground to open up and swallow me. You have very expressive eyes, you know."

"I don't hate you."

"Sometimes you do."

"It's the uniform that I hate, not you."

He was suddenly unbuttoning his jacket. Under my uncomprehending gaze, he promptly removed it, folded it inside out to hide the insignia and flattened it over his lap.

"There. Ordinary civilian shirt. Happy?"

"Yes."

"Thank God. I thought you'd make me strip bare, for a moment there."

I almost succeeded in hiding a smile. He almost succeeded at hiding his too… almost.

"I wasn't always a soldier, you know."

"No?"

"Believe it or not."

"What were you?"

"A customs officer in Dresden."

I lifted my brows. He shook his head. "Yes, I know. Sounds horribly boring. I'm a bureaucrat through and through, I'm afraid. First that, now – this. It's all paperwork that I do. I didn't make a good combat pilot, to be honest."

"Yes, I somehow concluded that from when you told me that you had to bail out quite a few times over Holland."

Instead of taking offense, he beamed at me, positively delighted. "You remembered that!"

"I remember everything you told me."

After I spoke those words, he grew serious for some reason. After a few moments of hesitation, he reached across the table and tentatively connected his fingertips with mine. I didn't pull away, just sat without movement for some time, deciding what to do. At last, I curled my fingers around his.

"See? It was the uniform all along," I tried to joke.

He was suddenly kissing my hand again, like the last time, only now he turned it over and kissed the palm as well, the wrist. With my heart pounding, I was instantly on my feet. He stepped closer and took my face in his hands.

"Stop it; you're mad," I whispered, or maybe just thought so to myself.

He pulled me against him and I made a half-hearted effort to push him away but then let him kiss me after all, even raising my face toward him, offering him my lips, my burning cheeks, the neck. Waves of harsh, intoxicating pleasure slowly radiated from my chest and spread down the spine, to the small of my back where one of his hands now rested, burning me with its heat even through all the layers of clothing. It was madness, obviously, and for which people got shot – on both sides. Yet, my arm coiled around his neck of its own accord and for a second, he made me forget what we were to each other. My first kiss, with a soldier…

I didn't hear the door open; only heard a voice which startled me back into reality.

"Schultz, where's that report that you promised me for—" The newcomer, who'd burst into the room without knocking, did a double-take. His brows climbed higher and higher as he gradually took in the table set for two, Schultz's jacket on the floor, and Schultz himself in a half-undressed state, his arms still circling the waist of one of the girls from his brigade. "Pardon. I didn't realize you had company, at this hour…"

"Have they not taught you how to knock, you miserable numbskull?" Schultz was suddenly furious.

Before the newcomer would remember himself, I swiftly grabbed my coat from the rack and slid past him into the hallway. I ran down the stairs as though the entire German army was chasing me; perhaps, it was worse than that. Who knew who in the blue hell that officer was? I didn't take my time to make out the insignia on his uniform.

"Ilse! Ilse Stein!" It was his voice and his steps behind me, not Schultz's. *Gott, please don't let him be the SS!*

I ran faster, at one point nearly taking some unsuspecting officer off his feet.

"Ilse! Wait up! Schultz said you forgot the ration cards!"

I finally stopped, almost at the doors, gasping for air.

The officer in a blue uniform – *Luftwaffe, praise God!* – seemed to be also catching his breath as he waved a stack of cards in his hand. He was laughing, I noted, with immense relief.

"Blast it, can you run!"

"A habit," I muttered under my breath.

He handed me the cards but when I tried to take them from him, he held them tighter, refusing to release them.

"Now I see what all the fuss was about. *'Ilse this, Ilse that. An extraordinary girl, Ilse. Ach, Otto, if you'd only seen her!'*"

"I don't understand what you're talking about."

We both were still holding onto the ration cards. Otto, which as I presumed was his name, was a handsome young man in his early thirties with curly chestnut hair which was smoothed down with pomade to the point where it was just wavy, mischievous hazel eyes and wide, expressive eyebrows. On his chest, quite a few awards gleamed; I noticed that and the absence of the Party pin.

"Don't worry, I won't tell," he said at last and let go of the stack. I pulled it to my chest as though afraid that he'd take it away. "He's mad about you, you know."

He clicked his heels, bowed his head slightly and headed back towards the staircase.

We both must be mad, I thought to myself as I watched him go *and such madness never ended well.*

*

The ultimatum day. The silence of the columns, marching into the ghetto from their respective working places, was tangible, intense. Guarded looks were exchanged among some, the ones who wondered if the SS would go through with the threat; if they should say something. Next to me, Liza walked. In her eyes, with a cold, faraway look in them, I read the same question. She, too, knew where Boris was. She, too, wondered if one life was worth several others.

An *Einsatzkommando* squad met us near the *Judenrat,* rubber truncheons tapping their legs in anticipation. Superintendent Richter strolling along the line of the *Judenrat* members; checked his watch theatrically.

"Five forty-five. Time's almost up," he announced casually, to no one in particular.

Condemned men – he'd even gone through the pain of dragging ordinary clerks out – stood looking at their feet, positively refusing to make any eye contact with the crowd. To my right, Liza fidgeted, her anguished gaze riveted on the martyrs living out the last fifteen minutes of their lives. The raven flew low overhead, croaking his death song before setting off in the cemetery's direction. His kin would have plenty to feast on tonight. I knew that the SS would leave the corpses lying in the snow until the morning.

"No one knows where Boris Makarsky is," Superintendent Richter stated, staring derisively into our faces. Brass-colored sunset painted his face with a rusty shade. "Isn't it amazing? Even his fellow *Judenrat* members don't." In a harsh move, he turned on his heel to face them. "Do you really wish to die for that communist rat?"

They didn't deem him a single look. Their proud, noble faces said it all.

"*Ach*. That's correct. I entirely forgot that you're all communist rats. Fucking musketeers; only instead of a King's lily, a yellow patch on your capes. *One for all and all for one,* blast you all, you Bolshevik numbskulls!" He bared his teeth in a snarl as he spat out the words.

"Why are you so mad, Herr Superintendent?" It was Meir Levin, former Elder Mushkin's right hand. His head cocked mockingly, hands in pockets, he had reconciled with imminent death it appeared and had decided to spit in its face before he went down with a fanfare. "Because your own praised *Kameradened* isn't as tight as we are, *the Bolshevik rats?* Is that why you never announced the reason for Mushkin's execution? Because he was hiding your own SS officer, who couldn't stand looking at your face another day and asked a Jew – a Jew! – for help to join the partisans. How rotten your ranks must be, how rusted the entire system, from inside—"

The gunshot silenced him at last, but, with immense satisfaction, we all saw that Richter's hand, with the gun still smoking in it, was trembling slightly. He whipped around, unnerved, but mad with fury, aiming his gun at our workers' columns this time.

"What is it?! A revolt; is that what you want?!" We tensed instantly, ready to drop down to the ground at a moment's notice. "I'll let you have a revolt you'll remember, you filthy scum!"

He began walking towards us, emptying his gun into the thick crowd. A few screams, women's voices, short; they died right away. We fell down but he walked among us now, replacing the magazine with a fresh one, shooting again at random heads. Richter's dog, held by one of the SS men, was choking itself as it strained on its leash, smelling blood. My face in the snow, I wondered if he would order to release it on us. It was one of his favorite pastimes, after all, strolling through the ghetto on a fine spring day and letting his Alsatian tear small children apart, who didn't run fast enough.

He was behind us now. I looked up at Liza but she had her eyes fixed firmly on the man in a dark coat, tall and distinguished, standing next to his fallen comrade Levin's body. She lifted her head higher, as though imploring him with her eyes. He was looking at her too; saw her tear-stained, strained face and shook his head ever so slightly. *Don't even consider it, Liza. Boris must live, for with him, our cause will live. I'm only a cog. I'm replaceable. He isn't.*

She understood it all too well and dropped her head into the dirty melting snow. I only saw her shoulders shaking with sound-less sobs.

A delegation suddenly emerged, hands promptly drawn up, all three gasping for air.

"He's dead! Herr Superintendent, Makarsky's dead!" Their leader, his head uncovered and close-shaven, maneuvered his way through the sea of the bodies – most still alive – and bowed deeply, offering blood-smeared papers to the uniformed, savage God. "We were burying the bodies left over from the latest *Aktion,* and recovered this passport from one of them."

Richter hesitated, turned the passport in his gloved hand this way and that.

"And you're certain it was him?" He looked at the man with suspicion.

The latter nearly rolled his eyes with enthusiasm before breaking into frantic nodding. "On my mother's grave, it was him, Herr Superintendent. The rats got to his face and hands overnight, but he's still identifiable. We left him unburied, in case you want to make sure of it yourself but I'd cover your face with something if I were you. It appears, he was sick with typhoid when he got shot. His chest was all covered with—"

"Go bury him then!" Richter threw the passport back at the man with a mortified look of utter disgust. He dug into his pocket, extracted a handkerchief and thoroughly wiped his gloved hands. It could have been an illusion, a shadow cast by a setting sun but I could swear that the fleeting outline of a coy smile passed over the old man's face. "Or, better off, burn him! Burn all typhus cases from now on! Filthy scum…" Richter muttered under his breath walking away.

One of his soldiers stepped forward, saluted, inquired on account of the *Judenrat* members.

"Let them all go to the devil for all I care!" Richter barked in response.

Next to me, beaming, Liza was looking at the equally grinning young man. He winked at her after the SS waved them all off.

"A fine friend you are," I grumbled in mock reproach as we stood up, dusting off our clothes from the snow. "Teased me about Schultz till you were blue in the face yet about your own dear friend you kept quiet as though he was a state secret."

"You're picking up more and more Soviet expressions, I see," she retorted in place of an actual answer.

"Is it bad?"

"Good. It'll help you once you get to the partisans."

"You think we'll get to the partisans one day?"

"Now, we will. *He's* our connection to them. *He'll* get us out."

She didn't have to pronounce Boris's name. Everything was understood without words among us.

"I almost told," she whispered in horror.

"But you didn't."

"No. They were hiding him in the hospital. Now that they aren't looking for him any longer, he'll be able to leave."

Soon, we will follow, his eyes said.

Chapter 12

April 1942

The air was thick with thaw that morning – the first warm day of spring. Beads of water dropped from the trees – tears of the land mourning another year of enslavement. With the melting, familiar frames came into view, still in their khaki-brown uniforms, still stiff with ice, still embedded into the dirty whiteness, out of which the digging brigades were working to pull them out. We marched past the frozen corpses, past the fallen statue of Lenin – now, not only his outstretched arm but half of his torso crept into view, much like the dead Red Army soldiers who died in his name and now lay in the eerily same direction in which their leader was pointing. The leader of the dead, also dead and unburied.

At night, wrapped in layers and layers of clothing and blankets – whatever was possible to procure on the black market – women slept soundly. That morning, however, with the first whiff of spring, they marched with faces lined with worry, cursing the spring that somehow stole past them and caught them unawares.

"Look at them, Fritzes," Sima, the only other Soviet woman from my brigade besides Liza, motioned her bundled head in the direction of the SS who supervised the corpse-carriers' work. Even though that morning 'supervised' would be quite too strong of a word to describe what precisely they were doing. Much like schoolchildren on a spring break, they were busy throwing snow-balls at each other, using partially-unearthed corpses as barricades. Whenever a snowball missed its gray-clad aim and hit one of the Jews from the digging brigade instead, they would nearly choke

with laughter and order him to drop dead for *he was now killed*.
"They're in a good mood. Faces out in the sun, grinning like cats."

"It's a fine day." I also removed my shawl from my mouth to
take in some fresh air, alive with melting snow. "Let them enjoy
themselves. The more they enjoy themselves, the better for us."

"For you, maybe. You don't depend on the weather. Your Fritz
will find you something to do regardless of the time of the year."
A few women snickered but most began grumbling their support
for *their Fritz – didn't he just double our rations, you miserable cow?
And you're still ungrateful?* Sima wasn't impressed. "Rations? For
how much longer? Do you, a bunch of blind geese, think of the
future at all? What of us? What will happen to us once it's warm
and they don't need our services anymore? To the pit with us all?"

Silence fell over the column. A few inquisitive gazes darted in
my direction. To be honest, Sima was right, at least in part. I hadn't
quite thought of the future. The truth was, pogroms, searches, and
random shootings happened so often that I didn't quite count on
making it to summer and when one awaits death daily, one doesn't
acquire the habit of worrying about the future.

"They will need us again in October," I began, not too convincingly.

Sima sensed it and snorted with contempt. "In October, she
says. In October, they'll bring more of you Hamburgs here. By
October, all of us will be dead."

I didn't argue because there was a big chance that she was, in
fact, right.

"I'll talk to Leutnant Schultz today," I promised, in a conciliatory
tone. "He'll figure something out."

Inside the Government Building, bones didn't ache any longer
from the sudden change of temperatures. By the time I reached
the seventh floor, I had shed my coat and shawl. The night brigade
was truly giving it their all; perhaps, also sensing the spring, and
with it – changes.

Schultz sat at his desk staring at a paper uncomprehendingly.

"An order just came through," he said instead of a greeting. "A furlough."

My heart suddenly dropped. My hands turned numb and cold, despite the coziness of the room which was even warmer than the corridor.

"Congratulations, Herr Leutnant." The words came out weak and strangled. "For how long, if I may ask?"

"Three weeks."

He was still perusing the paper as though trying to find a mistake that had crawled into the order and lodged itself between the lines. After a few moments of the most thorough inspection, his scowl grew deeper. Apparently, he didn't find any such mistakes.

"I'm supposed to be leaving in one week."

"Congratulations," I repeated again, a broken record. In spite of myself, I tried to muster a smile. "Furlough is always great news, is it not?"

"I haven't been home in a while…" he agreed, with a faraway look in his eyes. He didn't see me any longer. I wondered what it was, precisely, that he was seeing.

"Your family will be thrilled to see you."

I suddenly realized that I didn't know if he had any children.

His thumb touched the wedding ring without him realizing it, a soldier's instinctive gesture to remind himself that there was still a civilian life somewhere beyond the barbed wire and anti-tank trenches, someplace where people wore no uniforms and when the snow melted, the blades of grass fought their way toward the sun, not the stiff hands of dead soldiers.

"I will leave Leutnant Weizmann, the officer that you met before, in charge."

"Otto?"

"Yes, Otto. He's a grand fellow. We used to fly together until our command realized at last that, unlike him, I make a lousy pilot." He tried smiling at me but the grin came out almost pained, water-downed, and miserable. "You're early today. Marfa hasn't brought breakfast yet."

"It's all right. You don't have to feed me every day. I'll wait till lunch. They give us a lot of soup and even bread now. Thank you for saying a word for us in the kitchen, Herr Leutnant. All the girls are very grateful."

"Those ration cards are a joke. What they give you is hardly enough to feed a street mongrel, let alone a grown person. They won't agree to anything more though. I tried."

"I know you did. Thank you."

He was lost in his thoughts once again, his gaze riveted to the official paper, next to which more letters lay, still unopened. Near the neat stack of ration cards, his letter opener glistened in the sun, a miniature copy of a sword with a swastika on top. He didn't notice when I collected the cards or even when I silently closed the door after myself.

Foolish, foolish, foolish girl! I ran down the stairs – just to be out of there, the sooner the better. *What have you been imagining yourself all along? That he was any different from them all? That he would fall in love with you and save you from this hell? And Vati always thought you were the savviest of all his daughters. The shrewd one, the survivor. Shrewd, my foot. A lonely soldier, who hasn't seen his wife in months, kisses you once and you go thinking it's the romance of the century.*

I pushed the front door open and wiped my cheeks angrily. *Street mongrel is right; that's what you are to him. And he loves dogs too much not to feed even the filthiest mutt. And you're worse than a mutt; you're a Jew and an idiot. A sentimental idiot, on top of everything else.*

In the boiler room, my appearance was met with a few raised brows.

"Why are you so early today?" Stepan demanded, the only man in our brigade. He had a face lined with wrinkles, in which coal-dust soot always sat, yet always smiling and ready with a joke. "We usually don't see you till eight."

"Get used to it," I barked back. It came out much ruder than I intended. "Here's your card, Abramov. And less jawing on the work. Adelman!" I shouted the name written on the second card.

"Present, *Frau Kommandant*." It was Sima. She took the card out of my hands and crossed her arms over her chest. "You *are* early. I see the conversation went well with Schultz, didn't it?" Her raised brow added words she left out of her question. *I told you he didn't give a hoot about us. Or you, for that matter.*

I was suddenly incensed.

"Mind your business and keep your mouth shut, why don't you? All you do is gossip instead of working!"

She pulled herself up. "If your Schultz is in a bad mood, don't take it out on me."

"Shut your trap, or I'll report you right this instant!"

"To Schultz?" From Sima, a mocking sneer.

"To the SS." I made a step toward the exit.

The sneer vanished, just like Sima, within seconds. I still heard her, *Go on; you're just like them,* that she muttered under her breath on her way to her working station. Our exchange of pleasantries didn't go unnoticed by the rest of the workers in the boiler room. Their usual banter subdued and soon died out completely. I pretended not to notice their peering eyes as I distributed the rest of the ration cards before going out in the street and giving the remainder to the rest of the brigade. They all sensed that something was wrong, and knew all too well that their well-being presently depended on Schultz and if something happened between their benefactor and the mediator – me – it would be them who'd suffer in the end.

Stupid lot. My vexation didn't disappear in the warm April wind, only grew stronger and more bitter. *Only thinking about their stomachs and what will happen to them. I won't talk to him now, I*

*won't beg for our lives. The whole thing can go to the devil! Let the SS
come and shoot us all and get it over with.*

Away from everyone, I climbed into the furthest wagon with
lumber and began dragging the heaviest planks towards the edge.
Liza clambered inside after me, blocked my way, positively refused
to move even when I began shouting at her; only inched her way
to me among the wood and caught my hands in hers. Under her
kind, penetrating gaze – *what happened?* – I dropped my heavy
load and fell in a heap right next to it, hiding my face in my hands.

"Ilse, it's all right, you can tell me. Did he say something to
you? About summer? Did he say no?"

"I didn't get a chance to speak to him about summer." I couldn't
quite understand why I was sobbing like a moron. "He's leaving
in a week."

Her fingers clasped my shoulder tighter. "A transfer? Where to?"

"Not a transfer. A furlough. For three weeks."

Her grip relaxed. I looked at her in stupefaction – she was
laughing.

"And that's why all the crocodile's tears? He'll be back in no
time. You won't even notice."

"Like I care when he is back! He can stay in his Reich with his
wife if he wants to! No one will miss him here."

"That one could have fooled me but that's a topic for another
discussion. Is that why you're crying? Because of the wife?"

I sat upright and wormed myself out of her friendly embrace.
Tears suddenly dried on their own; wounded pride does that to
people.

"I'm crying because he made me believe that he cared for us
when in fact, he doesn't give a damn. If they shoot us all in his
absence, he'll just go into the ghetto and hire himself a new brigade,
in October most likely. In summer, he won't even need us, as Sima
correctly stated."

Liza looked at me in an odd way.

"*Doura ty*, Ilse," she finally said in Russian, shaking her head. I've heard the 'courtesy' far too many times, hurled at each other among the workers to not understand its meaning.

"Why am *I* an idiot now?"

"He's in love with you, that's why. And out of all people, you're the only one who positively refuses to see it. Even Sima noticed it long before you and she's as sensitive as a brick wall."

I had just opened my mouth to tell her that it was her words that sounded like so much utter rubbish but she silenced me in her usual no-nonsense way. "I know that you'll start arguing now, the pigheaded thing that you are but Schultz told me himself."

"He told you that?" I rolled my eyes and made a motion to get up. *Not in the mood for your tales, Liza.*

"Not in those exact words, perhaps but…"

I hesitated in between wood planks.

"Last Tuesday, when I went up to clean his room – he's never asked *you* to do it, have you noticed? – he asked me why the SS kill the Jews. I thought he was joking at first but then realized that he was very much serious. So, I said, I wouldn't know. You're the German here, you fight along with them, you should know better. He said that they, the Luftwaffe, aren't supposed to poke their noses into the business of the SS and that he didn't know anything about the ghettos or pogroms until he got transferred here. He told me, they tell them all in Germany that the Jews are all relocated here, to the east that is, to work on farmlands. He only saw what's really happening once he received this appointment."

I was listening.

"Then he asked what can be done to help you."

"Me?"

"Yes, just you. He knows he can't get all of us out so… I said, nothing. The best chance would be to get to the partisans but you don't speak Russian or Byelorussian. You won't probably even make it to the forest. You wouldn't know how to ask directions from the locals and wouldn't pass for a local in case a German patrol stopped you."

"And what did he say?" I barely heard myself when I asked her that.

"He said he'll have to find a way."

Chapter 13

The following morning, Schultz made a point of having Marfa serve the breakfast thirty minutes earlier than usual. I actually ran into her as she was leaving with her tray muttering in Russian under her breath, undoubtedly on account of *the cursed fascists and their whims*. Schultz rushed to take my coat and moved the chair up for me, attentive and apologetic as ever. *I must forgive him for yesterday. He wasn't himself.* I assured him that it was really all right and he had nothing to apologize for.

"I thought everything through." He served me today, with infinite gallantry and something else that I couldn't quite pinpoint. "I'll tell you everything after you eat. Weizmann will look after you; I have already arranged everything. I'll show you everything later. Now, eat, please. You must be starving."

He never touched what Marfa had set on his plate. He watched me eat instead, subtly and with a soft smile and only shook his head to all my questions as to whether the eggs were not to his liking that morning.

"You oughtn't to worry about me. I really am not hungry."

I wolfed my portion down and then his as well after he delicately moved his untouched plate toward me. After the second cup of coffee, again, served by my suddenly attentive host – *no, no; don't move please, let me do it for you* – I folded my hands on my lap and patiently awaited explanations.

Schultz rose to his feet and motioned me to follow him.

"Do you know how to type by any chance?" he asked, opening the door to the room which served as his bedroom. I shook my head negatively. "I thought so. It's quite all right. It's very easy actually; I will teach you in no time. Weizmann hates typing reports so he'll need someone to do it for him. All the paperwork, all the 'administrative nuisance' as he calls it and what I usually do, you will be typing in my absence."

"But the brigade—"

"Liza Gutkovich will be in charge of it while you're busy here. She'll be getting a double ration for it, so I don't believe she'll complain."

I didn't think she would. One ought to have been quite barmy to complain about a double ration nowadays.

Schultz, meanwhile, was already arranging a typewriter on a desk next to the wall and motioned me to it. Reluctantly, I lowered to the chair in front of the black beast with a single word *Continental* written in its center and a big winged *W* just above the keys.

"First, you'll have to insert a sheet of paper in it. This is how you do it. Slide the top of your paper between the roller and paper table. You'll know when to stop – it just won't go any further. Then you turn this knob counterclockwise to feed the paper into the roller." Leaning over me, with his hands above my shoulders, he expertly arranged a sheet of paper inside the typewriter.

He stood so close to me that I could smell the scented starch of his uniform, the cologne on his cheeks, the faint smell of the cigarette smoke – the good kind, not the atrocious Soviet makhorka of which every man in the ghetto stunk. I silently thanked God for the soap Rivka helped me steal, even though I had to scrub my garments and myself in the ice-cold water and a small communal basin. At least I was clean.

"Now you'll have to set the carriage. Move the roller as far to the left as it goes – it'll stop itself. This will also set the margins. And after that, you just type the words, simple as that." He typed the date in the top right corner. The typewriter made a dinging noise. "When you hear this sound, you need to return the carriage to begin a new line." He pressed the silver lever on the side of the typewriter and pushed the roller to the right. "See? The carriage stops itself where needed. Now you try."

He straightened behind my back. My fingers hovered over the keys.

"*Office of an Administration Officer of the Minsk Air Supply Unit Leutnant W. Schultz, Luftwaffe HQ,*" he dictated. I pressed the first uncertain *O*, which came out much too pale. "You have to hit the key harder. Don't be afraid, it won't break." He got a smile out of me. After a good minute, I finally had the first line down and looked up at him inquisitively. "You're doing great."

I knew I wasn't. "It's a bad idea. I'll never learn how to type in five days."

"Of course, you will. I'm a good teacher and you're an excellent student."

I was grateful for the encouragement even though his statement about my being an excellent student was quite far from reality.

"Now, next line." He patiently waited for me to adjust the paper. Surprisingly, I got it right. "Perfect. Now type, *To General-Kommissar Kube, Reichskommissariat Ostland, Minsk HQ*. Next line. *Gauleiter!*"

Little by little, I got the hang of it. Typing wasn't that bad of an affair but I still spent too much time puzzling over the keys and searching for the right one.

"You'll pick up speed later," Schultz advised, seemingly pleased with the progress. "All you have to do is practice."

"What do I do if I make a typo?"

"You'll have to retype the entire document, I'm afraid."

"I'll be retyping a lot of documents," I remarked, examining my latest effort and spotting at least three typos just in the first line.

"You'll do just fine," Schultz assured me once again, with the same affectionate smile.

"Leutnant Weizmann will hate me. He'll think me to be a right moron."

"No, he won't. You will have all day to retype them all. As a matter of fact, the longer you type them, the better. You'll always look busy in case someone from the SS headquarters makes an appearance."

My smile faltered. I knew that they were stationed in the same building but didn't know that they had free reign over other departments. "They can come in here without permission?"

"They like to stick their noses where they don't belong. So, yes. Don't look so frightened now; I told their commanding officer about you and God knows, everyone around understands that Weizmann needs a secretary. He's a first-rate pilot but the lousiest administrative worker you'd ever want to come across."

"Are you good friends?"

"Very good, yes," he replied fondly. "He'll be your guardian angel for the time of my furlough. He'll see to it that nothing happens to you."

From that day on, I stayed in Schultz's room daily and typed whatever he dictated to me from his chair by the round table covered by an embroidered tablecloth. He would drink his coffee and from time to time go for a cigarette into the hallway so the smoke would not bother me after I made the mistake of coughing in his presence – the ghetto air didn't exactly do wonders for one's lungs.

Weizmann would make frequent appearances now, which invariably led to hour-long breaks during which Otto – as he insisted I should call him (I never did, much like I never called Schultz, Willy) – instead of listening to Schultz's instructions would rummage through his friend's cupboard, hunting for a bottle of cognac and make the two of us drink along with him and laugh at the stories of his exploits. It was an odd and almost surrealistic situation, my sticking out between the two uniformed comrades like a sore thumb and toasting along with them to their victories – well, *Weizmann's victories and Willy's brains,* as Otto had wittily put it once.

I soon learned why the two were such tight friends; Weizmann, much like Schultz, didn't have a mean bone in his body and despite his having to set off on his deadly sorties on a weekly basis, he appeared to pity each and every one of his victims, genuinely. *Poor devil, he didn't have a chance against me. The fellow couldn't even turn his fighter properly; what sort of dogfight are we talking about? Seventy-two training hours behind him and years behind me in experience. Blast it all... killed someone's son. Teufel, pour me another one, Schultz. Sad business this war. They're good lads, too. Their cause is righteous, as Comrade Molotov had so correctly stated. And ours...* He'd sigh and throw a sidelong glance in my direction, invariably in tandem with a shake of his head. He looked at me with infinite sorrow, a constant reminder of a future world he was fighting for. He didn't like what he saw. Neither did Schultz, yet none of them could change a damned thing.

"He's a communist, you know," Schultz suddenly announced after one such visit.

I looked at the door, behind which Weizmann had disappeared, in stunned silence.

"In his heart, not officially," Schultz explained with a sly grin. "He's not that stupid. Was never caught at any meetings, nothing of that sort. All very clandestine and hush-hush. Reads books a German ace shouldn't be reading and listens to the radio waves he shouldn't be listening to... Thinks of bolting across the enemy lines, if I'm entirely honest."

"You shouldn't be telling me all this," I said quietly.

"It's all right. I trust you. Besides, didn't you tell me about Boris? It's only fair if I share my secrets with you now."

My chest felt instantly warm – from his words, not the brandy this time.

"Still, Herr Leutnant. In the ghetto, people from the underground trusted each other too. And no one would ever sell anyone out, willingly, but it so happened that someone got caught and the Gestapo are famous for untying tongues."

"You're just an ordinary girl. No one would suspect you of any underground activity."

"They kill women, too." Rivka's image floated in front of my face, together with her Yasha. "And children."

"Yes." He gave me an odd look. "And that's precisely why you're here."

He was afraid that I would die; I suddenly understood it.

It appeared amazing to me, at that moment, that women in motion pictures which I had seen in some obscure past life of mine, wished to hear the confessions of love and assurances of passion from their suitors. How absurd, how insignificant and superficial such worthless words now seemed. *It's good to know that one loves you, I suppose but how much more powerful and tremendous it is to realize that someone is mortally afraid that you will die.*

My nervous fingers toyed with the tassels on the tablecloth. He was gazing at me but I couldn't look at him for some reason. I suddenly couldn't imagine this room without him in it. He was still here but already gone and I was suddenly all alone in the entire world and the very thought of it terrified me to the marrow of my bones. I wanted to fall on my knees before him and implore him not to leave and I knew it in my heart that he wouldn't, if I only said the word and for that very reason I remained stubbornly silent. He didn't belong to me. I had no right to ask him anything.

An open suitcase lay on top of his bedcovers. The second set of his freshly cleaned uniform and a few changes of shirts, just delivered this morning by a Byelorussian washerwoman, lay neatly, in stacks, next to the suitcase, yet for some reason Schultz found reason after reason to delay the process of packing it. Now, he was staring at it oddly once again, almost with hatred in his eyes.

"Do you want me to help you with that, Herr Leutnant?"

He looked at me as though at a loss and shook his head slowly. "No. Later. I'll do it in the evening. I still have plenty of time."

"As you wish."

"Better, talk to me. Tell me something about your childhood, or about your parachute factory – anything you like. It'll give me something to think about while I travel." He was suddenly on his feet. "Wait right here! I'm such a blockhead, I swear! How did I not think about it earlier?" He disappeared into his office and soon returned with a Leica in his hands. "Please, type something and I'll take a picture of you if you don't mind. I would so love to have a photo of you, Ilse! It'll keep me company while I'm away."

A glance passed between us where no words are spoken yet everything is understood. I turned away and set to typing but the connection didn't break; it was still there, the invisible force that ties a man to a woman once and for all. The thought of it terrified me, not because I was afraid to be mistaken but because I knew for certain that I wasn't and the gravity of that unspoken oath nearly crushed me, for I knew that from now on we could only exist as a single entity, something that wouldn't stand separation.

He snapped a picture of me, then another one, a few more, from different angles as though wishing to create a multidimensional black-and-white ghost of the girl, who could have possibly been dead by the time he returned. He lowered into his chair with a heavy sigh and examined the camera in his hands, his face a mask of melancholy.

"Is the lighting bad?" I asked him sympathetically. I sat against the setting sun.

"No, it's a good camera. The light will be all right. It's just…" *It's not the same thing,* his face said it all.

I rose from my chair and walked over to him, sat at his feet and took his hands into mine. "Don't be upset now, Herr Leutnant. Think about how happy everyone will be to see you at home. Your children…"

"I don't have any."

I started for a second but then smiled again, for him, not because I wanted to. "Your wife then."

"Hedwig," he pronounced the name slowly, as though trying to conjure the right image out of the depths of his memory.

I wondered how long he hadn't seen her.

"Yes, Hedwig. I'm sure she misses you terribly."

He didn't react in any way.

"Your sisters," I tried again.

This time he smiled and brought my hands up to his lips to kiss them.

"You're so kind to me, Ilse."

"No, it's you who's the main benefactor here, Herr Leutnant, not me."

"How many times have I asked you to stop calling me *Herr Leutnant?*"

"Not enough," I tried to joke in spite of my swimming eyes. "Please, let me help you pack. We'll type the rest of the documents later."

Neither of us heard the knock on the door – if there was one, that is; only intentional shuffling in the passage. I leaped to my feet at once. Schultz turned in his chair in visible annoyance. A young officer with a sharp, handsome face stood leaning on the door frame with his arms crossed over his chest, an SD diamond visible on his left sleeve. The thought of how long he had been standing there turned me cold with horror. God knows what he imagined himself from our conversation.

"The oddest habit you have, Herr Untersturmführer, bursting into people's living quarters without knocking."

The officer chuckled in apparent amusement and smoothed his light blond hair with his hands. "The nature of our department, I'm afraid, Herr Leutnant. Besides, I did knock. But, I see, you were busy."

I didn't like one bit the wry look he threw my way.

"Now that the courtesies are out of the way, is there anything specific that I can do for you or have you just stopped by to wish me a safe trip?"

The officer advanced into the room and roved the gaze of a professional around it, taking in the desk, the table with an open bottle of cognac and three glasses on it, the bed. "Leaving tomorrow morning?"

"Your office stamped my papers." Schultz gave him a pointed look. *Why ask me then?*

"So, it did." Another inquisitive gaze in my direction, followed by meaningful silence.

"It's Fräulein Stein, Weizmann's secretary. I told your commanding officer, Sturmbannführer Bröger, about her. He said it was all right."

"Herr Sturmbannführer thinks a lot of things to be all right when he drinks. And you happen to have some good, French-imported Hennessy."

"The nature of the department," Schultz supplied with a malicious triumph in his eyes. "Anything else I can do for you? If not, I'm afraid I will have to ask you to leave. I have a lot of work to finish and a suitcase to pack."

Never before had I seen that side of him. Just now I did recall Liza's first words that I heard about him. *Efficient and superficially polite, like the rest of them, but nice? No.* He was clearly annoyed with the intruder and it showed, in his narrowed eyes suddenly hard as granite, in the contemptuous curve of his tightly pressed lips and in the purposely adopted posture – legs thrown impudently on the table, blocking the SD man's way to me.

The officer, unimpressed, perched on the side of the table as though such situations were nothing new to him.

"Will she have access to all the documentation then, as long as Weizmann substitutes you?"

He made a point of not calling me by my name, just *she*. *A Jew. Why bother remembering their names? We'll kill them all regardless.*

"That is correct," Schultz replied icily.

The officer made a face. "And you're quite sure she's not in any way connected to those underground types?"

Schultz looked at him as though the man had just said something incredibly idiotic. "Fräulein Stein is a German. Those underground types of yours, as you call them, are all local communists. She doesn't even understand their language."

"A lot of them speak Yiddish. It's not the same as German but makes it quite possible for them to understand each other. I, for one, understand it too. I'm sure, so do you. You somehow communicate with that other Jew who comes in here to clean, Elizaveta Gutkovich if I'm not mistaken? Now, Gutkovich is actually a communist. Her name was on the Party list when we had just begun going over the documentation left by the local *politruks* last June."

Schultz was visibly growing annoyed. "Gutkovich only cleans the room and leaves. She doesn't see any documents. Besides, I'm always here with her."

"You never know. These two are said to be good friends." He plucked an invisible hair off his uniform sleeve.

"Again, to bring to your attention if you missed it the first time; your superior officer, Sturmbannführer Bröger, permitted Fräulein Stein's working here. If you have any problem with it, why don't you tell him about your concerns directly?"

The officer laughed, positively delighted. "*Ach* no, why such drastic measures? You two are such good friends; he'll take your side and we both know it. Instead, I'll tell you a little story and I'll leave you two to it."

Schultz let the insinuation pass.

"There was a Jew in the Soviet part of the ghetto, a sculptor, who once drew a portrait of one of the Wehrmacht soldiers, just for fun. The soldier found it marvelous and went to his superior to boast about it. The superior was amazed at the Jew's talent and summoned him to his office to draw his portrait. The Jew goes out of his way and it's even better than the first; such a remarkable likeness, such vivid colors – that second officer even got him an actual easel and brushes, the whole business as it should be. In no time, the Jew was drawing portraits of the entire officers' mess while they were drinking, talking, generally, having a good time. And what do you know? Soon, each operation they planned and discussed, each planned trip to the forest to clean out that partisan filth, they get beaten and shot as though someone is supplying those damned partisans with information. The file had the fortune to land on my desk and after long hours of interviews and even suspicion of our own officers tipping the enemy off – not that there was never a precedent, right? – I finally put two and two together for those morons in the Wehrmacht. The sculptor confessed on the fifth day but refused to give the names of his accomplices. I have just hanged him, just this morning, with these very hands." His light-gray eyes fastened with a somewhat awed expression on his own palms.

"What do I have to do with the Wehrmacht and your sculptor?" Schultz pretended not to understand the moral of the story.

"Nothing. Absolutely nothing. I just thought it was quite an anecdote and wanted to share it," the SD officer replied with a wolfish grin. "Well, have a safe trip and enjoy your leave, Leutnant Schultz. I'll keep an eye on your little Jewess for you."

He sauntered out of the room, leaving the air charged with tension. Schultz drove the heels of his palms into his eyes and cursed under his breath.

"Do you know him?" I finally found my voice despite my heart still beating in my throat, one hundred beats per second.

"We're old enemies. That bastard would hang his own mother on orders."

"I figured as much."

"Don't be afraid of him. He won't do anything to you." He somehow didn't sound convinced by his own words.

The day was ruined. I helped him pack in silence. When it was time for me to leave, he pulled me close and held me tight against his chest until Liza's tentative knock on the door brought him out of his reverie.

"Just one more minute, Liza," he called out to her through the door.

"You'll have to let me go at some point, Herr Leutnant." I knew that my smile came out weak and pitiful but it was the best I could do at that moment.

He nodded but only seized me tighter instead.

"If we're late for the line-up," I began, lifting my face to his. "The SS will beat us."

Another nod. He kissed me on my forehead, with infinite tenderness. "Yes, go. I'll see you very soon. I'll bring you something nice from Germany. What would you like?"

"Nothing. Just hurry up and come back, please."

He kissed me on my mouth this time and I readily opened my lips for him so he wouldn't forget me in those infinitely long three weeks. For some reason, I couldn't stand the thought of parting with him any longer.

Liza was knocking again, her voice urgent, apologetic and pleading. "Herr Leutnant, we really must be going now!"

With great reluctance, he let go of me.

"Goodbye, Herr Leutnant."

"Not even now?"

I wiped a nuisance of a tear off my cheek and smiled at him. "Goodbye, Willy."

From him, a bright answering smile. "I'll see you soon, Ilse."

The following morning, I knocked at the door as it was my habit and stood in silent stupefaction when it was him who'd opened it.

"Surprise!" he announced, by way of greeting.

"What happened? Did you miss your train? Did you oversleep? Did they cancel your leave at the last minute?"

"I've never missed a train in my life and no, they didn't cancel it. I canceled it."

He didn't explain anything but I saw it all written in his infinitely blue eyes; the SD man, the hanged sculptor, and the three weeks during which we would have been apart from each other.

Chapter 14

May blossomed outside, the purple May with its incessant thunder-storms; the green-gray May, with summer uniforms; the red May, but not with May Day banners this time. Out of the window of Schultz's private quarters, I watched a group of soldiers hammering away at their grisly task. By lunchtime, the gallows stood in the center of the square with two SS men guarding it as though it was an ancient idol. Perhaps, to them it was; their God demanded bloody offerings to sustain its hateful being. Their God's name was War, and it had the face of a skull, with empty eye sockets, wickedly grinning. To justify their actions, they had to invent their own religion. They wouldn't get too far with any other, pacifistic God.

I pulled the blackout curtains closed and turned the lamp on to type the rest of the paperwork.

After the incident with Untersturmführer Schönfeld – I finally learned his name – Schultz (*Willy*, I mentally corrected myself) positively refused to allow my resuming my work along with the brigade. I never found out how much exactly he paid his "friend" from the SS but it must have been enough for that "friend" to concede that Leutnant Schultz indeed couldn't do without a secretary. In addition to my new office-worker position, Willy managed to bribe him for an *Ausweis* that allowed me to walk freely through the streets of Minsk running whatever errands he invented for me.

"This folder needs to be delivered to the field post office. Actually, it's only a five-minute walk from here but take Sovietskaya Street down to Komsomolskaya and turn onto Internatsionalnaya after that; it's beautiful out, take a nice walk. If anyone stops you, show your *Ausweis* and tell them you got lost."

Hardly anyone ever stopped me. Around the same time he'd gotten me this *Ausweis,* he managed to persuade his comrade from the SS that his brigade needn't wear yellow stars on our clothes since the risk that we would run away was minimal. *And where will they go and how they will get there? They don't speak Russian. Fat chance the locals will help anyone who speaks German. I truly hate to see those yellow patches on our compatriots, don't you?* That logic, washed down by some fine Hennessy, French-imported of course, somehow found the needed response in the SS official; we were permitted to part with our yellow stars.

And so, I wandered around the city from time to time, an invisible civilian who could finally see life, not through the barbed wire. I learned to distinguish the types of the troops and their insignia and knew when to keep walking ahead or quickly turn into a side street, *Ausweis* or not. Field-gray-clad Wehrmacht officers with their local girlfriends on a stroll never paid me any heed. Ordinary privates, marching in columns along the streets, sometimes called out to me and waved but so they did to all other women and I soon learned to ignore them the same way that those women did. The gray-blue uniforms I greeted with a smile. By now, I knew most of the local Luftwaffe office staff by name; almost all of them reported to Willy. Black-clad tank troops hardly appeared in the streets – their quarters were on the other bank of the river, away from the forest and its inhabitants. They were growing bolder, the partisans; they ventured into the outskirts of Minsk now. The SS, which I tried to avoid like the plague, was growing more annoyed with such a turn of events. All of their efforts, all the pogroms, and massacres were in vain. Survivors slipped through their fingers like sand and much like quicksand, they'd drown them soon, or so they promised in one of their latest leaflets which were published by the underground and circulated around the ghetto up until three weeks ago.

"Richter was grinning like a cat who's got the canary," Liza spoke with a snarl after one of our Sunday 'concerts,' which have become customary now after the very first one. The band consisted mostly of German Jews, who were allowed to live, solely due to their ability to play classical music and brassy marches – whatever Superintendent Richter fancied hearing that day. He thought such concerts to be a great success. On his good days – the SS had their good and bad days also – he would settle on Austrian waltzes. On his bad days, he took cruel pleasure in forcing the orchestra to play *"Heil Hitler Dir"* and anti-Semitic songs which were in such favor with the SA not that long ago. He took his mocking even further when he organized a choir out of his former compatriots and made them sing one such song: *Put the Jews up against the wall, Throw the Jewish gang out of our German Fatherland, Send them to Palestine, Once there – cut their throats so that they will never come back.* Yet, such verbal cruelty was still better than any *Aktionen.* We learned how to ignore it for the most part. "He thinks he took the last hope from the people by arresting Efim and the rest of the printers."

"In that case, he succeeded," I noted broodingly.

Liza translated those leaflets for me since they were mostly in Russian; in her clear, hopeful voice she read to me about the Red Army's fighting back, of liberated towns near Moscow, of partisans destroying a platoon in Staroselskaya Pusha – *so very close to us, a walking distance, really!*

"No, he did not." She squared her shoulders, a proud Soviet woman. "In no time, people will start working that press again. Our people are everywhere. It's not some Committee now, it's all of us, the people. And he can't kill us all at once."

I wasn't quite sure about that last part.

With thick curtains blocking out the grim view behind the window, I sat lost in my thoughts with unfinished documents still stacked next to the typewriter. Besides the small circle of light cast by a lamp, the room was shrouded in darkness. My heart thumped heavy in my chest; much too heavy for a young girl who should only know joy in her life. Shadows crept from every corner, threatening, haunting. The clock measured the time far too loudly. Everything around was hostile and frightening, even this room without the light, without Willy in it.

I've always been strong, brave, I thought with a shudder. *What have they done to me? Afraid of the dark and even more afraid to open the curtains.*

There was no getting used to this place. I was forced to live with this fear; it was a part of me now, just as real and tangible as one's limbs.

I will feel better once they remove the gallows, I told myself, clenching my fists. My palms were cold and clammy. *As soon as the gallows is gone, I will be brave again.*

I swung round on my seat. The sound of the lock turning in Willy's office startled me back into reality. He always locked the door whenever he left me.

"So that I wouldn't run away?" I joked once.

"Everything precious must be kept under lock and key so that other people wouldn't get to it," he replied, with an odd note to his voice.

I went to meet him, glad to be finally saved from that unbearable, mortifying solitude, from the invisible gallows behind the window. *He's back, and I can breathe again.*

"Why the blackout drapes?" He looked, mystified, at his darkened living quarters. "Are you expecting Soviet Ratas any time soon?"

"The sun is too bright," I lied for his sake. He walked in, so warm with sun and smelling of blossoming trees and here I stood grim like a warden of the graveyard. "All that spring business outside…"

"I didn't know you were so prejudiced again the sun and the spring; else I wouldn't have gotten you this." With a conspirator's smile, he presented me with a bundle wrapped in brown paper and tied with a cord.

"What is it?"

"We're going for a ride to the airbase. I thought you might want to wear this."

I looked at the parcel, in hesitation.

"Well, go on, open it up. It's for you. A present."

"Too many presents lately."

"I didn't give you any presents at all!" he protested at once.

"The food, the *Ausweis,* my new job, and no more yellow star."

"Those are not presents. I was just trying to create a semblance of a normal life for you."

"Those were very dear presents," I countered. He didn't argue.

I tugged at the cord and unwrapped the paper. It was a two-piece suit, a jacket, and a skirt, sky-blue and with a German label on the jacket's collar. I stared at it incomprehensibly. Thoroughly trying to conceal his enthusiasm, Willy held up the sleeve to my eyes.

"A perfect match," he declared.

"Where did you get it from?"

"The Fatherland. Asked one of my sisters to send it to me."

"She didn't ask any questions?"

"She gave me a Gestapo-worthy third-degree if I'm entirely honest but I managed to concoct a story that satisfied her in the end. Spring is here. I thought you could use something new for your wardrobe. Now, what's with the tears? That's not the reaction I was expecting. Do you really loathe *all that spring business?*"

"I don't. Spring is my favorite season." I quickly wiped my eyes. "You are too kind to me, that's all. I'll go change at once. I don't want you to be late for your appointment because of my sentiments."

I closed the door after myself and laid the suit down on his bed, to admire it for a few more moments. Yes, it was obviously a product of Germany, not a local seamstress. I used to see such suits on mannequins in the windows of Frankfurt's department stores, into which I wasn't allowed any longer. With bitter irony, I was putting it on now, an Aryan product for Aryans only, bought by a Party member for his Jewish lady friend he liked to kiss.

It hadn't gotten further than that yet; stolen caresses here and there, his hands on top of my legs but not further than a certain point, his mouth on top of mine that drove me to insanity... Still, he never insisted on anything as soon as I'd press my hands against his chest and push him off, for I could swear that a few more moments and I wouldn't have the presence of mind to resist him any longer. He'd only look at me with infinite longing and ask, between the small kisses with which he'd cover my fingertips, "Am I frightening you, Ilse?"

"Yes. But not like you think you are."

And how easy it would have been for him to just take what was now rightfully his, for what he had paid the SS and therefore could do as he pleased... They, for one, never even considered paying for such favors when they would come, drunk and looking for a good time, into the ghetto. They simply took the prettiest girls they could find and left with them in the direction of the cemetery and the following day the diggers would have a few more bodies to bury. The SS weren't so racially selective when it came to that and the dead Jewish girls couldn't quite report anyone, could they? Yes, he could have done just the same, yet, he courted me instead as though it was not wartime, as though I didn't owe my very life to him, as though it wasn't me, who was the helpless side in all of this twisted equation.

I opened the door of the bedroom.

"What do you think?" Tentatively, I smoothed out the skirt with my fingers. I didn't know how to wear all of these beautiful things anymore. I had long lost the habit of being a proper woman.

He didn't say anything just caressed me with his eyes with unconcealed admiration in them. Finally, he uttered with a sigh, "How I wish..."

He never finished the sentence only shook his head at all this rotten business around us.

"Yes, me too."

The sunshine outside was outrageous, mocking and grotesque, pouring down its glorious beauty on the corpses, swaying slightly in the wind. Thank God for the curtains; I didn't have to witness the hanging itself.

There was no avoiding the grim view, even in the staff car. The SS ensured the strategic placement of the gallows so that everyone would come face to face with dead "criminals." It served two purposes. To demonstrate a job well done, to their German superiors and to warn the locals who were stupid enough to go against them. I turned my face away from the window. Willy drove straight ahead, his mouth pressed into a hard line.

Though there wasn't any escaping from death, that day. The gallows had been erected on all squares, on most populated intersections, right along the route that we were taking, like a dark premonition of our common destiny.

"Sadistic bastards."

In spite of myself, I followed Willy's gaze to the nearby gallows. We stopped at the intersection, letting a column of Wehrmacht trucks pass in the direction of the forest. The gallows stood within twenty steps of us; there was no avoiding seeing it. Now, I saw for myself what he was alluding to – unlike the usual, *"We're the criminals who are guilty of spreading anti-German propaganda,"* a new sign sat crookedly on one of the hanged men's necks – *"Happy May Day!"*

"It's nothing new," I commented, averting my eyes.

I would really rather look at the trucks with soldiers in them, most likely driving to their certain deaths. There was no winning in the forest. They didn't know the terrain like the locals did; their maps were useless just like the directions given by the peasants, slyly pointing them to a marsh instead of a partisan brigade's location. There was no fair fighting in the forest; the partisans booby-trapped the trails, placed snipers in the trees, and showered the Germans with the machineguns of their own production, smuggled by the

Jews out of the factories. Now, it was more and more such Jews who were shooting at them. I wondered how they liked it.

"Herrgott." My voice was suddenly hoarse, breath stuck in my throat.

I didn't hear Willy's question, just yanked on the door handle and rushed outside, towards the road, charging right between the passing vehicles, one of them nearly crashing into me – the driver slamming his brakes on in time. I didn't see him and didn't hear his horn blowing; I was running like mad toward my little sister, who walked along the road as though she had a business to be there. The new dress on her thin frame – the one I gave her for her birthday, a cardigan from someone else's shoulder, blonde hair in two plaits, no yellow star.

I clasped her arm and pulled her forcefully toward myself.

"Lore…" Words suddenly failed me. I couldn't get my breath.

She looked at me in stupefaction, then quickly regained her composure and shifted what seemed like a schoolbag on her shoulder. *She got involved with something. Someone. How did I fail to notice it?*

"Let go of me," she said through gritted teeth. "You're making a scene."

"How did you get out?" That was all I could manage to say. "Did someone give you a special pass?"

Please, say yes, I beg of you. Please, be here on some official business. Please, tell me you are an informant for the Gestapo, whatever it is, just don't let me be right.

Lore inched away from me, her gaze already darting in the direction of an SS patrolman, making his way towards us. His face and the hand on his holster meant business.

"Let's try to run," Lore whispered. Before she could, I grabbed her firmly by the collar of her cardigan and held her tightly despite the withering glances she was throwing my way. Her hands were clenched on the straps of her bag. I instantly guessed why she wanted to run; just being outside the ghetto without a pass would earn one a simple beating in most cases. Whatever she had in that bag was far more serious.

It was too late now. The SS man had just yelled the terrifying *"Papiere!"* and unfastened his holster. I felt as though the ground had just gone from under my feet.

"It's all right!" Willy was shouting at the SS man making the same way as I had, in-between the trucks, which had now stopped, the soldiers in them observing the scene, half-curious, half-ready to shoot the participants. "It's all right; she's my wife."

The SS man forgot his gun for a few moments and pulled himself up to salute a superior officer. Willy replied to his enthusiastic Heil Hitler with the same and, still out of breath, turned to Lore instead.

The silence was suddenly grave and threatening. I had to think of something credible and fast but all I could think of was gallows; gallows right across the street from where we stood; gallows from which my sister and I could be swaying mere moments from now.

"She ran away from me again," I said, unable to keep the tremor out of my voice. Under my new suit, I was wet with sweat. The heat had nothing to do with it; my flesh was creeping with terror.

Willy's shouting startled me even further. "The first day in a new place and you're acting out?! Shall I send you back to your grandparents? To work in the fields all summer – is that what you want, young lady?!"

He was so convincing, Lore reddened and lowered her eyes without any effort, the scolded, unruly child.

One of the Wehrmacht officers, one from the truck column, approached us as well, seemingly not pleased with the interruption of their movement.

"Heil Hitler." After receiving the same greeting from Willy, he inquired, "What's going on?"

"My apologies, Herr Hauptmann." Willy lowered his head. I swallowed a lump in my throat. The Wehrmacht officer was a

Captain; Willy, just a Leutnant. The SS man wouldn't dare ask him for any papers; this one could. "My wife was trying to catch our daughter and almost caused you an accident. I apologize again."

The Wehrmacht Hauptmann looked at me closely, then at Lore.

"Your wife?" he asked again and raised his brow just enough to express a doubt. I looked barely twenty; Lore was a teenager.

"Yes. My wife, Ilse." He sensed the officer's hesitation, no doubt, and turned to Lore again. "Do you see the trouble you're causing me, you ungrateful brat?! Why did you run away from your mother?"

"She's not my mother," Lore grumbled back with all the defiance of a typical teenager, the smart girl, and gasped, so very naturally, when Willy slapped her hard on her cheek.

The Hauptmann blinked a few times, then grinned in understanding. *Ach, that's what it is. Herr Leutnant found himself a young wife, the pretty little thing and the daughter is not too happy about it,* it read in his eyes. He glanced me over once again. *Expensive clothes; he spoils her and the brat is jealous.*

"Apologize to Ilse at once," Willy's voice was steely.

Still holding her cheek with one hand, Lore turned to me, her eyes still riveted to the ground. "I'm sorry."

"I'm sorry, who?" Willy repeated.

"I'm sorry, *Mutti.*"

"That's better. Now, apologize to these two officers as well for causing all this mayhem."

"I'm sorry, Officers."

The SS man grinned, mighty pleased at the address form.

"You shouldn't be running away from your parents in this city—" The Hauptmann looked at Willy, who supplied him with the name and turned back to the girl, his tone getting more conciliatory. "You shouldn't be running around here, Lore. It's not Germany; there are partisans and other criminals here on every corner. You're putting not only yours but your parents' lives in danger."

"I apologize, Herr Hauptmann," Lore mumbled again, looking thoroughly ashamed.

The officer turned to Willy, who offered him another apologetic smile. "I have four brats myself, all girls." He rolled his eyes emphatically.

"I don't know how you manage them all. I can't manage one."

"I left my wife and their BDM leaders to the task. I'd rather be here with this riff-raff," the Hauptmann motioned his head toward the trucks, laughing, "than with those four princesses. I manage a company better than them."

"Don't even say—"

"God's truth! As true as I'm standing here—"

"And one can't even punish them properly!" Willy spread his arms in a helpless gesture. "They get in veritable trouble but then they give you those eyes, *Vati this, Vati that; I didn't mean to, Vati; it won't happen again, Vati; Vati, you're the best Vati in the world—*"

"The whole song and dance," the Wehrmacht officer agreed in a most emphatic way, smiles chasing one another across his face.

Willy's hand now rested on top of Lore's blonde head, the same color as his. *Vati's girl.* Satisfied with his performance, Willy began patting his pockets.

"*Ach,* I'm forgetting myself. You wished to see our papers?" An innocent look in the SS man's direction. "Here's mine. Leutnant Schultz, Air Supply Unit." He offered the Hauptmann his hand, which the latter thoroughly shook.

"What papers? Forget the papers." The Wehrmacht officer protested loudly, clapping Willy on his shoulder and pushing Willy's Luftwaffe-issued ID away. "I'm Bruckner, with the 67th company." He turned to me, all smiles and gallantry. "Are you and young Lore staying for long in our God-forsaken parts, Frau Schultz?"

"Lore is only joining us for summer. She's going back as soon as school starts. And I, for as long as my husband is here, Herr Bruckner."

He nodded appreciatively.

"They should make a special Cross for wives like you, Frau Schultz. Very few follow their husbands to the front. Most sit it out in Germany, in peace and comfort. I can count on my fingers the officers' wives that currently live in Minsk."

"I couldn't imagine being apart from my husband," I said, looking at Willy.

He gave me the most tender smile, brought my hand to his lips and kissed it with infinite affection.

"You must be newlyweds," the Hauptman noted, looking slightly embarrassed.

"Yes, we are. My first wife passed away a year ago. Ilse and I got married in March."

A bit of a white lie. We *met* in March but were inseparable since.

Apparently, it was enough to convince everyone present. The Hauptmann left, expressing his regret that they were leaving Minsk to join the frontline forces of the 6th Army in Ukraine, promised to visit us if he happened to be in our parts again; the SS man simply disappeared after yet another sharp salute. The column with troops even waited for us to cross the road back to our car before they resumed their movement.

As soon as we were far enough, Willy outstretched his arm toward Lore, who occupied the back seat.

"Give me everything you have in that bag."

Reluctantly, she pulled out a stack of papers, smelling of fresh ink. I stared at them in stupefaction while Willy gave them a cursory perusal before stacking them under his seat. So, Liza was right after all. They did resume printing them only three weeks later, while the bodies of the former printers still swayed from the gallows. And my little sister was now one of them. How did I miss that? How did I fail to notice her preoccupied ways, her suddenly serious eyes, her knitted brows as she worked something out in her mind? I was too busy daydreaming about Willy when I was away from him and I almost lost my sister because of it.

"Do you understand that you could have gotten shot?" I asked quietly.

Lore only nodded, very calm and collected. She did. She understood everything and decided that hope for the people was more important than her own life.

Willy never said another word, only slowed the car down and honked once he saw a column of the *Ostjuden*, repairing the road that the partisans had recently damaged. Their supervisors were nowhere to be seen, at least from where we were standing. Beckoning one of the workers, Willy lowered the window, quickly shoved the papers into the man's hands and sped away almost at once. In a rearview mirror, I saw how the man just as promptly shoved the stack into his jacket before returning to work. From the back seat, Lore saw it too and grinned. She was afraid Willy would throw them away and it was so difficult to type them!

"I'm sorry for hitting you," he finally spoke to her directly.

I'm not like them, his eyes said as he looked at her through the mirror.

"You had to; otherwise they wouldn't have believed you." *I know you're not.* She didn't say it, but it was evident in her voice.

Chapter 15

"It is impossible to estimate the loses, but…" Liza's brows were tightly drawn in concentration as she translated what sounded like complete and utter gibberish to me, at the same time marking things down on a piece of paper. "Marshal Timoshenko says they underestimated the 6th Army's potential and overestimated their own forces… Over two hundred thousand casualties." She shook her head, her hands lying limply in her lap. Abruptly, she turned to the radio, which we shouldn't have been listening to in the first place, and switched it off. "And those are censored numbers; Soviet *Informbureau* always ensures that they make Red Army loses appear smaller than they are. *Nakrylos kontrnastoupleniye mednym tazom,*" she added in Russian, with a note of desolate finality in her voice.

I understood her without understanding her language. The Soviet counteroffensive near Kharkov, in which the *Stavka* had such high hopes, along with our kin in the ghetto, resulted in a decisive German victory. When Superintendent Richter, who followed the events in Ukraine with great interest, read out the latest reports from the front last Sunday, we took it with a grain of salt. Didn't they lie to us in the same manner about the German troops taking Moscow and planning a parade in Red Square, just a few months ago, in winter? Perhaps, the Kharkov disaster was the same type of lie, another means of breaking our spirit? Liza nudged me in my ribs as we stood listening to the obligatory "concert" after Richter's address – it was Austrian waltzes that day, a good day for Richter – and inquired if Schultz's office radio could catch the Soviet radio waves. I pleaded with her to abandon such a suicidal idea but she simply barged in with her bucket and broom the next day, boldly lied to Willy that the brigade needed his attention outside and began working the radio knob until Russian speech poured out of the speakers.

I had sat with my back pressing onto the front door, my hand on the handle holding it fast, beads of sweat collecting under my collar, while she listened to stern voices, interrupted by mechanical rustling from time to time. Now, I let go of it at last and crawled toward her on my knees. For some time, we sat in silence.

"Will you put it in your leaflet?" I asked her, regarding her notes dubiously.

"I will. People need to know the truth, whatever it is," she replied with calm resignation.

"This is not the end of the war," I tried to console her. Judging by the sympathetic look she offered in response to my attempt, the consolation came out as rather pitiful.

"I know it's not, you innocent little baby." She touched my chin. "The whole trouble is, we're playing against time. Have you noticed how they keep pushing the borders of the ghetto towards the cemetery each month? New Gentile tenants had just moved into the houses, in which our friends used to live before they ended up in yet another pit. They'll clear it out entirely soon, the SS. Give or take another year. And if the Red Army doesn't come and liberate us in time…"

She didn't finish. The unspoken threat hung in the air, heavy as the smoke which came from the south whenever the wind changed direction. To rid themselves of the partisans, *Einsatzkommando* decided to burn as much forest as they could with flamethrowers. They didn't get further than the swamps and now peat bogs were burning, contaminating the air around the city with the stench of smoldering turf. Willy had a few choice words to say, on their account; now, at the end of May, days stood stifling hot and we couldn't even open a window to ventilate the room due to that smoke.

"What about the partisans?" I probed gingerly.

Liza only shrugged, sunk a rag into the bucket of water, twisted it and began scrubbing the floor. "What about them? We can't exactly up and move the entire ghetto into the forest, can we? We used to send as many people as we could through various channels but now after the Gestapo did away with the Committee in the Russian sector, it'll take time to establish a new connection to the partisans. It all takes time, which we don't have. You wait and see how they come up with yet another pogrom."

"God forbid, Liza!" I was knocking on wood like a mad woman.

"God may forbid, but the SS has special permission," she remarked with bitter irony.

"What is your Nahum saying? Do they know anything in the *Judenrat?*"

The grin, which brightened Liza's face at the mention of her beloved, didn't escape me. She had guarded him fiercely at first, from that day when I first saw them exchange those few glances in Jubilee Square but then, as habit has it, among young women, she couldn't help but talk about him, for long periods and invariably with a dreamy expression.

"The *Judenrat* is a rotten affair as of now, with all the collaborators Richter has appointed there. Except for Elder Yoffe, who replaced Mushkin, Nahum, and Dr. Kolb from the hospital, they're all on the Gestapo's payroll. Nahum says they can't sneeze inside without someone reporting it to Richter." She snorted in disdain. "And what of your Schultz?"

"He doesn't know anything. That is, he's in charge of the Luftwaffe supply and such. He doesn't know much about the military operations or the SS except for the bits he gets from this department or that and official reports which their political leaders read out to them every week."

"The Luftwaffe has their own Richter?" Liza broke out into mirthless laughter. "A veritable anecdote."

"You don't say."

"When did we become such bitter old women?"

"You tell me." I tried to pull the rag out of her hands. "Let me wash at least the other room. You never let me do anything!"

"Leave off, you princess. Your hands will reek of dirty water. Your duty is to look pretty and keep Schultz happy. Look how he's changed since you appeared. So kind to everyone, so generous with ration cards as though it's his own soldiers he's feeding and not some Jews from the ghetto. He used to be so stern with everyone and now look at him, all smiles and compliments. Jokes with us even, imagine that! So, keep doing whatever it is that you're doing. It's working."

"I'm not doing anything," I muttered, applying my utmost to conceal a smile. "Just a kiss here and there."

"Nu y zrya," like all of her pearls of wisdom, Liza expressed this one in her native language. "It's not the peaceful times when things should follow a certain order. Meeting, courtship, parents' blessing, all that rot. We can all die tomorrow for all we know. I should know what I'm saying; I lost my husband not even a year ago. Yes, call me a shameless wanton or what not but if I can feel alive in a man's embrace for one more night, you can bet your ration card, I'll do it. I'm still a woman; at least that they didn't take away from me. Live a little, Ilsechka, while you still can."

"Women will talk…"

"Women talk as it is. They think you are already lovers. Their opinion of you won't change a bit as long as their stomachs are full. Trust me, they are all very grateful."

In no time, she finished her daily cleaning routine and left with a wink.

Lovers. I brought my hand to my lips and touched them, remembering how his mouth felt on mine, how my heart was pounding whenever he held me in his embrace, how my body instantly responded to his caresses whenever he pulled me against him, his eyes dark with desire. I would always stop him before it would get too far between us but, instantaneously I would miss his arms around my waist and almost resent his respectful compliance. What if I didn't stop him next time?

Not quite myself from both Liza's words still clouding my mind with all sorts of inappropriate thoughts and my own confused feelings, I kneeled in front of the radio, working the knob and firmly set on distracting myself with some brassy propaganda pouring from a German station. But as luck would have it, instead of Goebbels's shouts, I came across Lale Andersen singing the ode to all lovers on *Soldatensender Belgrad* – *"Das Mädchen unter der Laterne"* – in her beautiful voice.

> *Outside the barracks, by the corner light*
> *I'll always stand and wait for you at night*
> *We will create a world for two*
> *I'll wait for you the whole night through...*

I turned my gaze toward the door as it opened, a grinning Willy appearing in the threshold. The fates just had it against me that day, it appeared.

"Who listens to this type of music in such a manner?" He scowled in mock-confusion, walked up to me and offered me his hand. "When a song like this is playing, you ought to dance."

I rose to my feet, smiling and placed my hand on his shoulder. He gently pressed my other palm, enclosed in his.

"Is everything all right with the brigade?" I asked.

"In exemplary order, as always. It is my profound conviction that Liza simply wished to be rid of my persona so you two could gossip in peace."

"You are not far from the truth," I admitted, smiling in embarrassment.

"You girls always gossip about us, poor miserable muttons."

"It's only natural. What else to discuss for two young women in love?"

Only when he stopped abruptly, did I realize what words had just escaped my lips. I looked at him in utmost horror unable to take another breath and cursing myself for such an idiotic slip of the tongue. Of all the things to tell him! My cheeks burning feverishly, I was ready to admit that we were listening to the Soviet *Informbureau;* anything to make him stop staring at me the way he was, in utter stupefaction, with a bare outline of a hopeful smile already forming on his face.

> *When we are marching in the mud and cold*
> *And when my pack seems more than I can hold*
> *My love for you renews my might*
> *I'm warm again, my pack is light,*
> *It's you, Lili Marlene*

"It's you, Ilse Stein," he sang along with Andersen, changing the name of the girl every soldier sang about in-between grisly fights of both wars. "I love you."

Not waiting for my answer, he drew me to himself and kissed me with unrestrained desire, nearly crushing me in his embrace. I clung to him and kissed him back with the same primal hunger, not hearing anything any longer except for Liza's words. *Live a little Ilsechka, while you still can.*

It can be my corpse that a black SS boot shoves into a new pit tomorrow and I want to die a woman who's known love at least for a few stolen moments.

With my fingers tangled in his hair, I found his belt buckle with the other hand and stumbled over it, unsure. He moved my hand gently to the side and unfastened the belt himself, letting it drop with a dull thud onto the carpet. His jacket followed – he threw it impatiently onto the chair.

"Not here. People." His whisper burned my ear as he pulled me after himself toward the bedroom, locking the door to the office as we passed it by.

He closed the bedroom door as well. I leaned against it, my entire body feeling as though engulfed in fire, either from my shameless behavior or even more shameless desire, reflected in his eyes that now shone with unspeakable brightness, on his suddenly pale face. It was unbearable to look into them for the intensity of the longing in their ice-blue fire terrified me yet excited me at the same time. His fingers trembled with impatience, undoing the buttons on my blouse. The tender cloth gave way and tore when he pulled it down my shoulder a bit too forcefully.

"I'll get you a new one," he whispered by means of apology, already claiming my mouth again.

I didn't particularly care for such trifles, too consumed with his hand caressing my bare breast he'd just released from under my shift after pulling a strap down. *Yes, let them kill me tomorrow; tomorrow, I will gladly die by their hand as long as they let me have my today – here, with him.*

I worked my way out of my skirt and let it drop next to his boots and a shirt. He took my hand and pulled me closer to the bed, his clouded gaze full of desire and tenderness.

"You are impossibly beautiful."

I must have been quite a sight, in mended stockings and a cotton undershirt which was so thin it might as well be non-existent, hanging off one shoulder. My hands moved instinctively to cover myself up.

"No, don't," he pleaded with me and pulled the blackout curtains closed at once, creating an artificial twilight in the room. He took me in his hands again and I lowered mine. "I don't want you to be shy around me. You have the body of a goddess. I promise I will worship every inch of it."

I grinned and hid my face in his neck; in spite of myself, flattered.

"You say such things to me…"

"It's true. All of it."

Both straps slid down my bare arms, guided by his hands. The undershirt stopped at my hips; he kneeled in front of me to remove it along with my underwear. I closed my eyes when he moved his lips along my inner thighs and grasped the iron frame of the bed as he parted them gently and put his mouth on me.

"Willy…" I hadn't the faintest idea of how many times I whispered his name in the course of the next few deliciously tormenting minutes and how many times I moaned it, my fingers clutching at his hair when I couldn't take it any longer.

I was almost relieved when he pulled me, barely coherent and still gasping for air, on top of the bed for I could swear my legs would give in had he not put me down. His hand in between us, he looked at me closely one last time.

"Are you sure about it?"

There will be no going back.

I didn't want to look back. I wanted only the future, with him, exactly where I belonged.

I nodded, kissed him instead of a reply and inhaled sharply as he guided himself in.

"Am I hurting you?"

I shook my head slowly, smiling. He could never hurt me and particularly now.

"I didn't know it would feel this way. So… amazing." Feeling you inside of me, the closest two people can get.

He beamed at me before covering my entire face in kisses. He began moving slowly, letting me get used to the sensation. I suddenly understood Liza and her invariably burning eyes each time she'd meet me at our "exit"; I knew she always saw Nahum before "smuggling" me inside her part of the ghetto. She teased me good-humoredly, implying that *I was missing out a lot* and I refused to believe all the fuss she made about it.

He was moving faster, harder now. I clasped the metal post behind my head with both hands and bit my lip to stop myself from making any sounds. Willy hid his face in the pillow as well, right next to my face.

"Ilse…" His hot breath burned my neck.

I only pressed my jaws tighter and wrapped myself around him, my legs, my arms; I couldn't hold it any longer either. He clutched me tightly one last time; along with him, I released a shuddering breath.

We lay together, my back against his stomach, for what felt like a blissful forever. We drifted into sleep at some point and I woke up to his lips covering my neck and shoulder with light kisses.

"It's almost five. I have to go and make a call to the airbase. They'll be waiting." The reluctance in his voice was palpable.

"Is it five already?" I rose on one elbow too to check on the alarm clock at the bedside table. "I have to go too. The brigade—"

"To hell with the brigade; stay here tonight." He was holding me fast once again.

"I can't."

"You can. I'll write a note for you and give it to Liza. She'll show it at the gates and they will mark it down so that there will be no trouble with the inspection if they check on your house tonight."

His tone was just short of begging.

"You have a solution for everything, haven't you?" I grinned, in spite of myself.

"Not for everything yet. But I'm working on it, I promise."

Chapter 16

June 1942

"Looks like your *bandit-partisaner* were quite busy lately."

I looked up from the handwritten report that I was typing. Willy, who sat at the round table beside me, couldn't quite conceal a sly grin as he perused the local *Minsker Zeitung*. I glimpsed the date on the front page, printed in the usual German Gothic, *June 22*. The longest day of the year. The anniversary of the beginning of the war with the Soviets.

Willy sipped his iced coffee. The air barely circulated through an open window and he sat in his shirt only, leaving his jacket on the back of his chair. "Another derailed train, just outside Minsk. They're getting closer."

"You seem to be far too pleased with the situation for a representative of the occupying forces," I noted, hiding my smile. The heat was sweltering and my hair was pulled up high to expose my neck and allow at least some coolness to pass over my skin. For the hundredth time, I pulled the thin cloth of my shirt away from my back to which it kept sticking.

"Not just me. Weizmann is quite pleased with it too."

"Speaking of Weizmann, you should have gone with him to the lake. It's far too hot to be indoors today."

The Komsomol Lake had been opened to the public exactly a year ago as well. I'd never seen it myself, only heard about it from Liza who had a chance to dip her toes in it a few days before the Germans occupied the city. Now, the lake was mostly frequented by said Germans. Even ordinary Byelorussian civilians preferred bathing in the river Svisloch rather than risk the company of their new masters.

"And leave you here alone? A fine fellow that would make me." A shadow passed over his face; he was suddenly serious. "He thinks about defecting."

I regarded him in astonishment. "Who, Otto? You're joking, most certainly."

"No, *Liebchen*. I'm very much serious. Apparently, he's had enough of this rot."

"But…" I couldn't summon any words. How bad could it have been for them, the air forces? Most certainly, sprawled out in the sun right now, still wet from swimming, getting their golden tan to match those sky-blue uniforms of theirs. Or playing ball with their comrades and emptying beer mugs delivered by the local Byelorussian's cart. And Otto, out of all people – I just couldn't quite take it in. He was a decorated officer, highly regarded by his superiors. But again, so was Willy and look who he had taken to his bed. "Why?"

"Doesn't fancy the regime he's protecting. He's always leaned towards the red side but now, after he's seen the ghetto with his own eyes and met you…" He paused. "He suggested an idea to me."

"What kind of an idea?"

Willy was biting his lip for some time, working things out in his mind. It seemed he was deciding whether to tell me or not; not because he didn't trust me but out of fear of putting false hope into my heart. "If he takes the radio box out of the back of his Messerschmitt, two people can fit in there. It'll be a little tight but… It's not that we have to fly far. Only across the frontline." A ghost of a smile passed over his lips.

I was already shaking my head. "No. No, no, no; it's a bad idea, Willy. It's a terrible idea."

"Not so terrible, if you think of it." Excited, he pulled forward. "We can take the staff car and drive to the airbase—"

"What will you tell the Field Police when they stop you and ask you what a Jew is doing in your car?"

"Same as I said the last time. I'll tell them you're my typist, and I'm a lazy bastard who can't be bothered with writing down his own reports. It worked last time, didn't it?"

"All right. What about when we get to the base itself? I doubt they'll let Otto take out that massive radio box in broad daylight. He has to do it at night then. Most likely they have sentries on that airbase, don't they?"

"Those can be distracted with the right amount of alcohol."

"Suppose they can. What about us? How can we loiter there all day without causing suspicion? And even if we do and even if we manage to get inside that plane, don't they have any anti-aircraft batteries positioned there that can shoot down anyone who takes off without proper authorization?" He wanted to interject something but I wouldn't let him. "And let's imagine – the best-case scenario – we *do* take off and they *don't* shoot us down, by some miracle. How are we to let the Russians know that we aren't an attacking aircraft but merely want to defect? Without the radio, that is?"

Willy cleared his throat in apparent embarrassment. "He has just recently suggested this. We didn't quite think the entire affair through."

I rose from my chair and sat at his feet, taking his hands into mine. "There's nothing to think through. It won't work."

He took my face into his hands. "I need to get you out of here."

"I know. But not like that. We'll just get killed, all three of us."

"I don't like the speeches our political leaders are making lately." He pulled me toward himself, sat me down on his lap and cradled me in his embrace. "*Judenrein* Occupied Eastern territories, by the end of the summer," he finished in a barely audible voice. "They say, we should follow Estonia's example. They're in the lead. Completely clean of Jews, as they have put it."

I buried my face in the stiff collar of his shirt. His hand was gently stroking my back. My blouse was stuck to it again and I was creasing his shirt and his neatly-ironed jodhpurs by leaning into him but for some reason, neither of us paid the slightest attention to any of this.

"Do you think they'd take us?" I asked at last. "The Red Army, I mean."

He gave a shrug. "They take the Jews, so you'd be safe. Partisans or ordinary Red Army, no matter."

"What about you?"

Another shrug. "It depends on luck, I suppose. Sometimes they put defectors into special camps; sometimes, kill them on the spot. It depends on their mood."

He spoke about it so calmly as though his life was of no matter to him any longer. I kissed him, with infinite tenderness, on his mouth. It was of matter to me though.

"So, the Red Army is not an option," I concluded softly. "Partisans it is."

A scowl replaced his beaming expression at the sound of persistent knocking on his office door. I quickly fled back to my chair and began typing; whoever it was on the other side, let them hear me working.

Willy went to open the door. For some time, I listened to subdued voices, soon replaced by Willy's apparent protests.

"Don't worry, Herr Leutnant." Blood left my face when I recognized the voice of the man who'd advanced further into the office and soon stood before me, regarding me with the eyes of a cat watching a canary – Untersturmführer Schönfeld. "I'll watch over your little Jewess while you're collecting those papers from the Reichskommissariat."

Willy didn't move an inch from the door, his arms crossed over his chest.

Without turning around, Schönfeld said in a sing-song voice, "The Reichskommissariat officers don't appreciate the wait, Herr Leutnant."

"I'll be right back," Willy said to me and, after snatching his jacket from the back of the chair and throwing yet another withering glance at Schönfeld, quickly left the room. I didn't hear the door close – he must have left it open on purpose.

"Ilse Stein, isn't it?"

So, he knew my name after all. I rose from my seat and smoothed out my skirt. "That's correct, Herr Untersturmführer."

"How old are you?"

"Nineteen."

"Much younger than his wife."

"I wouldn't know about his wife. We don't talk on personal subjects."

"What do you talk about then?"

"Work-related issues."

He pulled the chair out, in which Willy was just sitting and positioned himself quite comfortably in it. "Is that so?"

"Yes."

"You spend an awful lot of time here."

"He has a lot of reports to type."

"A convenient excuse." His mouth twitched in disdain. His gaze was growing dark, impenetrable. "Do you type at night, too?"

My hand gripped the back of my chair instinctively, searching for any kind of support. I felt as if I was falling, falling straight through the ground and into the pits of hell and the devil himself was now grinning at me.

"Sometimes I have to stay until after six and by then it's too late to return to the ghetto. The curfew…"

"*Ach,* the curfew." His artificial laughter echoed off the walls. "That's awfully convenient too. And where do you sleep when you stay for a night?"

"On the floor in his office."

"He wouldn't let you sleep on the sofa?"

"No. The sofa is for Aryan officers only when they come to visit."

"I smell horse manure." A sneer cut across his handsome, cruel face. "I bet you sleep right here." He motioned his perfectly coiffured head toward the bed. "Together with Schultz."

Steps in the office promised the salvation of Willy's face but to my horror, it was another SD officer, Schönfeld's superior judging by the way Schönfeld jumped to his feet and greeted him with a snappy salute.

The newcomer, dark-haired and looking positively bored, was tall and considerably older than his subordinate. The belt hugged a visible paunch and his bloodshot eyes and reddish complexion betrayed his fondness for a drink.

"Well?" He didn't bother returning the salute, only leaned against the doorframe and put both thumbs into his belt instead. "You dragged me here; now what?"

Schönfeld stole a quick glance in my direction. A pleasant smile now replaced his previous poisonous smirk. "Just tell Herr Sturmbannführer the truth concerning your and Leutnant Schultz's relationship and we'll all be on our merry way. There will be no consequences for you, I promise."

The mere thought of what they'd do to Willy if I only uttered one careless word turned me cold with horror. It might as well have been winter outside; my entire body had begun to tremble.

"There's nothing to tell. I type reports and orders for him…" I shot a hopeful glance in the Sturmbannführer's direction. He stifled a yawn before arching a brow at his subordinate.

The latter turned to me, the previously pleasant mask vanished, as though by magic, as he shouted at me in a loud, wild voice, "You sleep here, you Jew-whore! The truth, I said!"

I jerked and instantly froze where I stood, a helpless rabbit before the uncoiling cobra. I couldn't bear that shouting, for that infamous SS shouting was invariably accompanied by vicious beatings and shootings and I had grown much too tender while away from all that. Tears were stinging my eyes without spilling, only burning like acid instead. I was terrified of these two men, beyond any measure.

At last, I managed to speak in a miserably weak voice, "I sleep on the carpet in the office—"

In an abrupt motion, Schönfeld leaped forward, seized my arm and twisted it behind my back with such force that I yelped in pain. Still holding me fast, his hand pushed me face down onto the table; with the other one, he undid his holster and took his gun out.

"I don't have time for your games!" Beads of spit landed on my face as he bellowed in my ear. "The truth I said!" He shoved the gun into my temple. I squeezed my eyes shut. "I shot twenty Jews, personally, just yesterday; I have no problem shooting one more! Tell me the truth!"

My entire body shook with sobs and unspeakable horror but I refused to say a single word. *Most likely he'll shoot me when he doesn't get what he wants to hear out of me and in front of his superior on top of it.* But my fate was sealed – I would be dead in any case by the end of summer; Willy said so himself. *Nobody wants to be worse than Estonia, do they? But him, him they won't touch now, as long as I keep silent.*

"Say it!!!" He nearly dislocated my shoulder after yanking on my arm once more while his knee was pressing into the small of my back.

I cried out in pain but shook my head adamantly, looking at Sturmbannführer's polished boots instead. "There's nothing to say… I'm only a typist, I swear!"

The older man rolled his eyes. *Let her go, don't you have anything better to do?* His red-rimmed eyes read as he looked at his subordinate. He was ready to walk out. Most likely, he, too, had a cold beer waiting for him in his office, which interested him much more than some Jew-girl.

His face twisted with fury at his so far unsuccessful interrogation, Schönfeld moved the gun away from my head and shoved it into my ribs instead, right next to my breast. "You're telling me he doesn't take advantage of such a situation? That sounds like a waste if you ask me. You have some nice, appealing assets here." His gun circled round my breast and moved down my stomach, then along the hip. "I bet he fucked you quite a few times in the same exact position you're currently in. It's not that I blame him – you're pretty for a Jew. Just nod your head if I'm correct."

I shook it instead, as much as the table, to which my temple was pressed, allowed.

He leaned even closer to me, refusing to give up. "It's very lonely here, away from home. And you're telling me he never shoved his dick in you, not even once?"

Something snapped in me that very moment. "No, he didn't! Only your SS men do that, in the ghetto, at night, when their superiors are asleep," I growled back.

He had wanted to make me speak but those were clearly not the words he'd expected. Out of the corner of my eye, I saw his superior straighten in the doorway, his face losing its bored expression for the first time.

"Put that gun away," he commanded. Apparently, there were precedents when Schönfeld showed himself to be a bit too trigger-happy for his commanding officer's liking. "Now, I said!"

"Herr Sturmbannführer—"

"You hold your tongue now and release her arm. I can't quite talk to her from this angle."

Reluctantly, Schönfeld released my arm. I pulled it toward myself and made a motion toward the older man when Untersturmführer grabbed my shoulder and pushed me down onto the chair. His superior now stood in front of me.

"What is it that you were saying about our SS men in the ghetto?"

Still cradling my arm, I stared at his brass buttons. We were not allowed to look into their eyes. It took Willy a good few weeks to persuade me in the opposite, for him. How many times, after we had just met, had I been staring at my food or the papers on his desk – anywhere but directly at his face. He had finally succeeded in breaking that hateful habit but now the words, drilled into our poor heads, beaten into us until we were covered in bruises, were back with a vengeance. *No Jew is allowed to approach an Aryan. No Jew is allowed to touch an Aryan. No Jew is allowed even to look an Aryan in the eye; the Jew can only look at the Aryan's feet and kiss them if needed. This is your place; remember it for the remainder of your short, vermin lives.*

The SD senior officer was waiting. I forced myself to part my lips. "They've been coming at night from time to time, ever since we've arrived here. They come drunk, select the prettiest girls and make them dance for them."

"Did they make you dance for them?"

I nodded. "A couple of times."

"What else did they make you do?"

"Me, nothing. But they did take some girls with them and people who work in the cemetery would later tell us that they found their naked corpses the following morning."

"That's a lie!" Behind my back, Schönfeld bellowed. "It's a shameless lie! She's only trying to divert the issue from herself, the cunning bitch! No SS man—"

"What part of the, 'hold your tongue' order did you not understand?!" his superior roared, his face growing even redder – from rage this time. "How long has this been going on and why have I never seen a single report about it?"

"Because it's not true, Herr Sturmbannführer…"

The older officer looked down at me. "Would you be able to recognize the men who came into your house if I showed you their photos?"

"Yes, Herr Sturmbannführer."

Already turning his back to me, he motioned for me to follow him. I did, putting as much distance between myself and Schönfeld as was possible. In silence, me trailing behind him, we walked along the carpeted hallway and up the marble staircase. On Sturmbannführer's floor, SD field-gray uniforms replaced the Luftwaffe blue ones. I stuck to him like glue, refusing to meet any of the curious gazes.

His office was larger than Willy's, with a portrait of Hitler occupying a big part of the wall. Below it, countless cabinets stood, instantly reminding me of the library catalog. Something told me though, it wasn't anything literature-related that was hidden there, numbered in succession and assigned its respective letter. He motioned for me to sit down while he searched for needed files behind my back.

"Ilse, isn't it?" He sounded calm, almost amicable.

"Yes, Herr Sturmbannführer."

"Schultz says you're a very good typist."

I didn't reply anything, just guessed by that remark that the man interrogating me must have been Sturmbannführer Bröger, Willy's acquaintance from the SD. He wasn't twisting my arm like Schönfeld but instinct, instilled by years of dealing with his SD kin reminded me, at once, that I had to watch myself with him even more.

"Is he a good boss?"

"Yes," I replied carefully.

"Does he give you extra rations?"

"He gives me scraps of his own food sometimes," I lied, putting as much humility in my voice as possible.

"Hm. That's nice of him. Is he kind to you?"

I considered carefully before responding, "He's demanding but just."

"Demanding?" He arched his brow, taking the chair next to me and laying out a stack of folders in front of him.

"He doesn't like sloppy work. Typos that is."

"Makes you retype the entire document until it's perfect?"

I faked reluctance before answering, hoping for the needed effect. "He hits my hands with a steel ruler when I make them. Sometimes he hits me on the head too because he thinks I do it on purpose. Just today he told me that if I keep sabotaging his work, he'll send me back to the brigade." I lowered my eyes, brimming with tears.

Another *hmm* from Sturmbannführer, more thoughtful than the first. "That's odd. He never appeared the type, to me, that would hit anyone. Let alone a woman."

"Oh no, that's not 'hitting,' it's more of a…" I pretended to search for the right word, "disciplining, that's what it is. It's my own fault, too; I should have been much better at it by now but…"

"But what?"

"He makes me nervous when he stands above me like that. I keep fearing he'll hit me again."

"Are you afraid of him?"

"A little."

He relaxed his posture a bit, seemingly satisfied. "I'll talk to him. I'll tell him to go easy on you." He moved the folders toward me. "Now, let's finish with this rotten business. These are the personal files of all SS men who have access to the ghetto. Go through them and tell me if you recognize any of them."

He patiently waited while I was sorting out the files. It took me a good thirty minutes, perhaps more. There were so many of them, perfect Aryans, most of them of my age, looking smugly at the camera, proud and arrogant in their uniforms. I thought of adding a few of them to the small stack but decided against it. No need for anyone to catch me in lying if I happen to point out the wrong man.

"These twelve I recognized. They all came to our house, on a few different occasions. You can ask the women who live with me – they'll confirm it."

"I will. The Field Police doesn't bring up anyone on charges unless it's proven by multiple witnesses. Anyone else?"

"No. Not out of these files, no."

"Any officers among them?"

"I think they were all privates."

"Regular SS men?"

"Yes."

He rose to his feet. I followed suit.

"You can go back now. I'm sure Schultz is looking for you already. And don't be afraid to tell him that you were here helping me with things if he starts threatening you with that ruler again." He even allowed a little smile onto his face.

I smiled timidly at his joke and wished him a good day before making off.

When I knocked on the door to Willy's office, it opened within seconds. He pulled me inside and shut it closed before drawing me into the tightest embrace. I still felt his hands trembling as he patted my arms, shoulders, searched for the marks on my face.

"Are you all right?"

"I'm fine, yes," I rushed to assure him.

"One of my men told me that Schönfeld came here with Bröger. He heard you screaming."

"Schönfeld twisted my arm," I admitted.

"What did that bastard want?" His voice was steel now; eyes, hard as granite.

"He wanted me to tell Sturmbannführer Bröger that you and I... that we were lovers. I didn't say anything, don't worry." I caressed his cheek with a smile. "I said you beat me with a steel ruler sometimes, so don't get too surprised if Bröger brings it up."

He covered my face with kisses. I looked at him in surprise when I felt wetness on my cheeks. He wiped his face quickly and offered me a somewhat guilty grin. "I thought I'd lost you."

"I'm here. It's all right," I repeated again. *The tears? Because of me?*

He only shook his head again. "Usually, when Schönfeld leads people away, they never come back."

Chapter 17

Thunder rolled in the distance, following remote flashes of lightning. It hadn't begun raining yet but the air was charged with electricity, dark violet clouds outside ready to burst into July showers and wash down the night. I lay awake again. One nightmare or another wakened me; I could never remember them once I opened my eyes with a start.

Willy stirred in his sleep – his arm must have gone to sleep under the weight of my head. I tried moving gently away from him but only found myself wrapped in his arms again.

"Stay, *Liebe,* stay," he muttered through sleep, without opening his eyes.

His face was tanned and relaxed against the whiteness of the pillow. A strand of hair fell over his forehead; soaked with a metallic glint of the lightning, it shone silver for a few moments before the darkness absorbed the room once again. I brushed it away gently and drunk in his features – the man who loved me more than he loved himself.

"You are getting out of here and I am coming with you," he said to me with grave resolution in his voice not two days ago. He wouldn't listen to my protests. *No, he didn't care one way or another he would be considered a deserter. No, he didn't care that he would never see his Fatherland again. No, he didn't care if the partisans decided to kill him.* "As long as you're alive and I'm with you." That was all that mattered. Everything else was dead to him; the family, the army, the loyalty.

He blinked his eyes open and grinned at me.

"What are you up to, Ilse Stein?"

"Just watching you sleep. Like you always watch me."

"How do you know I watch you?"

"I feel it." I brushed my fingers on his chest.

"Another thunderstorm?" He was looking at the open window. A curtain was floating in the wind like the great sail of a ghost ship. The time and the matter didn't exist any longer. We were the only people alive in the entire universe. "Come close to me. Why is your body so cold?"

Perhaps, because I'm already dead.

I only smiled and draped my leg over his. "I'm always cold. That's why I need you to hold me."

"I'd hold you every night if I could." I leaned my face toward him so he could kiss me in the way that would make me forget everything, for a few moments at any rate. "I'll hold you every night once we're out of here."

"You promise?"

You and I, we both know that it will hardly work, but say the words, lie to me, tell me about the future that will never come true.

"I swear."

He sat up with me still straddling him and put his lips on my breast. I lifted my hips up when he reached down and drew in my breath as he slid inside of me. I needed this tonight, needed to feel alive again, for one more night at least.

I didn't tell him how, two days ago, as I was marching together with the brigade back to the ghetto, Schönfeld emerged out of nowhere, seized me by my arm and pulled me to the sidewalk, on which we weren't allowed. People parted upon seeing his uniform – even civilians didn't wish anything to do with the dreaded SD.

"Twelve of our men were brought before the court-martial for the *Rassenschande* yesterday," he growled, his voice full of venom. "This morning, they were executed."

I was afraid he'd break my arm if I implied that they got what they deserved, so I kept my mouth shut.

"Twelve of *my* men are dead because of you." His face was suddenly split by a vicious grimace of a smile. "You watch what I do to *your* people now."

With that, he shoved me back toward the road. I ran as fast as I could to catch up with the column.

*

July 28, 1942

I didn't hear the first shots due to the noise of my typewriter. Only when the trucks with wailing people sped down Sovietskaya Street, did I yank the curtain open and shuddered at the sheer number of them. Some men tried to jump off and were mown down by the machinegun fire at once – the SS escort was more than vigilant. The civilians scrambled out of the trucks' way, out of the SS troops' way, as far as possible from the Black Police shouting loudly in Lithuanian as they savagely clubbed the ones, who were only wounded, with their batons.

I rushed to the office and tried the front door – it was locked, as always. After the incident with Schönfeld, Willy positively refused to leave any chance for the situation to repeat itself. I heard the people running to and fro in the corridor; where Willy was, it was anyone's guess.

Back in his bedroom, I pushed the window open and leaned outside, hoping to locate my brigade. At the end of May, when the need to heat the complex of buildings had disappeared, Willy came up with quite an arrangement for them; they were gardeners now, cultivating and creating the most beautiful floral ensembles around the Government Building and various adjoining headquarters. To the SD commanders, who took to the idea rather dubiously at first, he soon proudly demonstrated a *Großdeutschland Adler* arranged out of decorative bushes and flowers, which could now be seen from Sturmbannführer Bröger's window. Bröger beamed and thought it to be a delightful idea and toasted to it, with Willy's imported

French cognac. Both of my sisters joined the brigade as well, on Willy's insistence. "It's easier to keep an eye on them this way," he explained in an off-hand way. *It's easier to save their lives once the SS come,* he actually meant.

The gardening brigade observed the movement of the trucks, with their tools still in hand, exchanging wary glances. One of the Lithuanians with the Black Police armband strode toward them. The supervising policeman from the *Ordnungsdienst* showed him some paper, pointed at the Government Building, then at the women again, moving the paper closer to the man's face. The latter stalked off, disappointed. I could almost hear the collective sigh they all released.

Rapid bursts of gunfire and screams now echoed through the streets, coming from the ghetto itself. Soon, blasts of exploding grenades joined in, accompanied by the maddened howling of the dogs. I shut the window closed and sank to the floor right under it, my hands rising to cover my ears of their own volition. That's precisely how Willy found me when he returned to the office, his face as white as chalk.

"What's happening?" I barely heard myself say.

"I don't know. An *Aktion*."

He stood in front of the window. His boots were covered in dust.

"Have you tried going there? Are they liquidating the ghetto? Are they going to kill everyone?" I raised my head to look at him but he was still staring straight ahead, his brows drawn tightly in concentration. Not getting any reply out of him, I tried again. "Willy, was there any kind of order? Is this the end? Is this because of me? Schönfeld said that because I reported those SS men to Bröger, he'd do something horrible to my people now. Is this all truly because of me?" I felt as though my nerves would snap any second now.

Willy's hand found my shoulder and squeezed it slightly – that was all the reassurance he could give me, as of now.

"Why would you put such a silly idea into your head? It's not because of you and it's not Schönfeld's doing. His rank is not high enough to sanction anything like this. There must have been some high order from above. Don't fret; you're safe here," he said, at last, his voice as weak as his promises.

I pulled my knees toward my chest and hugged them tightly.

"If Schönfeld comes here—" I began.

"Schönfeld won't come here," he interrupted me at once.

"If he comes here or one of his people," I repeated, catching his wrist, "I want you to do it."

He stared at me in horror.

"I want you to do it, not them," I tried to smile pleadingly through the tears. "I want you to shoot me. Don't let them take me away. They will hurt me. With you, I know I won't feel anything."

He sank to the floor next to me as though his legs refused to hold him. He found my hand and kissed it softly.

"If it comes to that," he spoke, suddenly very calmly, like a man who had finally looked death in the face, "we'll both go, together."

I wanted to protest something, to talk him out of it but one look into his eyes was enough to understand everything. He couldn't shoot at the enemy, as a pilot, choosing to get shot at instead and crashing several aircraft just to avoid taking another man's life – Otto told me that himself; would he really be able to execute a woman he loved in cold blood and live with himself after that?

The shrill ringing of the telephone in the office pulled harder on the nerves, already strained to the utmost. Willy watched it ring with suspicion, then decided that it would be worse not to answer it altogether. His posture visibly relaxed after a few moments. He gave me a reassuring smile. *It's not for me then that they're calling; not yet. A few more minutes to live. A few more hours if I'm fortunate enough.*

Hours dragged on, interminable, full of unbearable tension, interrupted by the odd phone calls and visitors who brought reports, which Willy threw irritably, without reading, onto his desk until it was littered with them. *The people are dying in their hundreds outside and they worry about spare airplane parts!* The sun was rolling towards the west, still high enough to offer salvation. The wait was growing intolerable. The uncertainty was impossible to bear any longer. *He would try to go outside and see what the SS's exact orders were,* he explained, putting his gun into my hands.

"Do you know how to shoot it? No? It's easy. Click this safety catch off – now it's cocked. Then, all you have to do is pull the trigger." He held my face in his hands as though memorizing it for the time being. "There are eight bullets inside. You have seven to spare for their stomachs. Got it?"

I nodded and bit my lip not to break down. He needed me to be strong for him, just like I needed him to be courageous. He kissed me, desperately and deeply, as if for the very last time and quickly stepped out of the door – while he still could bring himself to leave me. The key turned in the lock. He showed me where to aim if they began breaking it in his absence.

*

He returned in the evening, pale as death, and began rummaging through the drawers of his desk until he pulled out a ring with several keys on it.

"Ilse, you're going to have to come with me." The keys jingled ever so slightly; he clasped them in his fist to stop his hands from trembling. "They will listen to me better if you're with me. They trust you."

"Who?" I still held his gun clumsily pressed against my stomach. I'd spent the entire day in this position, with my arms wrapped tightly around my waist for I could swear I would fall apart if I let go of myself even for an instant. He took the weapon from my hands. It was wet with perspiration.

"The brigade. We need to hide them for tonight. The SS are taking skilled workers in trucks to some special camp they installed next to the ghetto, supposedly to keep them separate from the others while they clean the ghetto out but whether it's true or a trick of some sort one can only guess. I'd rather keep them away for the time being."

"Where are you going to hide them?"

"In the cellar. It's big enough."

"Won't you get in trouble if they find out that you're hiding the Jews?"

He hesitated with his response.

"Those SS men got executed for the *Rassenschande* after I told Bröger about them. Is it worse of a crime than that, what you're planning to do?" I pressed.

Anyone found guilty of interfering with the SS Aktionen or aiding or concealing any person of Jewish nationality is subject to immediate execution; we knew the words by heart now for they glared at us, in angry black letters, from every corner of the ghetto, from every corner of every street in Minsk. Was it meant only for the eyes of the civilians or the occupying forces as well?

He was silent for a very long moment. "No," he said at last with a ghost of a smile, not having the heart to tell me the truth. "It's nothing, what I'm planning to do. Just a minor misdemeanor."

He'd get shot if they found out; that much was clear. What was also clear was the fact that he knew it and purposely chose to go through with the risk, much like he used to do with the enemy fliers, by offering them his aircraft to strafe instead of doing away with theirs.

I caught his sleeve when he was already at the door.

"Ilse, your sisters are there," he reminded me softly, "and Liza."

He was so much calmer than me, so much braver.

"What about you, though?"

"Don't worry about me. I know my way around their laws."

"Willy, let us all go with the trucks. Maybe there is indeed a camp and we all carry the cards of skilled workers—"

"What is this? Defeatist talk, Ilse Stein. We're having none of that tonight. No taking chances, little soldier; not on my watch. Tonight, we all live. Understood?" He smiled at me in spite of himself. I nodded, putting on a brave face for him.

I didn't ask any more questions, only followed him along the corridor, down to the ground floor, then – even lower, into the damp and barely lit cellar. We walked through its maze for a good few minutes until he pushed the door open and whistled softly into the staircase. A hint of freshly-cut grass and earth wafted through an open door – it must have led to the outside, at the back of the building.

Hurried steps followed Willy's signal. I recognized Stepan and Liza as their leaders. Liza rushed to hug me tightly. Soon, the cellar was full of women, all two hundred of them. I kissed both of my sisters with immense relief.

After ensuring that all women were accounted for, Willy locked the entrance and motioned for them to follow him. He brought us down one more level, where the walls were covered with mold and moisture and tremendous pipes ran along the walls, wrapped in some sort of insulation. At the end of this labyrinth, was a former boiler room, which was no longer in use.

"Sit down by that wall," Willy commanded. The women dutifully obeyed, a sea of frightened faces. "I know you think you will have it worse if you don't return to the ghetto tonight but I assure you, if you do so, you will most definitely die. The *Aktion* will continue throughout the night. The SS have orders to liquidate all ghettos in all occupied Eastern territories. The order for the executive action was given to the heads of the *Einsatzgruppen* by Reichsführer Himmler himself, just two days ago. What it means for you is that only a handful of skilled workers will be left alive – for now. All women, children, the sick, and the elderly are subjects for immediate execution."

A collective moan echoed through the room. Some jumped to their feet and tried to run past Willy and out of the cellar – half of the women had children in the orphanage and elderly relatives in the ghetto.

"Sit down!" In the narrow passage, he was shoving them back toward the wall until the situation threatened to get out of hand. Pulling his gun out, Willy pointed it at the nearest woman's stomach. "Sit down and shut up this instant, I said!! Don't you understand what's going to happen if they hear us here? We'll all get shot; is that what you want?!"

Suddenly, he didn't look any better than them, his forehead glistening with a film of cold sweat. It wasn't the gun or the dreaded uniform that produced the desired effect; it was the inhuman, desperate tone of his voice, which was just short of begging. For the first time, through the crack of the carefully erected façade of a confident officer, *one of the masters of the world,* fear showed itself and it terrified everyone around into submission better than any gun would. If the officer was afraid, the business was indeed serious.

"Please, sit down and keep quiet." He passed his hand, with the gun still squeezed in it, across his forehead, suddenly looking very tired. "All of your relatives are already dead. Your Sonderghetto has been liquidated. There's nothing that can be done about it now. You can't help the dead; you can only help yourselves as of now. Please, stay put where you are. Give me a few hours, just till the morning… I'll tell you when it's safe to come out…"

He didn't know what else to tell them and looked at me help-lessly.

"Herr Leutnant is good friends with Sturmbannführer Bröger, the chief of the SD here, in Minsk," I turned to the women. "Remember how we were all afraid that the SS would shoot us all as soon as the heating season was over? Herr Leutnant kept us alive, didn't he? Now, he'll help us again but he needs you to stay as quiet as mice down here, do you understand? He's risking his own life hiding you all here; please, please, stay put and quiet until either of us comes down here and lets you out. We'll try to bring you food and water when it's safe. My own sisters are among you – we'll never just abandon you but please, stay quiet while Herr Leutnant is working things out with Sturmbannführer Bröger, will you?"

They murmured their agreement. Most still cried softly. In the corner, Liza was biting her nails to the quick.

"Do you know anything about the *Judenrat*?" she asked Willy, in a straightforward manner. She also couldn't take the uncertainty any longer.

He gave her a pained look. *Why are you asking?*

"They executed Elder Yoffe; that's all I know. The SS wanted him to assure the people that it was safe to board the trucks which they had brought into the ghetto and he instead told the people to run and hide. The SS shot him on the spot. I don't know about the rest. Weinstein is alive though."

"Of course, he is. Collaborating pig!" Liza spat out.

"If I find out anything tomorrow, Ilse will tell you the news." He softened his tone, sensing her pain.

Liza smiled bravely at him. "Thank you, Herr Leutnant. Forgive me for the outburst. The nerves…"

He nodded his understanding.

"I'll lock you here. Please, be as quiet as possible," he asked them once again instead of a goodbye.

I kissed my sisters and Liza before following him outside.

"I can lock you here as well, if you think it to be safer than upstairs, in my office," he suggested, fumbling with the keys.

"No. I feel safer with you."

He brushed my cheek with infinite tenderness before turning the key in the lock.

"Thank you, Willy." In the meager light of the cellar, he suddenly seemed aged by ten more years, only the eyes shone brightly, blue with the steel of resolution, just barely tinted with a shade of fear. "I know what it will mean for you if they find them."

"They won't find them."

I didn't know who he was trying to persuade more, himself or me.

"They will kill you if they find them."

"It's my life to live and my life to lose." He cupped my cheek once again. "Be brave now, *Liebchen*. We have to hope for the best."

With tears of gratitude, I nodded and kissed the hand which granted me life, which granted all of us lives – for a few days perhaps and probably, at the price of his own.

Chapter 18

The shooting continued throughout the night. Tracer bullets were visible if we stood close enough to the window – the SS were shooting from their positions on the roofs, from watchtowers, at the unfortunates who crawled out of their hiding places hoping for the cover of the night. An animalistic, drunken howling of the Black Police *pogromshiks* drowned in the bloodcurdling screams of their victims – we could hear it all even through the tightly shut windows, streets away from the massacre itself.

We sat, fully dressed, on the bed with our backs against the wall, a half-empty bottle of schnapps between us. It was impossible to sleep just like it was impossible to get drunk that night. No alcohol in the world would be enough to silence that orgy of death outside.

I put the neck of the bottle to my lips but couldn't take another swig. I put it back, searching for his hand in the darkness instead.

"Talk to me, Willy."

"What about?"

"Anything. Tell me about your childhood."

He was quiet for some time, gathering his thoughts. It was difficult to concentrate on anything but the carnage outside. "Let's see. I was born on September 3rd, 1899, much to my father's delight. He'd already had three daughters by then and had all but given up hope that he'd have a son. Not that he didn't adore them; if anything, I'd say they got away with mischief for which he usually administered me a veritable thrashing." He smiled fondly at the memories. "He was a career officer, so I believe he only wanted a son so that he could discipline at least someone in his family. My mother, however, ruined even that idea for him; whenever I was caught at any mischief, she always took my side and my father loved her too much to insist on punishing me when she would ask him not to."

"Did he serve in the Great War, your father?"

"He did and in the war of 1870 before that. I lucked out on the Great War's account though. As soon as my infantry training finished as a new conscript, the Armistice was signed. I didn't see any fighting at all. Only what happened later." His voice took a different tone.

"Was it difficult for your family after the war?" I asked carefully.

He considered for some time before replying. "It wasn't all that bad, I suppose. That is, it was worse for the others. Much worse. My father was fortunate enough to secure himself a position as a policeman through an old comrade and we weren't starving at least. I was studying and doing odd jobs whenever I could. You don't remember the twenties, I suppose? You were just a baby then."

I shook my head with a smile. "No, I don't. I remember starting from '26 or '27 and then it was already all right. Besides, when you're a child, you don't really notice those things. Your head is full of air when you're young and all you want to know is fun and games. Besides, we lived in a very small town surrounded by farmlands. My parents were grocers, so we never starved."

"Small towns fared better than big cities. That much is true."

"When did you decide to join the Party?"

I didn't want to ask him that, yet I did. It was one of those truths that one better face, no matter how hurtful it may be.

"When I was told that the position of a customs inspector which I was eyeing was for the Party members only," he explained almost apologetically. "It was 1933. Hitler had just come to power and they began securing it all starting with the government and on down. The customs department was on the priority list. I didn't think it to be a big deal back then. I didn't care one way or another about politics, you see. All I knew was that I was engaged to Hedwig and

I needed a job to provide for us both. She had expensive tastes." Another apologetic grin.

It was the first time we spoke openly about both – the Party and Hedwig.

"Women will be the downfall of you, Willy Schultz." I nudged him with my shoulder in jest. Gallows humor, it surely was but he obliged me with a chuckle.

"So, it seems." He circled his arm around me and pulled me even closer. "Tell me about your childhood now."

"There's not much to tell. I was born in Nidda in 1923, the middle sister of three but that much you already know. My parents were grocers and my best friend's name was Ursula Bosch. Usch Bosch, she was called and she was a tough sort. She was very tall, taller than me even and very athletic." I paused at the memory. "She was one of the few girls who still remained friends with me after 1935 and she would beat anyone who would be daft enough to tease my sisters or me in front of her, be it boys or girls." Catching a blank stare from Willy, I specified. "The Nuremberg Laws. After they came into effect, we realized for the first time that we were actually Jewish, different from Aryan Germans. Before, we thought we were all the same. My family wasn't religious at all; if anything, we even had a tree put up for Christmas every year. Though, it didn't matter in the end. You probably didn't pay much attention to any of that."

"Not really," he admitted, looking pensive. "I suppose one doesn't pay attention to the matters that don't concern them personally."

"It wasn't all too bad at first. We only had SA soldiers gluing papers to our store window from time to time, which we weren't allowed to rip off under the punishment of imprisonment. You know, those posters that said *Jewish-owned business; don't shop here* and everything else to that effect."

"There were plenty of those in Dresden as well."

"Yes. People didn't particularly care though; we always had the freshest produce and my parents were hospitable people and never denied anyone credit. So, people still shopped in our store till the SA destroyed it in 1938."

"The *Kristallnacht*?"

"Yes. How was it in Dresden?"

"People thought the war had started. Then, Goebbels addressed the nation and reassured us that we had nothing to fear." He paused before adding softly, "And that the Jews would have to pay for all the damage they caused."

"Ironic, isn't it?"

Willy sat quietly for a few moments.

"Why didn't you emigrate after that?" he asked.

"We didn't have any money. Only enough to move to Frankfurt. There, Lily and I worked as maids and later, in the factory. You know that part of the story."

I looked at him. He sat in the darkness, with his brows knitted tightly together, as though trying to grasp something, to understand the inconceivable, to pinpoint the moment when everything suddenly got out of control and the point of no return was officially passed by both sides – the future murderers and their victims. The new Reich sorted us into two kinds and now he suddenly found himself among those who held an ax above our miserable heads.

"Don't blame yourself for anything," I answered his unspoken pleas. "You couldn't have possibly known where all this would lead you, in the end."

"Do you know what interested me the most in 1938?" He spoke at length. "How wonderful the new autobahn was because I had just bought a new car and loved taking it to the countryside, to take my jacket and tie off and drive as fast as possible along that endless road. Another big problem was where to go for summer because Hedwig wished to go on a cruise in the Mediterranean and I wanted to go to the Baltic Sea. I let her have her way after all and spent all two weeks cursing myself and her because it was hot and humid like in a sauna and I can't tolerate the heat. Then, one of my sisters had her fourth child and named him after me – felt sorry for me most certainly. I always loved children yet didn't have any myself. And so, I was rather too preoccupied with being a spoiling uncle to notice that the world was ending for certain people around me and I hadn't the faintest idea. Not even that; we preferred not to see it. Businesses closed, then reopened under a new name; people just disappeared – our own neighbors sometimes. We shrugged it off and preferred to think that they moved to a different city or a different country perhaps. The genocide was starting under our noses, yet we thoroughly pretended that we didn't smell anything. How terrifying it is, Ilse! How positively terrifying!"

It was, the way it started and the way it was ending now – in the massacre right outside our windows.

*

At dawn, silence at last. It was only interrupted by the odd crackling of automatic rifles – the SS was finishing off whoever survived the night in their hiding places. Unshaven, with bloodshot eyes and wrinkled uniform, Willy motioned for me to follow him downstairs. The building was deserted still – the officers never bothered waking earlier than seven.

One step at a time, we were making our way to the cellar. After talking the entire affair through last night, Willy came to the conclusion that there was no explaining – neither to Bröger nor to anyone else for that matter – what he had done. There was only facing him directly and taking the gamble.

"Aren't you afraid?" I took his hand. Today, it was warm and steady.

"I've been allowing them to intimidate me for too long," he spoke with calm resignation in his voice. "A seventeen-year-old girl – Masha Bruskina – I still remember her name, a Jewish partisan, wasn't afraid of them when she stepped on the gallows. I had just arrived in Minsk and the first thing I saw was three teenagers, two young men and a young girl, being led through the street with placards around their necks: *'We are the partisans who shot at German troops.'* My staff car couldn't pass through the thick crowd and the driver stopped right across the street from the Minsk Kristall, a distillery plant in front of which the gallows had been erected. My first day in the city and I was watching an execution. Do you know what stunned me the most though? The girl's face, calm as it could be, as though it wasn't her neck that was being put in the noose. She wasn't afraid and I couldn't understand it back then. We had been taught to live with this fear, to constantly watch ourselves, what we do, what we say, just not to end up like her. I thought her to be mad then; now, I think of her as a hero. If more of us refused to be intimidated by them, this all wouldn't have happened. So, no, *Ilschen,* I'm not afraid. If Bröger shoots me, let him. I'd rather die than continue living like a coward."

Down in the cellar, the women looked as though they hadn't slept at all, eyes red and weary, hair and clothes in disarray. Without saying as much as a good morning, Willy motioned them silently after himself and headed for the same exit through which he'd let them in the day before. Liza, an irreplaceable leader in front of the column, hesitated before coming out.

"What do we do now?" she asked Willy.

"We walk out and act as if we belong there," he replied simply.

He led the brigade himself to their usual working place in front of the building and waved them to the flowerbeds. "Well? What are you waiting for? Go ahead, pick up your tools and get to it. There's still time for you to use the facilities and wash up before everyone wakes up but as soon as they do, you all must be right here, where I can see you."

Stumbling and unsure, the women spread out among the flowers, digging aimlessly, with trembling hands, into the earth.

After observing them for some time, Willy lowered to the ground and leaned against the building's wall. His eyes were closing; he dug the heels of his palms into them and rubbed them vigorously. I stood next to him, deadly tired yet inexplicably alert.

The first people appeared in the street. The first officers made their way through the carefully organized pathways framed by blossoming flowers, hurrying to a neighboring building with a report. Willy straightened out and watched them, like a hawk, with his hands clasped behind his back. The blue-clad ones from the Luftwaffe saluted him and shook their heads while rolling their eyes emphatically as they passed us by. *What a damnable night! Blasted SS and their Aktion! I barely slept an hour,* their annoyed expressions read. The gray-clad ones from the SD were still curiously absent, most likely either busy planning yet another massacre or sleeping off the previous one.

By lunchtime, Sturmbannführer Bröger stepped out of the staff car, scowled at the brigade incomprehensibly and made his way toward us, still standing at our post.

"Heil Hitler, Schultz."

"Heil Hitler, Sturmbannführer."

"Where did these come from?" A nod in the women's direction.

"You gave an order yesterday not to let any working brigades back into the ghetto until you're finished there and there were no more trucks left to transport them to your special camp," Willy answered. "I only followed your orders."

"Those orders were for factory workers and suchlike." Bröger grinned.

"The heating season will start again soon," Willy said quietly.

"In September only." Bröger obliterated him with a wave of his hand. "I'll give you new ones, from France or Czechoslovakia. Fresh ones, eager to work."

"These are very good workers. I'm used to them."

Bröger regarded him closely. "Schultz, do you really care that much who plucks the weeds in your garden or who shovels the coal into the boiler room? What's the difference between one Jew or the other?"

Willy just stared at him without saying a word, stared long and hard until the smile faded from the SD officer's face and he shrugged nonchalantly. "*Ach,* keep them if you like; it's all the same to me. They're being fed by your department, not mine."

"Allow me to tell any of your subordinates that these women are permitted to stay on premises in case they inquire on whose orders?"

Willy's pleading gaze promised all the best goods in the entire Occupied Eastern territory he could only get his hands on, to Sturmbannführer Bröger for his generosity. Bröger moved his shoulder – a monarch granting a life. "Tell them. Only don't tell them that it's because I have a soft spot for your company that I permitted this. Or we'll both be heading to the front the next day, Schultz, and I won't forgive you that, trust me."

"I swear, Sturmbannführer. I'm a grave."

"You look like one." Bröger gave Willy a once-over. "Go take a shower and change for Christ's sake. My men, who've been working all night, don't look half as miserable as you do."

Willy obliged him with a crooked grin. Bröger could abuse him for an entire day for all he cared, as long as his brigade was safe.

"I'm serious, Schultz. Go put yourself in order and I'll be waiting for you for lunch in thirty minutes."

"I'll be there."

"You'd better. And bring that Hennessy, if you still have it and the sardines. We're celebrating today."

Willy nodded his compliance. He'd bring him the cognac. He'd bring him everything he had, his soul if needed, just to adhere to what he had chosen to ignore, just to save a couple of hundred out of hundreds of thousands that were already dead.

Chapter 19

The ghetto had been sealed, by the SS, for four days. For four days, the brigade slept in the cellar – this time, though, with Bröger's permission. On the fifth day, he made a personal appearance and, red-faced and jolly, announced that since the brigade was allowed to live, the SS would have to get something "for their trouble."

"No gardening for you today," he said. "March to the ghetto and clean up the mess there. Off you go!"

Willy was absent that morning. He'd been summoned to the airbase on an urgent matter and left me behind to watch the brigade.

The SS men were already counting the women as they lined up, obedient and meek, in the usual rows of five, on the street. I threw a glance at the building. I didn't have to go with the brigade; I knew that, even though Willy's office had been closed, any of his comrades from the same floor would let me stay with them until he returned. They had all been familiar with me by now and called me "our Ilse." Even Liza gave me a sign to stay put where I was – who knew if the SS received another order to do away with the working brigades as well and where best to do that, if not in the ghetto itself. I contemplated the entrance, then the brigade in front of me.

"You don't have to join them, Fräulein Stein." Bröger looked at me in surprise as I slipped into the last row of women. "You'll only bring typhus back."

"She won't. Our people dispatched the entire hospital." His adjutant tried to conceal his chuckling by coughing but the wry, mocking smirk still sat, ugly and crooked, on his young, clean-shaven face.

"You really can stay," Bröger repeated, ignoring him. I began wondering how much exactly had Willy paid him for him to express such concern for my well-being.

"Thank you, but it's all right, Herr Sturmbannführer. I'd like to go with my sisters."

"As you wish." Bröger raised a brow and snorted with amusement before setting off.

It was early morning, yet the heat was rising from the asphalt as we marched on. New shoes, still tight and unbroken, pinched my feet. I looked ridiculous among them in my attire and I felt it. I hadn't the faintest idea why Willy had insisted on dressing me up in all these ridiculous outfits from the German department stores. First, that suit; then shoes, underwear, stockings – the best of the items for a corpse who would soon be buried. But after all, wasn't that how the tradition had it? Only the best for the dead, even though they may be still living. Still, he dressed me with some obstinate obsession, as though all of these clothes, shoved into an endless black hole of hatred from which time was leaking out, corroding everything on its way, would be enough to stop its relentless, inevitable course.

Near the gates of the ghetto, a bored sentry looked on from his watchtower as we were being counted before being admitted inside. As soon as he took his attention elsewhere – no doubt, to two sharply dressed Wehrmacht *Helferinnen* walking past with their Alsatian on a tight leash, on their low heels, in their ironed skirts, with their beautiful hair put under the caps in fashionable rolls – one of the men from another working brigade inched his way toward ours and slipped something into Liza's hand.

Her eyes lit up at once as she recognized the handwriting. With a beaming smile, she hid the note in her pocket. The man from the neighboring brigade had already rejoined his ranks and thoroughly pretended to be immersed in reading the only sign that "graced" the gates of the ghetto and which we all knew by heart: *Warnung,*

Bei Durchklettern des Zaunes wird geschossen. Warning, people who climb through the fence will be shot.

"What is it, Liza?" I guessed what it was but was too afraid to jinx it.

"Nahum has managed to escape," her reply came in a hushed, excited whisper. "He's alive. He's with the partisans already. He writes he'll get us out as soon as possible but until then, he says not to talk to anyone and not to trust anyone except Sergei." She stole another grateful glance in the man's direction. He was still perusing the sign with what appeared to be the utmost interest. "They left only collaborators in charge. Sergei, he's a good comrade, a longtime friend. We worked together at the same power plant before the war – I know him quite well. He could have run too but he stayed to keep the connection between the ghetto and the partisans."

I regarded the inconspicuous man with newfound respect. To purposely remain in this purgatory, that took more than most of us had in us.

"I've never met him before," I confessed.

"You've never met many of them before and that's the way it should have been from the very beginning," she replied. "It's because everyone knew everyone in the fall that already in the spring the Gestapo killed Rivka, Styopka-Kaznachey, Zyama, Eli; through them got to the City Committee, then hanged Efim and almost all of his fellow printers and almost caught Boris himself."

"That's what I say."

I swung around and came face to face with Lore, my baby sister with a wise, grown woman's eyes who didn't even try to conceal the fact that she was listening to our hushed conversation the entire time.

"Discretion should be our utmost priority," she uttered again.

My brow clouded at that "our" of hers; she had never severed her ties with the printers or whoever she was in contact now – she wouldn't tell me that just like Liza preferred to keep quiet on some people's account, not because they distrusted me but solely because it was the only sensible thing to do. The less one knows, the less one will reveal under torture and who can tell how well they can tolerate the pain when they make an actual acquaintance with the Gestapo? I never told them about Otto Weizmann's communist inclinations and his defection plans he kept contemplating along with Willy; neither did I speak of any of that with Lily, my elder sister. Life had taught us all too well how to keep quiet.

"With Sergei's help, Nahum will get us out. You'll see how fast he will," Liza whispered again. "Nothing is lost yet, Ilsechka. Nothing is lost."

How I hope for you to be right, my dear Liza!

Our bright mood didn't last long. As soon as we stepped through the gates, the overpowering stench of blood assaulted our senses, metallic and instantly recognizable, even more pronounced on this hot summer day. As we were marched to our assigned sector, we stepped in it; it was inevitable since it was everywhere – in dried-out puddles and brownish streams, splattered against the walls and running down from the windows, from which half of a torso was hanging – *shot during an attempt to escape,* it was officially called in their reports.

Lore stared ahead, grim yet perfectly collected. She looked as though she was committing the entire grisly picture to her young mind. She was, most likely, to report the carnage to her cell members who would print it out and shower the city of Minsk with it, the villages around it; perhaps, dispatch it to Moscow even. Unlike my youngest brave girl, my poor pale-faced Lily was swaying slightly on her feet. My eldest sister couldn't bear the sight of blood and the streets around us had turned into a veritable charnel house which turned even my stomach with dread and I had never complained about the weakness of my nerves. I could only sympathize with her plight and offer her my elbow for support. I had the most

profound conviction she would have fainted had I not gathered
her into my arms in time.

"Start with the roofs and top floors." Our SS supervisor was all
efficiency; they all were. "Assemble all the bodies on the ground
along the sidewalk. The trucks will arrive by twelve to collect them."

A shadow passed over his face as he had fixed his gaze on us,
regarding us closely for the first time. "Why are you not wearing
your stars?"

"We're Leutnant Schultz's special brigade," I explained quickly
and offered him my *Ausweis* for perusal. "Sturmbannführer Bröger
said it was all right. We're German Jews; we aren't considered a
flight risk."

He gave my papers a cursory perusal, nodded with a measure
of respect at Bröger's signature and suddenly grinned brightly.
"Well, you're the only ones left. There's no more Sonderghetto. I
hope you won't mind too much, your future living arrangements
together with the *Ostjuden*."

"I suppose you won't make us suffer too long." I don't know what
bug bit me to say it; much too my relief, he only laughed again.

"No, we won't."

That was evident without his morbid confirmation. From our
vantage point on one of the roofs a few minutes later, we watched as
the men from the working brigades were tearing down the barbed
wire which formerly served as a border to the Hamburg ghetto
while the other unit was already erecting a new wall, much closer
to the cemetery. Our SS supervisors explained that this was where
we were going to live from that point on, in squat little houses with
typical Russian windows, framed in carved, painted white wood.

"Good neighbors. Quiet," Liza commented in a flat tone,
motioning her head in the Jewish Cemetery's direction.

Someone snorted next to us. I did too, in spite of myself. Soon,
our entire little clean-up *Kommando* was laughing hysterically

while tears streamed down our faces. We laughed at our own approaching death.

After a few hours, we learned to recognize when the person that we carried was killed. The most recent ones were stiff as boards; their arms and legs were impossible to maneuver into any sort of normal position and we carried them the way they fell, rigid and unyielding, to the blistering outside. Their skin was cold and clammy; we soon learned to hold them by the parts where their clothes covered them so they wouldn't slip from our grip.

The ones from the first two days of the massacre were bloated caricatures of their former selves, insects already crawling inside their mouths open in silent pleas. Each time we lifted them, the gasses inside their poor broken bodies made soft, sighing sounds, as though the dead were apologizing for causing us to look at their discolored faces and suppress retching at the stench they were emitting.

We lined them all up along the road regardless – the stiff and the bloated, the young and the elderly, the men and the women, until the streets were full of them. There were more dead in the ghetto that day than the living.

In the evening, after scrubbing the blood off the floors of our new lodgings, we washed our hands and headed to the Labor Exchange to receive our meager rations distributed by exhausted men who didn't look any better than us. After exchanging our ration coupons for some bread and soup, we brought the food back to the house. There were very few of us occupying it – we had been allowed even to choose our own quarters; that's how many wooden huts now stood empty and silent, with their windows staring at the street like the glazed-over eyes of the dead. We decided to wash them as well the next day; there was no blood on them but still, we wished them to be clean, just on general grounds.

In the evening, an hour before the curfew, Liza and I walked to the cemetery and sat on the ground, still warm from the day.

The burial brigade was still digging in the distance, dying sunset bleeding its last rays onto their uncovered heads.

"How many of us are left?" Liza wondered out loud.

"I don't know. A few thousand?" I squinted against the sunset.

"There were over two hundred thousand of us just last June. How is it possible? They killed almost two hundred thousand people in a little over a year. Just here, in Minsk. How many similar ghettos are out there, in Europe, do you think?"

I didn't say anything. It was inconceivable just to imagine the number. I didn't want to imagine anything today. I saw far too much for my much-too-short life to imagine things in addition to what I already seen. My head would explode if I began counting the dead that I didn't carry today.

The cuckoo bird started her mocking counting somewhere among the headstones. Liza, looking strangely concentrated, began counting along with it.

"What are you counting, you silly thing?" I nudged her with my elbow. "It's a Jewish cuckoo bird."

"Seven," she counted out loud. "Is there a difference between Jewish cuckoo birds and Gentile ones? Ten. Eleven…"

"There is; a big one. A Jewish cuckoo bird doesn't predict the years to live as the Gentile one does. The Jewish ones count the days until we die."

"Fifteen… I'll still take it. Two more weeks to live. Sixteen…"

"You're a silly old bat!" I barked at her, rising to my feet.

She didn't say anything, only chuckled and kept counting. Outbursts like mine were nothing new and she herself was prone to them. We were long past the days when it would offend us.

*

I was back in Willy's quarters. Upon returning from the base, he wasn't himself, wandering around with a lost look about him. I wrote it off to working matters and let him be, busying myself with all the lists and reports he had brought along.

I felt his eyes on me as I typed, miserable as they get. He rose to his feet, paced around the room like a caged animal, moved the curtain away, restless and searching for something he couldn't quite find.

"Leave it." He touched my shoulder gently at last. "Leave that paper; it's not important now. Let's go for a walk instead. The weather is beautiful and we don't have many summer days left."

I was grateful for that "summer" which he tactfully included in the sentence.

Outside, the air smelled of lilacs. Soft clouds drifted languidly across the sky, entangling themselves sometimes in crowns of the trees and turning into flowers of cotton. Willy bent down and twirled a leaf he'd picked up in his fingers, scowling at it with dissatisfaction.

"The first yellow one already?" I took it from him.

"The autumn will be here soon. It's good for the brigade. The heating season…" His thoughts were far from the brigade; I sensed it well enough.

"Out with it." I stopped and made him look at me. "What is it?"

"What is what?" He smiled weakly, pleadingly.

"You've been walking around with the face of a professional mourner ever since you returned. What is it? A new order of some sort you've learned about? Don't try to spare my feelings; it's worse this way. Just say it, so I'm prepared for whatever is coming."

He stole a glance around, took my hand and pressed it slightly before I pulled my palm out of his, giving him a certain look. *No need to risk it; those soldiers are much too close, and one of them wears a Feldgendarmerie Gorget around his neck, I can see it gleaming in the sun from here. Let them clamber onto their motorcycle first and drive away, the further, the better.*

"Walk with me some more, Ilse."

We strolled forward, circling the building. Near the intersection, the Field Police caught up with us on their motorcycle and sped ahead, ignoring the red light with astounding arrogance about them. An elderly peasant, who was carrying a heavy sack on his back, had barely managed to drop his precious cargo and leap off their path for they showed no inclination to slow down. Accompanied by their laughter and the roaring of their powerful engine that was now growing fainter in the distance, the elderly man dropped to his knees to gather as many potatoes as he could before the light would turn green and the staff cars would smash them to a pulp. The light changed and the horns blared their warning but the man positively refused to get away from the busy road. This pitiful sack was perhaps the entire harvest which he and his wife (if she were still alive that is) managed to grow this year and at this point getting hit by a car seemed much more preferable to him than slowly watch her die from starvation, or starving himself, all alone, for that matter. Tears were streaming down his heavily-lined, leathery face, as he continued to work at his task, with stubborn determination. All else simply ceased to exist around him.

Willy was already running toward him and signing for the cars to halt. With his usual efficiency, he summoned some teenagers who were loitering on the corner and, waving a pack of German cigarettes as a powerful incentive, motioned for them to help the old peasant. I collected whatever I could as well and deposited all of the potatoes into his sack, which he held open with trembling hands. When the last item was packed, Willy led him away by his elbow and, after handing the grinning youths their promised payment, inquired if the old man was hurt. The latter only grinned with his thin, toothless mouth which kept twisting into a tearful grimace despite all of his visible efforts to keep it straight. Fearful of offending, yet overpowered with the desire to demonstrate his gratitude, the peasant reached out with his crooked, arthritic fingers and patted Willy's sleeve ever so slightly.

"Spasibo, synok."

Not knowing what else to offer, he extracted two big, round potatoes and handed them to Willy. Not having the heart to refuse him, Willy took them.

He was still holding them as he watched the peasant shuffle away in the direction of the market.

"He called me *son*," he said finally and put the potatoes into his pocket.

"Since when do you speak Russian?" I smiled, thinking it to be positively splendid that he didn't throw the potatoes away but kept them despite having no actual need for them.

"I have just begun learning it." With those words, he extracted a small Russian-German military dictionary out of his pocket and demonstrated it to me. His smile, however, faltered. "I didn't have to go to the base. I made that up to make an excuse… I wanted to talk to Weizmann, you see. To try what he had suggested earlier, with his Messerschmitt. Yes, yes, I know your views on all that business and don't waste your words telling me now that it won't work. I was willing to try. Anything is better than this torturous *unknown*. But it's all finished anyway. He wasn't even there when I arrived; just a note and this dictionary he's left for me. They transferred him to the front two days ago. With such urgency, he didn't even get a chance to call, to warn me. I don't know anything anymore, Ilse. That was the only plan we had. Now, everything is finished."

"I didn't know you were such a pitiful defeatist, Willy Schultz."

He chuckled along with me, looking darn miserable. He leafed through the dictionary, paying closer attention to the words circled by Otto's hand, repeated some of them out loud. *Zdravstvyite, tovarish, mama, otets, reka, spasibo, doroga, pomogite pozhalyista, kak proity k, partisan…*

"Partisans… Yes, there are, of course, partisans…" He began musing out loud.

"Liza's Nahum had managed to escape to them."

"Did he really?"

"Yes. To Zorin's Brigade, she said."

"Lucky old chap," Willy sighed wistfully.

I regarded him incredulously.

"Are you telling me you're envious of an escaped Jew?"

He stared vacantly ahead before answering, "I am. He's a free man now."

"And you're not?"

He was just going to reply but suddenly stiffened and pulled himself up at the sight of Schönfeld – I saw him too now as he had just turned the corner and was making his way toward us in a purposeful stride. Grinning and looking positively happy with himself, he exchanged salutes with Willy and stood next to him, pretending to observe the workers as well.

"A splendid day, is it not, *Parteigenosse?*"

"It is," Willy said through his teeth.

"By the way, what happened to your Party badge? I haven't seen you wearing it lately. You didn't lose it, I hope?" His concern was anything but genuine. "I can get you a new one if you did. Such things happen."

"It's being cleaned," Willy replied venomously as he stared straight ahead of himself.

"*Ach,* then it is," Schönfeld consented surprisingly easily and clasped his hands behind his back.

"Is there anything you wanted, Untersturmführer?" Willy didn't care to conceal his desire to rid himself of the SS officer's company.

"Just wanted to express my sorrow concerning your comrade Weizmann."

Willy turned to him, suddenly pale. Schönfeld's grin widened.

"Such a shame about his transfer, eh? I understand you two were good friends. You will miss him terribly, no doubt."

"How do you know about his transfer?"

"How do I know, is one way to put it. Another way to put it is, what I had to do with his transfer."

Willy's hands closed into fists. I coiled my fingers around his wrist. *Do not hit him now. Do not make a scene. This is precisely what he wants, to provoke you.*

"What do you want, Schönfeld?" he finally growled.

"What do I want as in 'what is my end goal' or what do I want as in 'what do I want for me to stop pursuing that end goal of mine'?" He purred pleasantly. "You ought to be more specific, Herr Leutnant."

"Understand it as you like."

Schönfeld was suddenly serious. "I only want to serve my Führer, Leutnant. That is my end goal, just as it should be yours. Weizmann is already gone; there are rumors that Sturmbannführer Bröger is going to be promoted and transferred soon. It would be a shame if they sent you, along with everyone else, to Ukraine."

"I don't see it happening. You see, I'm the most terrible flyer. They don't allow me near their aircraft, anymore."

"So I heard."

"You're not even bothering to conceal the fact that you tried making my transfer happen?" Willy seemed to be amazed at such audacity.

"Why should I? You think of me as your enemy when in fact, I'm your best friend, as of now. You are heading someplace very dark with that Jewess of yours. Do you want to end up in the same pit, perhaps? A court-martial, is that what you want?"

Willy kept obstinately silent.

"I'm only trying to set you back onto the right path before it's too late, Schultz."

"Watch how you address a superior officer, Schönfeld."

"If you keep being a pigheaded numbskull, you will lose your rank along with your life, in the near future, Schultz. Think about it and do something about that broad before it's too late. There are plenty of very willing Gentile girls in Minsk. She's not worth dying for."

"What do you care? You're not the one to get shot."

"I'm the one to hold the rifle and I terribly hate shooting at my own fellow officer kin, you see. So please, be so kind, spare me such a grim responsibility."

"Go hang yourself, Schönfeld."

The SS man only shrugged and made off. The day had long ceased to be splendid.

Chapter 20

September 1942

"Damnable business, I tell you."

I was listening to the voices in Willy's office as I typed some report or the other – they had all morphed into a ceaseless infinity of numbers and letters a long time ago.

The officer who was talking was in charge of the newly arrived *Staffel* that Willy was to put up in the Government Building until he, as the administrative officer, could find a new suitable place for their quarters. The village that housed their previous lodgings had been razed to the ground by the SS – that much I had learned from the *Staffel* commander's half-indignant, half-astounded report, as though the man himself couldn't quite believe such a turn of events.

"Were they truly aiding the partisans then, your hosts from the village?" Willy inquired.

"Not from what I know but the most damnable part is that the SS didn't even bother with an investigation, of any sort, on their account. They simply rode into the village one morning, showed me the paper signed by General-Kommissar Kube, gave my men and me one hour to collect our belongings and got down to their business."

"Do they not realize that they're only making it worse for themselves?" Willy said incredulously. "When we first arrived in Minsk, some of the villagers and townspeople even welcomed us or at least didn't display any hostility towards the occupying forces."

"Indeed!" the other officer agreed emphatically. "We gave them food for cooking from our own field kitchen; we paid them for laundry and cleaning in occupation money—"

"And the partisans?" Willy interrupted him in the heat of discussion. "It all also began with the SS and their treatment of the Soviet prisoners of war. Have you stepped inside our Shirokaya camp? You'd be appalled by the conditions in which those men are forced to exist. I'm not even touching on the subject of the ghetto," he added very quietly.

"*Ach,* that. I've heard… People talked, in the village, about the entire affair. Some of them had friends in the city – they saw it all with their own eyes." The officer released a tremendous breath. "I'm ashamed to call myself a German after what our fellow countrymen are doing to those poor devils. The nation of Goethe and Wagner, aren't we? High culture and all that rot! And now those numbskulls from the SS wonder why the partisan problem is out of control. Because now, even the locals have turned on us, following their new policy. *If we only suspect a village of aiding the partisans, all of its inhabitants will be subject to immediate measures of retribution,*" he spoke in a mocking voice. "The forests have already been crawling with partisans since April; you watch how fast the rest of the formerly neutral locals turn on us as well. Even the ones who haven't been aiding the partisans, now will."

"I don't blame them."

"I don't either. Do you think you can find us something suitable any time soon, Schultz?"

"Give me a few days; I'll find you such a base, it'll be even better than the other."

"Not too close to the forest, though."

"I wouldn't think you'd want to be close to the forest." Willy laughed readily along with his guest.

"And with some flat field nearby, if possible. For the aircraft."

"Naturally. How many do you have there? Twelve?"

"Twelve."

"Any other machinery?"

"Two regular army trucks, in which we arrived."

Willy's mechanical pencil quickly jotted down the information on the piece of paper. I removed the finished report from the typewriter and stared vacantly ahead as I listened to his approaching steps. *Now, he'd place this new paper in front of me and I'd be typing a new report, in which the annihilated village would become yet another name, yet another number in the list of casualties of the Neues Deutsches Reich.* Through an open window, a gust of September wind burst, bringing with it the faint smell of carbolic and decay. Broodingly, I wondered which would happen first, our total annihilation, or their running out of paper for such reports.

Willy must have seen it all written on my face for he caught my hand before I could reach for the paper he'd just brought and kissed it.

"Leave it. It'll wait. Come have coffee with us. I'll introduce you to Hauptmann Greiser. He's a first-rate fellow!"

I followed him, with reluctance, into his office and hesitated before offering my hand to a tan, middle-aged officer clad in a somewhat faded, wrinkled uniform which distinguished frontline soldiers from "office pen-pushers," as Willy jokingly referred to his own kind.

I stiffened even more as Greiser plainly remarked, *You're not local* after I replied to his "How goes it," in perfect German. He gave me another once-over, noted the absence of the uniform, which all German secretarial staff posted in Minsk wore and smiled. "Jewish?"

I searched Willy's face instead of responding. He nodded calmly, so did Greiser and pulled up a chair for me as if such introductions were the most ordinary thing in the world. He not once, again, mentioned my Jewish nationality or position here but still spoke carefully choosing his words and topics for a conversation, much like healthy people talk with their sick relative who has already been sentenced by the doctors, with a diagnosis which can only be mentioned in a hushed manner and as far away from the doomed relative's ears as possible. I was still grateful for that; grateful that even after Otto had been sent away, there still remained other such *Ottos* who at least didn't hate us openly and were, if anything, apologetic. *We're sorry that you are to die and we are to live. We are sorry that the disease claimed you and not us. We will still visit you and bravely hold your hand and pretend that perhaps you will get better one day and walk out of here alive, even though deep inside we all know the truth... However, we'll still pretend; for your sake, we will.*

Only Willy never looked at me with that painful sympathy and pitiful compassion. His eyes were always frank and bright whenever he looked at me for he was the only one who stubbornly refused to acknowledge the diagnosis no matter how many second opinions or third ones were brought up before him. *Death? We're having none of that. No, my dear, you will live because I said so. I love you and therefore death has no rights over you. You were mine first and therefore it can't have you. I will fight it to the bitter end and you will see that I will win.*

To him, for those frank eyes of his, I was grateful the most.

*

By dinner time, Liza and I were tasked with arranging the newly arrived airmen's living quarters in suitable rooms. While the *Staffel* had their meal in the officers' mess, we made their beds – temporary cots promptly brought in by the soldiers summoned from their nearby barracks – and ensured that each had a clean, folded towel to use. It was all done in such an incredible rush that we were still hurrying between the rooms long after they had returned from the mess, writing down their requests and answering torrents of questions.

"The restrooms are at both ends of the corridor," I answered for the millionth time in the course of the past thirty minutes. The entire floor was in wild confusion, buzzing like a beehive as these *knights of the sky*, as they were good-humoredly addressed by their local administrative Luftwaffe counterparts, were settling in. Willy generously offered his own quarters to Staffelkapitän Greiser and his immediate staff. With the sofa and the additional cots, we managed to lodge not only the Staffelkapitän himself but his Staffeladjutant and three pilots as well. "The showers are on the first floor, left from the bottom of the stairs and you'll have time to shower only from seven to eight in the morning – from eight to nine Field Police use the showers. For the night, keep the windows closed and the blackout curtains drawn at all times; the Soviet aircraft don't often pass our parts but there were acts of sabotage when the local underground directed Soviet bombers onto the SS barracks with the aid of their signal installed on the roof. We have sentries on the roofs now but keep the windows dark in any case."

"Any casualties?" A perky, dark-haired pilot asked, his eyes alight with mischief.

"There were many casualties, yes," I replied carefully.

"Good," he concluded merrily, causing a burst of laughter from his receptive audience. "Those swine had it coming if you ask me. I hope you awarded the brave fellow who thought of the whole scheme?"

"He was never caught," I explained, hiding a grin.

"I bet it was one of ours, not Minsk underground," the Staffeladjutant supplied from his cot that we had squeezed in between Willy's bed and the desk, at which I usually typed. "Merkel, was that you, you cast-iron limb of Satan?"

The small room was once again in an uproar of laughter.

A blond pilot, who couldn't have been older than twenty, ceased his rummaging in his suitcase and straightened out with a grave look about him. "As much as I would love to ascribe such a feat to my modest persona, I'm afraid this time it was not me. But now that I think of it," he turned to face me, "how often did you say those sentries patrol the roofs of the new SS barracks and how easily are they distracted?"

"Watch yourself, Merkel, or you'll find yourself in the disciplinary battalion faster than you think," Staffelkapitän Greiser added his voice from the round table, which had been pushed close to the wall and at which he was perusing a map together with Willy. Despite the noise, the two were deeply in search of the new possible base location. "Those muttonheads share a building with us now. If they hear you, not I, not Göring himself will get your sorry face out of the court-martial."

"Chance worth taking, Herr Staffelkapitän."

A tall officer with raven black hair and pale face, who sat at my desk staring into nothing the entire time, suddenly leaped to his feet and stormed out of the room, bumping into his superior's chair in passing. The room was instantly immersed in silence.

"Nice going, numbskulls," Greiser muttered poisonously. "You had to go and bring the damned SS up when Konradt is still all out of sorts after what happened and joke about it on top of it. A lot of sensitivity you have on you comrade's account; nothing to say!"

"Sorry, Herr Staffelkapitän." Merkel made a move toward the exit, his previous playful expression all but gone. "I'll go fetch him at once and apologize."

"Let the poor bastard be." Greiser caught Merkel's sleeve. "You'll only make it worse. Let him walk it off. In cases like this, a man has no need for company and particularly yours, you miserable clown."

"I truly didn't think, Herr Staffelkapitän—"

"You never think." Greiser buried his head in the map again. I shot Willy an inquisitive look but he only shrugged his shoulders slightly. With that, the subject was dismissed.

Liza and I were to sleep in Willy's bed that night. He, himself, after much protesting from his guests' side and suggestions *to put the ladies on their beds while they slept on the floor,* insisted on using the bedroll as his sleeping arrangements for the night. *Ladies.* Even Liza eventually warmed up to the pilots after all of the harmless flirting and compliments they subjected her to. It was nice to be looked at and addressed as young women and not as sexless, nameless objects which were to be exterminated as soon as their usefulness had run out. In this respect, the Luftwaffe differed greatly from the SS.

While the men were settling down to sleep, we used the chance to slip into the now silent and empty corridor and headed for the restrooms to brush our teeth and wash up.

"Liza," I called out to her quietly. "Everyone's in their beds; shall we try the showers downstairs?"

"Are you quite mad, Fräulein Stein?" Her eyes glistened in the darkness as she regarded me in amazement. "I have no desire to get shot by some Field Police sentry on duty. Two Jews in the shower for German officers! That'll go down well with them! Say thank you it's the Luftwaffe floor and we're allowed to use their sinks. Showers, indeed!"

She snorted and proceeded to the restrooms. I halted in my tracks; she did too.

"Ilse, are you really considering it?" Her tone was serious now.

"I wouldn't have been if it was winter. But it's still an Indian Summer and I'll stink like a corpse tomorrow if I don't shower."

"Don't be daft!" she hissed at me and this time took hold of my hand. "Wash up in the sink – it's all the same."

"Not in the slightest is it the same."

"You smell just fine to me. Like a fresh lily. Now, come."

"I stink like a horse after plowing and it'll be even worse tomorrow."

"Schultz really spoiled you, you know! You didn't mind washing up in an aluminum basin in the ghetto, did you?"

"It was in the ghetto; we all smelled revoltingly there. Here, it's different. And we have people quartering with us now. I'm embarrassed, in front of them; you understand?"

"Hrenova kultura nemetskaya," Liza muttered under her breath, something on our *German culture's* account, from what I gathered.

I chuckled softly and released my hand out of hers. "You go, Liza. There's no one down there; everyone's asleep. Willy and I have snuck in there multiple times. I'll be just fine, don't worry about me."

"Suit yourself, Stein. If you get caught, I'll pretend I don't know you."

"Wench!"

"You certainly are."

After our exchange of pleasantries, I headed to the staircase and climbed down to the first floor, thanking whoever thought of mounting a carpet on the marble stairs – it muffled all sounds just perfectly.

The floor was shrouded in velvet darkness. After removing my shoes, I noiselessly padded barefoot to the showers, careful to tread as quietly as possible despite the abundance of thick runners, still left from the Soviet rule, here as well. I halted at the entrance when I thought that I heard some muffled noises coming from the inside and listened closely. It couldn't have been an officer deciding to take a late shower for the lights were off and no sane German (except for Willy, but he had a good excuse in the face of myself as his company) would shower at night and without any lights. I quickly discarded the idea of someone from the underground conducting their affairs there as well. In the cellar, to assemble a bomb as they had done just two weeks ago at the brick factory, that was one thing. In the showers? I think not.

A sudden noise of something crashing to the floor startled me. The unmistakable sound of someone struggling for breath – I've heard it far too many times for my liking – prompted me to charge forward without thinking twice. It was dark as pitch inside, the only source of light being a Luftwaffe-issued flashlight, the one that Willy used whenever we came down here, now lying on the tiled floor. In the amber shadows cast by it, I recognized legs of an overturned chair, one of those that lined the walls of the corridor. Above it, two boots dangled, unmistakably German. I dropped my towel and shoes and grabbed the man's legs at once, lifting him in the air as high as I could.

My muscles screamed in protest – the man was much heavier than any of the lumber I had to hurl in my early days in the brigade. A cold sweat broke out on my temples as I considered the situation, in horror. *Scream for help? Reach for the chair and take the chance of running upstairs for Willy?* The man was here by himself; no one hanged him, so putting him back onto the chair wouldn't do a lot of good. He wished to die – of that, I had no doubt. I couldn't hold him for much longer either; my arms were straining with the effort, as it was.

I shouted as loudly as I could. I screamed for a few interminably long minutes the way it felt, while he slipped out of my grip, while no sounds could be heard in deserted hallways, while everyone slept soundly in their beds. I held the man who wished to die because death and I had an old score to settle and for the first time I had a chance to look it in the face and claw at least one victim back out of its bony grip.

For the first time in so many years, I had the power to save someone, to become a rescuer and not a silent victim in need of rescuing that I swore to myself there and then that I would drop dead first before I let go.

My throat was hoarse with shouts. I didn't know the man; I couldn't even see his face but I suddenly understood Willy's disregard toward his own fate whenever he tested providence by helping me or Liza or the entire brigade for that matter. Saving someone's life was worth dying for; in this tiled shower room, I understood what no man could put convincingly into words, neither a ghetto rabbi nor an underground writer, in his leaflets.

At last, the metal clinking of hobnailed boots on the tiles. Blinding lights flooded the shower room – someone must have flipped the switch at the entrance. I still held on until a few pairs of hands wrenched the man out of my grip and moved me out of the way. Against the blinding light, the men were mere shadows, setting the chair, cutting the rope attached to the water pipe that ran along the ceiling. I couldn't tell which kind of troops they were, the Feld Police or the Luftwaffe. All they wore was their undershirts and underwear, and only one of them wore boots.

In cold terror, I recognized the man with the rope around his neck – the pale-faced, raven-haired Konradt, who had run out of the room in such haste not an hour ago. Dazed and half-conscious, he gasped and wheezed long after the rope was torn off his neck. Someone said something about fetching the doctor.

"You stay where you are," the voice commanded as I tried to slip quietly out of the room. "What's your name and how did you get here in the first place?"

"I'm Ilse Stein, with the Luftwaffe, fifth floor, Air Supply Unit," I promptly reported. "I know this man. He's quartered with my superior, Leutnant Schultz. Allow me to go fetch his Staffelkapitän?"

"I said, stay put where you are." The man in boots motioned for one of his orderlies to go upstairs instead.

Hauptmann Greiser was down in the showers along with Willy and all of the men now lodging with us in mere minutes. Soon, he was shaking my hand and thanking me profusely for saving that *damned Schweinhund* from certain death.

"I should have known," Greiser repeated for the hundredth time when we were back upstairs. Konradt was taken to the hospital even though he actually walked there on his own, supported by two of his comrades. "I wondered if that's what he'd do after what happened."

"Is he in some trouble with the SS?" Willy probed gently, making a conclusion from the bits of the overheard conversation.

All of the pilots nodded their gratitude as he generously poured cognac in their respective glasses. Liza refused hers and pushed it toward me instead. I must have been quite a sight; my hands were still trembling – from the nerves, not from the strain.

Greiser made an evasive gesture and downed his glass. "It's not that. He had a girl in the village, you see. Most of the fellows did, but Konradt actually loved his girl. Wanted to marry her once the war was over. She was madly in love with him too… The whole rotten Romeo and Juliet affair, blast it all to hell."

"Did the SS shoot her?" It was me this time who asked.

"Shoot? No. Even though, what difference does it make, eh? No, they didn't shoot anyone. Simply put them all in three big barns, locked them inside and set the barns on fire with flamethrowers." Greiser was silent for some time. "We saw it all from where we were. The fire that is… didn't realize at first what it was. Refused to believe, I suppose. Konradt charged forward at once. We grabbed hold of him immediately, wrestled him to the ground, held him fast. Eventually, he ceased his fighting when nothing was left of the barns, just smoldering ruins. He hasn't said a word, ever since. Didn't eat, didn't drink. Just sat there, like a ghost, staring into space and the eyes – dead already. I thought he'd come out of it in the new place. I should have kept him close at all times. We did take his gun, knife, and shaving blade away, but… I should have let Merkel fetch him…"

"Where did he get the rope, I wonder?" Merkel murmured, biting the edge of his glass with his white teeth. He suddenly looked like a child to me, a mere teenager whom someone dressed in a flyer's uniform and convinced that the war was a fine game. He suddenly looked as though he didn't understand its rules any longer, didn't comprehend why yet another of his friends had almost died.

"What difference does it make?" Greiser shrugged indifferently. "When a man wants to die, he'll find a way. Same as if he wants to live, I suppose."

It was long after twelve when we finally settled down to sleep. The dawn hadn't broken yet when someone began knocking on the door urgently. The visitor wore a uniform and an armband with the red cross on it. Greiser's face paled at once, as soon as he looked into the doctor's eyes.

"Konradt?" That was all he asked.

"I'm sorry, Herr Hauptmann. We assigned a nurse to watch him but she dozed off… He jumped out of the window."

"Dead?"

"*Jawohl*, Herr Hauptmann. The fifth floor. I'm sorry."

Greiser nodded several times and went back into the bedroom. Willy took the empty cot just to occupy the empty place, just so it wouldn't stare with its bare eyes into the eyes of the comrades who had just lost their brother. Still, no one could sleep for the rest of the night.

In the morning, when the men had gone to the mess, I found Willy standing in front of the open window, the cloud of a curtain billowing around him, obscuring him from sight.

"Willy," I called out softly. "Why aren't you downstairs with the others?"

"I'm going down in a second," he replied without turning around, clearly preoccupied with something.

"It's a shame about Konradt, isn't it?"

I approached him and circled my arms around his waist. He covered them with his at once.

"I love you endlessly, my Ilse. Do you know that?"

"Yes, I do. I love you too and it's because I love you so much that I want you to promise something to me."

"No."

"You haven't even heard my request yet."

"I know what you're about to ask me and I can't make a promise that I know I will break." He kissed me with infinite tenderness and held me close. "If something happens to you, Ilse…"

"Nothing will happen to me as long as I have you."

He pulled back and regarded me tragically. I brushed his cheek and kissed him softly on the corner of his mouth. *I'm sorry for burdening you with such a responsibility, Willy Schultz but it's true. I've grown to believe in you as one believes in some deity that will, without doubt, keep one alive as long as the faith is living in the one who's praying for salvation. You're all-powerful and merciful; you're the kind God, the all-forgiving God. You aren't blind to tears and you answer the prayers, unlike all the other Gods. I only pronounce your name with eternal love and reverence now. Have my soul as an offering – forgive me, for I have nothing else to offer you; my body, that has long been yours and forever will be, as long as you'll have me.*

"I can't promise you that I'll go on living after you die because we both know perfectly well that I won't," he began speaking at last. I'd never heard his tone to be so grave, so solemn. "But I can promise you this, as long as I'm alive, nothing will happen to you. We live together, or we die together."

I looked into his infinitely blue eyes and understood everything. *Because without the one who has faith, God is dead.*

Chapter 21

December 1942

Liza's excitement, when she approached us, was visible despite the fact that the lower part of her face was covered by a thick scarf. The temperatures had plummeted last night and now even the SS looked at the brigade of Jewish workers as a blessing from the sky. Without them, they would all freeze overnight in their private quarters.

Since early morning, I spent as much time as I could with them not only as their supervisor but as their comrade; the brigade could use every pair of hands these bone-chilling days and particularly nights and I made it my responsibility to ensure that all the Government Building complex was thoroughly heated.

Willy would come out to us, bundled in his winter overcoat, every now and then. In front of other officers, he would pull himself up and issue commands in a no-nonsense voice. As soon as the area around the boiler house was deserted once again, he would lend a helping hand to the women and our only male worker Stepan, who carried sacks, with coal, inside. We always had at least one girl taking a break from the back-breaking work and standing guard on the corner; she'd wave her hand as soon as she saw someone in a uniform approach and Willy was back to his tall posture and commanding. The officers saluted him and went about their business, none the wiser.

"Nahum sends his regards," Liza began without any unnecessary preamble.

We instantly pricked our ears. Nahum, Liza's lover from the underground who had managed to escape the July massacre, was with Zorin's Brigade ever since. It differed from all other brigades due to its unorthodox function; instead of the fighting, which was the primary mission of all other units, the Zorin one made it their business to save and shelter as many families as possible. They refused neither feeble nor old; pregnant women and small children were welcome there and that was one of the reasons why Liza's Nahum found it to be the most important one to join.

"But if we don't fight for our women, children, and elderly, what are we fighting for then?" he asked Liza when he returned in September to lead another few people from the ghetto under the cover of night. *"Who needs freedom if we lose everyone dear to us in the process of fighting for it?"*

He wanted Liza to go with him but as soon as he made the mistake of mentioning that the depleted underground needed a liaison with the Russian side, Liza, who didn't have to wear a star on her clothes as a member of Leutnant Schultz's heating *sonderkommando* and was therefore a perfect nondescript candidate, volunteered for the task and positively refused to listen to any arguments. She offered me to go with him but I refused to go without my sisters and Willy and Nahum could only lead five people at a time without arousing suspicion. And so, for now, we all remained in the ghetto until someone could come up with a better plan in which none of us would have to separate from the others.

"I also spoke with Sergei today," Liza continued, much too loud for my liking. However, the wind was howling with such savage force that day, hardly anyone besides us could overhear her words. I remembered Sergei from the day when he had slipped a note from Nahum into Liza's hands in front of the ghetto's gates where we had stood as a part of the cleaning commando right after the July massacre. Willy's mystified scowl indicated that he had not the faintest idea whom Liza was talking about and she quickly explained before continuing, "Sergei and I used to work at the same power plant before the war; now, he also works for the

Luftwaffe command but under some other officer's supervision." She scrunched up her face as she looked up at Willy.

He appeared to be going over different names in his mind. "Hallman?"

"No, doesn't sound like it."

"Müller?"

"No, I would have remembered Müller."

"Kemmerich?"

"That's it! Kemmerich!" Liza asserted at once.

"He's responsible for the radio communications and engineering," Willy clarified. "Go on."

"That's right! Sergei told me that he overheard Kemmerich and his staff discuss the situation with Stalingrad. Some entire Army Group is surrounded there, he said." Again, she looked up inquisitively at Willy.

"The 6th? Paulus' Army Group?" He regarded her in surprise.

Liza shrugged, as much as was allowable by her coat and layers of clothing under it. "I wouldn't know. He only said that they're completely encircled by the Red Army and now it's only a matter of time as to when they'll surrender. Do you know anything about it?"

Out of us all, Willy was the only one who stood with his face exposed to the harsh elements. A small smile formed on his pale lips. He lowered his gaze as if in an apology. "We have a political officer who addresses us every Sunday. In his last address, he announced that the shortening of the front around the Stalingrad area was almost completed, that General Rokossovsky's Don Front is all but annihilated, that our new counterattack positions are even more favorable than the previous, and that our counteroffensive will result in our ultimate victory."

Upon hearing two versions of the same news which positively contradicted each other, I shifted my uncomprehending glance from him to Liza and back.

"Sergei said he heard about the surrounded Army Group over the radio too," Liza said. "The Soviet *Informbureau*. It can be propaganda too, of course… No one knows what to believe nowadays."

"True. People in Germany believe we farm land, here in the East," I muttered.

"It's worse than that. They envy you, the Jews. *You have it nice. They have rationing in Germany now and you can eat all you want from your farms.*" Willy's voice was razor-sharp with sarcasm.

Liza snorted with disdain. "A veritable buffet; nothing to say! You tell them next time I'll happily trade my place with any of them."

"It was in the newspaper."

"Even worse! More people will read that nonsense and believe in it!"

Willy took out his cigarette case, pulled his gloves off with his teeth and lit up one. "What I wouldn't give to listen to the Soviet radio myself. Out of two sources, perhaps one can work out what's really going on. It's not like anyone would tell us the truth either."

Liza regarded him in amazement. "Don't you have a radio set in your living quarters?"

"I don't understand Russian and neither does Ilse," he reminded her with a smile.

"Blast it. I forgot."

Two officers, fur collars upturned and stiff, appeared on the stairs leading toward the boiler house. Liza began reporting some production nonsense in a loud voice. Willy nodded with the gravest of airs.

"Damned Russian winter!" One of the officers shouted through the layers of fur and gusts of wind by means of a greeting, as soon as they leveled with us.

"Byelorussian," Willy corrected him with a grin.

"All the same. Cold as Hades! Makes one want to ask for a transfer to the JG 52 – I bet they aren't freezing their tails off in the Caucasus!"

"To hell with that!" his comrade countered at once. "I'd rather freeze my tail off here in Minsk with our partisans than get it shot down over Stalingrad by the Soviet flak!"

"JG-52 isn't anywhere near Stalingrad," the first one argued.

"It is now; someone has to escort the Stukas that drop the supplies to the Army. At least part of it is transferred there, I heard."

"Nonsense! They're near Crimea, the Kerch Peninsula or some such, warming their bones in the sun as we speak!"

"Like hell they are! They're covering the 4th Panzer Army's retreat in Stalingrad; I'm telling you this on the most reliable authority."

"A breakthrough then; not retreat!"

"What kind of a breakthrough is it when one is trying to work his way out of an encirclement, I'm asking you?"

"They're breaking through the enemy lines, so it's a breakthrough."

"Same song, different words. They're surrounded, aren't they?"

"See that the SD muttons don't hear you or you'll quickly find yourself in one of their disciplinary battalions. *Surrounded*," he repeated mockingly.

"They are though!"

They made off, still bickering between themselves. I watched them go, marveling at the very idea that the occupying forces themselves had just as much idea as to what was happening around them as the local population. A lot of good their radios did, too; Willy couldn't bear listening to it for longer than five minutes before changing the wave to something that played music – *the music didn't lie,* according to him. Everything else, including newspapers, Goebbels's speeches, Hitler's promises, Göring's reports, and most of all, local political officers' announcements, was lies through and through.

"Liza!" An idea suddenly occurred to him, lighting up his eyes. "What if you listen to the radio in my office when you clean there? Ilse and I will leave the room while you clean and you can turn it on and learn more about what's going on. If the news is true, perhaps, we'll be able to do something about it."

"Like what?" She regarded him dubiously.

"If the 6th Army is indeed surrounded and is about to surrender, we're talking about hundreds of thousands of soldiers lost to the Soviet Gulag," Willy began to explain patiently. "As soon as Paulus surrenders, the OKW will need to take manpower from somewhere to cover that hole in the front. Most certainly they will start taking personnel from all the parts of the Occupied Territories, which is not involved with the active front. Including Minsk." He gave Liza a pointed look.

She wasn't grasping it, judging by her look. "But that's bad news for you, is it not?"

"Not for me personally. I'm a bureaucrat; they won't transfer me. They need flyers, not bookkeepers. Our Wehrmacht colleagues, however, will most likely have to take a hike, along with a few *Staffel* of the Luftwaffe and the SS. This will make their patrols and such much laxer since now they'll be lacking the manpower to man every single checking post."

A shadow of a smile lit up in Liza's gaze. "We'll be able to run to the forest."

"That's the idea," Willy confirmed with a conniving grin, which was soon replaced by a scowl. "You'll be taking a great risk with that radio though. I can't lock the room while you're in there; I can only warn the people against walking in there so that they don't muddy your freshly mopped floors but…"

"Don't worry on my account, Herr Leutnant, I'm not afraid. I'll talk my way out of it."

*

We were decorating Luftwaffe quarters for the approaching Christmas. The mess hall for the officers was adorned in fir tree branches and garlands, which Liza and I cut out of paper – layers and layers of artificial snowflakes of all shapes and sizes rested on the sharp-scented pine. The tables had been already moved into a bracket shape by a few orderlies and covered by the freshly starched tablecloths. From the forest, the woodcutters delivered a tree of such an enormous size that its top was reaching the ceiling without any additional decorations. Willy still ordered one of the soldiers to climb the ladder and snip the top a bit. *The Yule Tree is not a tree without a star,* he declared.

Much to my surprise, one of the officers delivered two large cardboard boxes filled with toys and decorations of many kinds.

"Requisitioned from the townspeople," he explained, a bit embarrassed. "A toy from each household. We'll return them all after the holidays, of course! Everything is written down and accounted for."

I had no doubt it was.

He soon returned with a box full of candles, this time simply depositing it by our feet and walking away briskly. Where that was requisitioned from, was anyone's guess.

Liza and I finished decorating the tree by four. Kitchen personnel began setting the tables and we went up to Willy's office to collect our coats and ration cards for the brigade – today we would be getting a double portion.

Willy was on the phone with someone. Abruptly, he finished the conversation with the *I'll have to call you back about that* and regarded us at a loss. "Ration cards? You aren't leaving, are you?"

Liza stole a quick glance in my direction, adding a slight nudge with her elbow. *The question is for you, kukla. Hardly he cares if I'm staying over to celebrate.*

"We have to go," I said, staring at my feet.

Willy opened his mouth but ended up saying nothing, only looked at Liza helplessly.

"You don't have to go." She understood his silent plea and gave me a bright smile. "I'll take the cards by myself just fine. What do we need two people to distribute them for?"

"Really, Ilse, stay."

"No, I can't." I tried to smile at him. "Surely, you understand."

"No, I don't understand. You said it yourself, your family always celebrated Christmas… Liza, you too. Didn't you tell me that you all celebrated Christmas here in Minsk before the war?"

"New Year. Soviet people don't celebrate Christmas. But yes, the tree was always up."

He shifted his uncomprehending gaze from Liza to me and back. It was Liza who finally sighed, collecting herself and began explaining, with infinite patience, the things that I couldn't quite put into words.

"Herr Leutnant, forgive me my directness please, but Ilse would never tell you this herself because she wouldn't want to hurt your feelings unintentionally. I know you're offering this with the best intentions but your Christmas, our New Year – both are family holidays. And you want to make her sit with people who are complicit in killing half of that family of hers. I know you're not the same as the SS but you all fight for the same Führer and you all wear his uniform. It would be positively heartless to make her sit among you."

Willy was looking at his hands. Liza gave my fingers a reassuring pressure and carefully picked up the ration cards from his desk. "Merry Christmas, Herr Leutnant."

"Merry Christmas," he replied automatically.

I was already closing the door after myself when he called my name quietly.

"Yes?" I paused on the threshold.

He was searching for the right words but none fit the situation, the entire predicament we found ourselves in. For an instant, it appeared that it was not only the door that stood between us but hundreds of thousands of dead and hundreds of thousands of living, with their eternal hatred, with their souls corrupted by the madman's words, with the lust for blood with which they desired to wash an entire race off the face of the earth. The entire world stood between us.

Willy rose to his feet and closed the distance between us in a few hesitant steps. Just as he was about to say something, Liza cleared her throat loudly in the corridor – someone was walking by.

"It's all right." I smiled at him. "You don't have to say anything. I know exactly what you feel." I quickly brushed his left breast pocket, behind which a heart was beating in rhythm with mine. "Merry Christmas, Willy Schultz."

"Merry Christmas, Ilse Stein."

I turned around and walked away before he could see that I was crying.

*

Stille Nacht, heilige Nacht!
Alles schläft, einsam wacht
Nur das traute, hochheilige Paar.
Holder Knabe im lockigen Haar,
Schlaf in himmlischer Ruh,
Schlaf in himmlischer Ruh…

Tears rolled down our faces as we sang. It was only a few of us, the ones who celebrated, gathered around a small table with the fir tree branches, decorated with paper and placed in a vase with a cracked neck, which Liza brought from somewhere. My sisters and seven more women from the brigade who belonged to the confused flock which wasn't quite sure what to make of itself. Not Jewish in the religious sense and proclaimed stateless nationality-wise. Whatever the hell we were, we didn't know any longer.

The beautiful melody which used to instill hope and serenity each time we sang it, now sounded more like mourning. The celebration of life turned into funeral by some evil, malicious twist of fate in our forgotten piece of the earth, shrouded in snow and silence. The latter, we couldn't bear any longer and so, we sang; we sang *"Stille Nacht"* and *"O Tannenbaum"*, *"Weiße Weihnacht"* and *"Alle Jahre Wieder"* just to hear something besides that deafening silence around us. Eventually, we ran out of songs.

Behind the window, the snow whirled and floated, landing softly on top of the tombstones. I couldn't see the gates of the cemetery from here but I knew that they, too, were covered in snow, just like the sign above them – *He who is born must die; he who dies enters life eternal.* The words were still there, invisible under the layers of snow and time, yet still true. I wondered who engraved them there and why. They offered both hope and an inevitable end, depending on the way one looked at them. Perhaps, that's what our entire existence was, a matter of personal perspective.

The women, who celebrated with us, remained in our house for the night in order not to risk wandering around past curfew time. In blueish light, provided by the snow outside, I kissed my sleeping sisters' temples, took my coat and stepped out, unnoticed by anyone. For a while, I stood facing the street, so velvet, so diamond-dusted and deliciously frosty. The snow melted on my cheeks; it crunched under my feet as I made the first few steps toward the cemetery. In the distance, the soldiers were shooting rockets into the sky against all regulations. I smiled at their defiance, much like my own and ventured even further away from our thatched-roof dwellings. For one night, they allowed themselves to believe that the Soviets wouldn't annihilate them overnight with their bombers; for one night, I allowed myself to believe that they would not annihilate us.

Making my way around the headstones, I eventually found the "exit" which used to be frequented by the underground members before the massacre. I was certain that it was still in use, only the underground members were so few now, no footsteps could be seen near it. Perhaps, it was just due to the fresh snow. Yes, it was much better to think this way. Gently probing the barbed wire, I discovered the place where it had been cut and carefully reattached, worked my way to the other side and put the wire back in order. On the other side, even the air was different. It smelled of freedom here, freedom and fresh snow. I wondered how far I could make it before anyone would notice me.

Round the cemetery, round the ghetto itself, the skeletal remains of it. The streets were deserted; only fresh burn marks from the German signal rockets marred the pristine whiteness around me. A new layer of snow was slowly covering, concealing both them and the ground itself, matted and pockmarked by hobnailed boots. The soldiers, who'd left them, were already sleeping in their beds. I was the only one left in the whole world.

Sovietskaya Street. No patrols here either. It's dead and abandoned, like a position which cannot be held any longer. I thought about soldiers in Stalingrad. I wondered if they had anything to eat for Christmas this year. I wondered if they remembered that it was Christmas. I wondered when we would all forget all the Christmas eves spent in ghettos, trenches, and forests. I wondered when we would become humans again.

A figure in an overcoat appeared in front of me, far away still yet dangerously close – depending on how fast he could run and how quickly I could hide. I stopped dead in my tracks, hesitated, wondering if he could see me. The figure stopped and hesitated also. We both had no business here, this soldier or myself. He watched me apprehensively – I could have been a partisan for all he knew. I watched him anxiously as well – I saw no rifle slung over his shoulder at least.

Him, half-a-step forward, half-a-step to the left; a pause. I mirrored his route but also to the left. A silent agreement passed between us; you go on your way and I go on mine and we'll both thoroughly pretend that we can't see each other. Blurry and mysterious, we watched each other closely as the distance between us shortened with each guarded step. He took his hands out of his pockets, just to demonstrate that they were empty, no weapons. Out of politeness only shared between the enemy troops, I produced mine, with difficulty though, as Willy's fur gloves tangled themselves in my coat's narrow pockets. He stopped again, abruptly. I turned both hands palms up, just in case.

"Ilse?"

I blinked a few times, my hands still up in the air, holding some invisible offering.

"Willy?" I finally whispered, so quietly, most certainly he couldn't hear me say his name.

In a few short steps, he crossed the road and stopped in front of me, bewildered. "Just what are you doing here at night?"

"I can ask you the same." I grinned in spite of myself.

He moved closer and took my hands in his. "I recognized you by the gloves."

"They're my talisman."

"I wanted to see you."

His face was sharp and white against the snow. His eyes were shining.

"How exactly were you going to see me?" I asked.

"I know exactly where you live."

"You weren't going to sneak into the ghetto in the middle of the night, were you now?"

"That's precisely what I was planning on doing."

"You are quite mad, Willy Schultz."

"But you were going to do the exact same thing, Ilse Stein."

His teeth glistened as he began to laugh softly, along with me.

"How do you know that I was going to see you?" I wrapped my arms around his neck. "Perhaps, I was just taking a stroll. Such a beautiful Christmas night outside. Perhaps, I simply felt like walking."

"One doesn't risk their life for a simple stroll in the middle of the war, you little liar."

"No. One only risks their life for something worth it. A stroll on the new snow on Christmas night when the whole world is asleep is very much worth it."

"Yes. So is sneaking inside the ghetto to steal a kiss from you."

"Good thing we met halfway then."

"I suppose."

I leaned into him and opened my mouth to his. He tasted of coffee and cognac and cigarettes and everything I grew to love so much.

"How far do you think we can make it tonight, before they catch us?" I asked him when he broke the kiss to replace it with soft and tender ones, with which he was covering my eyes and cold cheeks.

"Not as far as we need to."

"We won't make it to the forest?"

"No. But I'll try it with you all the same if you really want to go."

I held his face in my gloved hands. "No. Not tonight. Tonight is for dreaming only."

It all looked like a dream around us, the sparkling, pristine whiteness, the indigo velvet overhead, the windless, soundless night where only two of us existed.

"Did you make a wish at twelve?" he suddenly asked me.

"No. Did you?"

"I did. Do you want me to tell you what I wished for?"

"No, or it won't come true."

"That's right. Never mind then. You'll know exactly when it comes true. I'll tell you then." He pressed his lips to my forehead again and I closed my eyes for I couldn't bear how much I loved him at that moment.

Chapter 22

February 1943

A month had passed uneventfully. Then, suddenly, Liza crying on the freshly-mopped floor, by the radio through the speakers of which a Russian voice was still speaking excitedly as we entered. Willy rushed to switch it off.

"They surrendered! Stalingrad is ours!" Liza cried out and grabbed my legs until we both were on the floor, laughing and kissing each other. Willy observed us, positively beaming, then began working the radio again, only searching for a German state wave this time – he wanted to hear the news in his own language. Somber notes of "Adagio" from Bruckner's Seventh Symphony poured into the room instead of regularly scheduled announcements. He tried another German wave, the local one, for the troops. Again, mournful, classical German music and stubborn silence apart from it.

"They can't bring themselves to acknowledge it," he muttered, at last, his eyes alight with some inner victorious glow. "The very first major defeat. They refuse to face it."

They. His own superiors became "they" to him. The alien side, the hostile side. Somehow, in the middle of this war, he switched fronts without realizing it fully.

Liza, still smiling through happy tears, reached out for his hand and pressed it tightly.

"Dear Comrade…" Her voice broke. In her eyes, newfound faith shone.

For the first time, she dared to touch him, for that day he had forever ceased to be the enemy; he was one of "us" now, the future victors, whose cause was the right one, according to their *narcom* Molotov.

We all linked hands, alight with hope once more. It was all coming together just as we planned. We'd be able to get out of here now – we allowed ourselves to indulge in this selfish belief that brightly-lit February day.

For a few more weeks, still no news from the German radio. Willy reported that there were no official addresses from the political officers on account of Stalingrad as well. The German troops, along with the German people, were kept in darkness. The mail, exchanged by comrades who had been separated by a twist of fate, was monitored even stricter now. Entire passages in the letters coming from the South were blotted in black ink. Willy puzzled over his wife's letter as well, which was almost entirely black. The orderly who brought his mail only shrugged apologetically in response to Willy's uncomprehending look as the latter showed him the letter.

"From home?" he inquired sympathetically. He was an older fellow, with a kind face lined with wrinkles, most of them around his eyes and mouth. He must have smiled a lot in his youth, before the Great War. He carried the Cross from it, on his chest, along with the one from 1939. He held his left arm stiffly by his side and favored his left leg as he moved about. It was sad to see an old warrior in a messenger's role.

"From my wife."

"She must have complained about the bombing then. Or the rationing. Censorship office always blots that out."

"What bombing?" Willy regarded the old soldier in disbelief. Surely there couldn't have been any bombings in Germany?

The latter shook his head in a quick and dismissive manner – *you didn't hear me say a thing, my good fellow; I may have given an*

arm and a leg for the Fatherland but I'm not ready to surrender my
life for some reckless remark – and made for the door but at the last
moment took pity on his younger counterpart and asked him in
a mere whisper, "Where does she live then, your wife?"

"Dresden."

"No, shouldn't be that then. The RAF are mostly skirting the
borders now – Dortmund, Essen, Duisburg, Düsseldorf and such.
Dresden is safe from what I last heard. Though, no one can know
for certain now. Don't ask her that though; they'll censor it in any
case but the Field Police will be on your doorstep before you know
it to ask you who supplied you with such information. As long as
she writes, everything is fine."

I looked at Willy. His hand was clutching the edge of the desk
with such force that the knuckles turned white. With tremendous
effort, he collected himself, at last, passed the other hand atop
his head and nodded his gratitude for the truth. At least the old
soldier still had the heart to speak it when the new generation knew
nothing else but how to keep one's mouth shut. *Blind obedience,*
no questions asked – that's how it was now.

"Thank you. I won't mention it to anyone; you have my word."

"Good." The old soldier smiled. Fatherly kindness softened his
eyes. "And don't worry more than necessary, Herr Leutnant – it's
an old Army rule."

In the background, the German radio played classical music
with the obstinacy of a crew pumping the water out of a ship
that was steadily sinking, as the passengers on-board remained
blissfully ignorant.

*

February 15, 1943

The day dawned dim and gloomy, with the promise of a snowstorm
in the gray air. Even at eleven in the morning, it was still so dark
that the lights were on in both Willy's office and his living quarters,

in addition to the lamp that was casting a soft yellow light onto the paper as I typed under his dictation. His earlier predictions concerning the relocation of the troops turned out to be correct; even some of the administrative workers were being transferred to the Volga – "to shorten the front," no doubt.

We didn't speak about the new orders from the OKW, only smiled in the same hopeful and dreamy manner – him, as he dictated; me, as I put down his words on paper. No doubt, if the Luftwaffe was going, the SS was going as well. They needed much more Field Police there now, to keep the troops' morale at the necessary level and correcting their behavior by means of disciplinary battalions and a few court-martials thrown in for good measure, when the soldiers refused to exhibit the prescribed amount of enthusiasm on account of their "imminent victory."

After a polite knock, followed by Willy's *come in,* Schönfeld sauntered in and stood in the doorway, looking positively delighted at Willy's suddenly soured face.

"Heil Hitler, Herr Hauptman," Schönfeld greeted him amicably as Willy scowled at the wrong rank, already sensing some malice.

Schönfeld's face looked yellow and waxy in the artificial light of the room, only his eyes shone with triumphal light as he regarded a paper in his hands which he then laid out in front of Willy. "I suppose, congratulations are in order."

Willy pulled the official paper toward himself and read it carefully while I remained in my seat, staring at the floor under Schönfeld's fixed stare.

"A promotion?" Willy finally raised his gaze to the SS officer.

"Why, yes, of course. You've demonstrated brilliant results since your transfer here and I couldn't help writing an excellent reference letter to your superiors as one of your political officers. Told them what a conscientious civil servant you are, what a reliable officer, and a most convinced National Socialist." Despite his grin growing wider, it looked outright predatory now. "Speaking of National Socialism, is your Party badge still being cleaned?"

"It's in my desk drawer. I forgot to put it on."

"Don't forget to take it when you empty your desk then. I don't want your new superiors to think that I lied on your account and suspect you of not being loyal to the Party."

Willy's face grew pale at once. A passing shadow of fear crossed his features before they turned to granite as he narrowed his eyes at the man standing before him.

"What new superiors?"

"*Ach,* I can be so forgetful at times! Please, do forgive me." He tapped his forehead theatrically before extracting another paper from his pocket. "Here is your transfer order; it goes with the new promotion. You can receive your marching orders directly from your superiors here but your promotion order I wished to present you myself since I had so much to do with it. Tallinn, such a beautiful city! I envy you, Hauptmann Schultz. Serenity and fresh Baltic air and no partisans, of any sort, just waiting to shoot your head off at every corner. And the best part – no Jews, whatsoever, in the entire country. Imagine that? Yes, a paradise, no less. I bet it'll do wonders for your career as an officer. You're welcome now. Heil Hitler!"

He raised his hand in an exemplary salute and made his exit, whistling a jolly tune. Willy still sat at the table, looking as though he'd been shot.

An ice-cold wave of horror washed over me. I clutched at the side of the desk just to stop my hands from trembling. For the third time, Willy was re-reading the order as though in the hope that the words would somehow miraculously change their meaning before his eyes. He moved his lips as he read yet he made no sound.

"When?" I could only squeeze one word out of my throat, which suddenly was constricted with an invisible rope of the ticking clock around it.

He didn't appear to hear me.

"Willy, tell me when?"

Tell me how much longer I have left to live.

He read that last question, which I didn't dare utter when he finally looked into my eyes.

"April first," he replied, at last, his face still white as chalk.

"Six weeks."

He shook his head in denial, then counted in his mind and let his head drop to his chest in defeat.

"Six weeks," I repeated in a hollow voice.

"We still have time…" he whispered softly.

"We have nothing, Willy. We have nothing any longer."

I rose to my feet, swaying like a drunk. My feet were suddenly far too light to hold me. He tried catching my wrist as I passed him by but I pulled my hand away and picked up my coat on my way out. The air in this room turned hot and suffocating. I needed fresh air. Just a bit of fresh air to stop that pounding in my head.

Outside, the snow began falling in great fluffy flakes. The sentry who stood at the door was almost all covered with them. I passed him and stole my way through the snowdrifts, toward the boiler house, near where small, snow-covered figures were moving – I could see them from here. My people. This is where I belonged from the very beginning. Shouldn't have allowed myself to believe in any miracles; miracles were shot dead and buried in the pit along with babies from the Jewish Orphanage during the Purim pogrom. Last March it happened, almost a year ago. Nearly a year ago, General-Kommissar Kube stood at the edge of the pit, into which the SS was throwing the children, still alive and screaming and threw candy into their pleading hands. He thought it to be merciful, to give them something sweet to eat before the SS would start piling earth on top of their still-moving bodies. He thought a lot of things to be mercy. So did Willy. He thought it would be merciful to throw me candy as well when I was already one foot inside the same pit, already half-dead but he felt he could do at least something for me. I know he meant well. Perhaps, so did Kube. People said, he did love children and always gave bonbons to the orphans whenever he visited the ghetto on inspection. But then, the SS killed all the orphans and he eventually got over it. And so will Willy, eventually. He still has Hedwig at home and Dresden is still standing. As for me, I will turn into snow, snow and earth, from which I came and that's exactly how it all should have been from the very beginning. A rabbi in the ghetto once said that it was unnatural to intervene with the natural course of things; stiff luck I didn't realize it back then that the natural course of things didn't include Jews into the equation of the *Neues Deutsches Reich* anymore. My own fault for believing in something that was never meant to be. I really shouldn't blame him for anything.

I stumbled into the boiler house, stared without understanding at the woman who was trying to report something to me – she thought I was here on my supervising business. As though in a daze, I finally found my way around her and stumbled toward stacks of coal and into the corner, pulled my legs to my chest and buried my face in them. That's precisely how Liza found me after they fetched her.

"Ilse, what? Don't just look at me with such eyes as though someone died! Tell me what happened!"

Oh, Liza, my dear little Liza! You should have gone with your Nahum while you still could, for we will all die here soon.

"Willy's being transferred," I finally mumbled.

She pulled back at once. Her hand slid off my arm.

"When?"

"April first."

She tried to smile at me but only cringed instead. I felt my face twisting as well; I'd held it together so well but now the tears rolled out of my eyes of their own accord and there was no stopping them. My sisters came running from the outside, two bundles of coats, shawls, and rosy cheeks. I sobbed even harder at the sight of their beautiful, young faces. *You relied on me and I failed you both. I failed you, Liza, too. I failed everyone.*

"Ilschen, what happened?" They cooed around me, rubbing my shoulders and arms that were shaking with sobs.

"Did you have a row with Herr Leutnant?" Lily demanded, the stern older sister.

"Don't be daft!" Lore dismissed her with the wave of her hand. "When did they ever have a row? He loves her to death."

"You're a right romantic, Lore!" Lily pursed her lips in a defiant line. "People fight from time to time; it has nothing to do with love."

"It has everything to do with it! When you truly love someone, you learn how to sacrifice things for them instead of battling over them all the time."

"What do you know about it?" Lily was suddenly suspicious.

"Nothing for you to worry about," Lore threw back. She didn't tell Lily anything about Reuven, a teenager who worked as a doorman in one of the buildings of the General *Kommissariat,* the German headquarters in Minsk; she only told me because *I'd understand* and because I surely wouldn't betray her when she'd return just before curfew with lips still raw from kissing and a few pieces of bread soaked with honey carefully wrapped in a newspaper. I didn't ask anything but it was my most profound conviction that the Polish youngster was dabbling in some underground business too, judging by the goods he supplied Lore with. "What is it then, Ilschen?"

They both fell silent as they traced my gaze and saw Willy standing in the doors of the boiler house, with his coat open. Stepan, the only man working in the brigade, swiftly removed his hat and was now holding it in his hands, his head bowed. Liza and my sisters slowly rose to their feet and murmured their greetings. Only I remained on the floor for I just couldn't bring myself to move a single finger. The life itself was gone out of me.

He approached me and gave me his hand. "Come."

I shook my head slowly, through tears. *Don't drag me back there. I don't belong there anymore. Let me be, why can't you? Why torture me some more when everything is already decided?*

"Ilse, come," he repeated, motioning for me to get up, with his hand.

Still, I sat without moving.

He stepped back for a moment, took a deep breath.

"On your feet! Now!!"

I jerked from the unexpected shout but found myself standing before I knew it. Liza had long ago remarked that we, Germans, we were indeed curious creatures, who understood shouting much better than coaxing. We were used to orders, that's all; I explained it to her. Orders are easier to follow whereas pleading leaves you choice. We don't like choice. We need to be told what to do, by someone who knows what needs to be done. I was grateful for the shout even though it startled me at first, worse than a gunshot. Willy saw it too and nodded slightly, with a soft, apologetic smile. I looked at him and suddenly understood everything, this soft grin of his, that necessary shout, that coming back for me in the first place – he still had positively refused to abandon hope when I had already surrendered myself to the fate.

"Come," he repeated. "Liza, you too."

Obediently, we trailed after him back into the Government Building. Inside his quarters, he didn't say anything until he took a bottle of cognac out of the cupboard and poured three glasses, an even amount in each.

"Let's drink to victory. And then, we'll all sit down and decide what to do. No one will leave this room until we have a plan. We *will* have it."

He fetched the paper and we all stared at it long and hard, our minds as blank as the sheet itself. Outside, the wind pushed itself against the windows as though trying to force its way inside. In the corner, the clock was ticking, mocking and indifferent to our common suffering.

Eventually, cogs began turning in our brains. Willy started to speak, his words slowly gathering conviction. Something feasible soon began taking shape, outlined by Willy's determined hand.

"Partisans. Forest. How to get to the forest? Only by legal means. Legal means are brigades. Wood-cutting brigades. But we get wood delivered by train. Falsify a working permit then?"

"Do we have to?" Liza blinked, mystified. "Can't you obtain an empty blank?"

Willy shook his head. "No. I have access to ration cards but can only put the request for working permits through the Labor Exchange; however, it's them who approve the request and bring the filled passes back to me."

"Who holds the blanks?" Liza was all business now, the former Komsomol leader. The occupying forces might have stripped her of *the Komsomol* part of the title but *a leader* she remained and they would have to shoot her to take that away from her.

"The SD office."

We all leaned back onto our chairs in the same hopeless surrender. Another interminable stretch of prolonged, torturous silence descended upon us, shrouded us in its dismal cloak. The snowstorm was raging with violent force behind the window. It had grown darker. It was that particularly dismal, winter hour during which all colors are absent; when everyone's face appears leaden and lifeless; when it seems as though darkness will forever prevail and when brandy tastes the best.

Suddenly, Willy was on his feet. In a few short steps, he crossed the room and brought the lamp from the desk at which I usually typed, turned it on and, instead of keeping it next to him and his paper he pushed it to the center, sharing the light with everyone. With stubborn resolution, he turned to Liza once again. "Do you know anyone, a woman perhaps who washes the floors there, who can have access to the room where they keep them?"

"I don't know anyone who works in the *Kommissariat,* but I can ask Sergei. Maybe he does."

I felt my face brightening at once as the realization dawned on me. "*Kommissariat,* you said? I think Lore's new friend works there as a doorman. Yes, I'm quite sure she said it was the *Kommissariat* building."

"Don't jest with holy things!" Liza was suddenly afraid to breathe, afraid to jinx our luck; only regarding me with her wide-open eyes, her hand on top of my wrist.

Willy pulled forward at once as well. "That new friend of hers, does he have access inside?"

"He's a *mischling* from what I know, not a full Jew, so I think it's possible that they let him inside on one business or another. I'm convinced that he deals with someone corrupted there. Lore wouldn't tell me anything but I drew my own conclusions. He brings her far too many goods for them to come from an honest source."

"How serious is that young man about Lore?" Willy asked.

I grinned. "She's thirteen, and he's sixteen; I doubt they talk about the wedding and such—"

"No, what I mean is, would he do something for her if she asked him? Would he steal a blank from the SD office?"

My smile melted at once. One had to be serious about a girl to risk his very head for her in such a manner. From what I had heard about him I concluded that he was a savvy little weasel and a profiteer but then again, that's precisely the way Lily regarded Willy, all the while he risked his life for us.

"I don't know," almost apologetically, I replied. "I will have to ask her about that."

Willy nodded a few times. "Please, do. Perhaps chivalry is not yet dead and the young fellow will come through."

Next to us, Liza was suddenly crossing herself. Both Willy and I regarded her in utter astonishment.

"Just what are you doing, *comrade*?" I snorted with laughter after recovering my senses at last.

"At this point, this won't hurt." She shrugged nonchalantly.

"But you're not even a Christian!" Willy was laughing.

"I'm not Jewish either if we're speaking of religion. I've been raised an atheist but right now I'm ready to pray to whoever, as long as this affair pans out."

"You just believed in a cuckoo bird that lives in a Jewish Cemetery," I reminded her with a wry smile. Gallows humor, but that was all we had left.

"I'll pray to the cuckoo bird just as hard. Let's all pray." She suddenly grasped our hands and signed for us to link ours as well. "Let's all pray to some universal God of Goodness who still exists and perhaps just got distracted by something to let this all happen right under his nose. Let's pray one of his assistants hears an old communist scarecrow, like me, pray and thinks it to be a most hilarious affair and pats God's shoulder to point him at such a veritable anecdote. Let's pray that God sees us at last, even if just for the laugh of it and realizes how much evil has been done in his absence and decides to fix things. At least for us. At least because we made him laugh. I don't care what his reasons, as long as he decides to keep us alive. Let's pray, to whoever you believe in."

The entire bizarre scene was beyond any comprehension – a Luftwaffe officer, a Soviet communist, and a German Jew praying as hard as they had ever done in their lives – yet it felt like the most natural thing to do given the circumstances. We prayed to the Jewish God, to the Christian God, to the *mischling* boy, to the cuckoo bird, to everything that still bore goodness in it, in the desperate hope that at least one would answer our prayers.

Chapter 23

February 18, 1943

On February 18, the German government had finally broken its silence. The officers were ordered to gather in the mess hall for the official radio translation from the Berlin *Sportpalast*. Left all alone on the entire floor, Liza and I positioned ourselves in front of the radio in Willy's office. The transmission had just begun and the crowd was already cheering Propaganda Minister Goebbels who was to speak to them momentarily.

I disliked his voice immensely; he hadn't uttered a word yet and I was already dreading hearing his sharp Berlin accent. Unlike Liza, I knew precisely what to expect of him, the sardonic little being who managed to stir so much hatred just with those carefully chosen words of his, to instill such loathing and contempt into the hearts of the ones who didn't know any better and perhaps would have ignored certain matters entirely had their blissful ignorance not been broken by his artfully outrageous rhetoric, that I was expecting the speech with a faint incensed tremor in the very tips of my fingers. He reminded me so of my former school headmaster, with his thin mustache, with his Party badge, with his wooden pointing rod with which he'd jab in my direction – in those rare moments when he'd deign to acknowledge my presence in his class – and demand, with a disgusting sneer, which I had grown to loathe with such passion, "you, girl, from Palestine; what do you say to that question?"

No one called me *a girl from Palestine* before he had made his appearance and taken up the position of the "politically unreliable" headmaster Krupp; soon, half of the uniform-clad class was addressing me in the same mocking manner. No one had thought German Jews to be enemies of the state before Minister Goebbels went and announced them as such; soon, we were herded into ghettos by the uniformed-clad men and exterminated on a mass scale. Who would have thought that words could hold so much power, to stir so much hatred that it would eventually lead to genocide? I, for one, had always believed that we, the human race, were better than that. However, Minister Goebbels had gone and proven me wrong.

"I do not know how many millions of people are listening to me over the radio tonight, at home and at the front. I want to speak to all of you from the depths of my heart to the depths of yours. I believe that the entire German people have a passionate interest in what I have to say tonight. I will, therefore, speak with holy seriousness and openness, as the hour demands. The German people, raised, educated and disciplined by National Socialism, can bear the whole truth. The blows and misfortunes of the war only give us additional strength, firm resolve, and a spiritual and fighting will to overcome all difficulties and obstacles with revolutionary élan. Now is not the time to ask how it all happened. That can wait until later when the German people and the whole world will learn the full truth about the misfortune of the past weeks and its deep and fateful significance. The heroic sacrifices of the heroism of our soldiers in Stalingrad have had vast historical significance for the whole Eastern Front. It was not in vain. The future will make clear why."

As Goebbels made progress with his speech, Liza's brows lifted higher and higher as though the very idea was unfathomable to her that a man could speak with such graveness of *openness* and *honesty* and take himself seriously after he had kept his entire nation and, what was even more outrageous and abominable, soldiers at the front, in complete darkness, for the past few weeks. At last, she snorted with contempt. "He should have been an actor. Our Minsk *Dvorets Profsouzov* would have signed him up in a second."

I chuckled grimly at the joke. "You wait. He's just getting started."

Liza rolled her eyes melodramatically.

The radio crackled. I worked the knob to get a clearer signal.

"We face a serious military challenge in the East," Minister Goebbels proceeded. "There is no point in disputing the seriousness of the situation. It is understandable that, as a result of broad concealment and misleading actions by the Bolshevist government, we did not properly evaluate the Soviet Union's war potential. Only now do we see its true scale. This is a threat to the Reich and to the European continent that casts all previous dangers into the shadows. If we fail, we will have failed our historic mission. Everything we have built and done in the past pales in the face of this gigantic task that the German army directly and the German people less directly face."

"Historic mission?" Liza cringed with disdain. "Did that deluded half-an-actor truly just say something about a historic mission?"

"It'll get worse when he gets on the subject of the Jews." I decided to prepare her beforehand.

I knew what was to follow. I'd heard enough of that rot at home, in Nidda and later, in Frankfurt.

"Danger faces us," Gauleiter of Berlin Goebbels raised his voice and continued, after a dramatic pause. "We must act quickly and decisively, or it will be too late."

Liza suggested to switch the damned thing off. *Well, we did finally hear their admission of their defeat; what else was there to listen to,* was her line of thinking.

"No, wait. I want to hear it all." I moved closer to the radio.

"What for?" She was already on her feet, ready to get on with her daily chores.

"Before, he – well, all of them – thought that they would win the war." I paused and looked at her pointedly. "I want to hear what they're planning to do now that they know that they may lose it."

Reluctantly, Liza lowered onto the sofa next to me.

"The goal of Bolshevism is Jewish world revolution," Goebbels continued in the meantime. I gave Liza a certain look; *what did I tell you?* "They want to bring chaos to the Reich and Europe, using the resulting hopelessness and desperation to establish their international, Bolshevist-concealed capitalist tyranny. I do not need to say what that would mean for the German people. A Bolshevization of the Reich would mean the liquidation of our entire intelligentsia and leadership and the descent of our workers into Bolshevist-Jewish slavery. The German people, in any event, is unwilling to bow to this danger. Behind the oncoming Soviet divisions, we see the Jewish liquidation commandos and behind them terror, the specter of mass starvation and complete anarchy. International Jewry is the devilish ferment of decomposition that finds cynical satisfaction in plunging the world into the deepest chaos and destroying ancient cultures that it played no role in building."

"How is that we plunged the world into chaos?!" Liza exploded, at last, her face flushed and contorted into a fierce, livid mask. "Just who marched into our country first?! Who marched into France? Who marched into Norway, Netherlands, Poland, Denmark?! Us, the Soviets most certainly?"

I silenced her. I wanted to hear what new policies he had come up with to fight the Jewish Bolshevik threat – us.

"We also know our historic responsibility. Two thousand years of Western civilization are in danger. It is indicative that when one names it as it is, International Jewry throughout the world protests loudly. Things have gone so far in Europe that one cannot call a danger a danger when it is caused by the Jews. The paralysis of the Western European democracies before their deadliest threat is frightening. International Jewry is doing all it can to encourage such paralysis. During our struggle for power in Germany, Jewish newspapers tried to conceal the danger, until National Socialism awakened the people. It is just the same today in other nations. Jewry once again reveals itself as the incarnation of evil, as the plastic demon of decay and the bearer of international culture-destroying chaos. This explains, by the way, our consistent Jewish policies. We see Jewry as a direct threat to every nation. We do not care what other peoples do about the danger. What we do to defend ourselves is our own business, however, and we will not tolerate objections from others. Jewry is a contagious infection. Enemy nations may raise hypocritical protests regarding our measures against Jewry and cry crocodile tears but that will not stop us from doing that which is necessary. Germany, in any event, has no intention of bowing before this threat but rather intends to take the most radical measures, if necessary, in good time."

The crowd in the *Sportpalast* broke into thunderous applause. Their chants and shouts wouldn't let the minister speak for a few minutes during which Liza sat and looked at me in pure astonishment.

"Please, do not tell me they all approve of what he's saying."

"The audience for such meetings is always carefully selected. They want to make sure that no one starts whistling and booing in the middle of the live broadcast. But yes, the majority of the population does approve of it." I gave an indifferent shrug.

"There must be a minority though. People who disagree." Liza looked at me almost imploringly. "During my student years, they taught us that the German nation is the nation of great literature, great music, and great culture. I refuse to believe that it has been reduced to a nation of killers after that madman has come to power and brought all these hateful minions along with him."

"There was a minority," I replied after a pause. "In 1933, they began taking them off posts and putting them away in Dachau, the very first concentration camp. After they didn't come back, the others – who disagreed – promptly learned to keep their heads down. Then, there's Willy, of course."

She smiled in response to my little joke. Then, suddenly, she switched the radio off and leaped to her feet, catching my hand in hers before I could begin protesting. "Wait! Wait for just a second; they'll be clapping for five more minutes. Come here instead!"

She was holding the door open into the corridor. I approached her, utterly confused.

"Hear it?" she demanded, excitedly.

"Hear what?"

She grabbed my wrist and pulled me after herself into the corridor. We ran along it until we reached the grand staircase. She bent over the railing, motioning me to do the same. The mess hall was only two floors below us and we could clearly hear the applause coming from it.

"What?" I regarded her, scowling.

"Listen closely, you silly cow!"

And then it dawned on me, the mechanical crackling which interrupted the steady applause and cheers from time to time. It was coming from the speakers, not the mess hall. The mess hall listened to the transmission immersed in graveyard-like quiet.

Goebbels began speaking again and we remained where we were, riveted to the spot, blissful smiles now sitting on our faces. Nothing was lost yet while at least a few officers didn't cheer the madman. Hope could still be heard in their defiant silence.

"The tragic battle of Stalingrad is a symbol of heroic, manly resistance to the revolt of the steppes. It has not only a military but also an intellectual and spiritual significance for the German people. Here for the first time, our eyes have been opened to the true nature of the war. We want no more false hopes and illusions. We want bravely to look the facts in the face, however hard and dreadful they may be. A merciless war is raging in the East. The Führer was right when he said that in the end there will not be winners and losers, but the living and the dead. The German nation knows that. The German nation is fighting for everything it has. We know that the German people are defending their holiest possessions; their families, women and children, the beautiful and untouched countryside, their cities and villages, their two-thousand-year-old culture, everything indeed that makes life worth living. Total war is the demand of the hour. I ask you – is your confidence in the Führer greater, more faithful and more unshakable than ever before?"

More mechanical cheering from the dynamic and nothing from the men seated in the mess hall.

"Are you absolutely and completely ready to follow him wherever he goes and do all that is necessary to bring the war to a victorious end?"

The mechanical crowd in the radio erupted in applause. It was them, who bellowed *"Führer command, we follow!"* and *"Sieg Heil!"*; not the officers who sat silently two floors below us. Next to me, Liza was looking at me with swimming eyes. I squeezed her palm tighter.

"The nation is ready for anything. The Führer has commanded and we will follow him. In this hour of national reflection and contemplation, we believe firmly and unshakably in victory. We see it before us, we need only reach for it. We must resolve to subordinate everything to it. That is the duty of the hour. Let the slogan be; now, people rise up and let the storm break loose!"

Someone switched off the obligatory broadcast below. Almost at once, officers poured out of the hall and flooded the staircase, bearing the expressions of schoolchildren, relieved at the sound of the bell at the end of the dreadfully monotonous class. Someone had distributed black armbands to them before the assembly to honor their fallen and captured comrades, no doubt; only, if the mourning had been more timely and not presented under the guise of yet another veiled stab in the back by the Bolsheviks, Jewry, and whatnot that Minister Goebbels could come up with. Stalingrad *was* a stab in the back – a stab in the back of the German army by its own Führer who had no trouble sacrificing hundreds of thousands of young men solely in the name of some abstract idea that it was more honorable for a German man to die rather than retreat. Some officers still grumbled their discontent on account of such an unsound order as they ascended the carpeted stairs. Some offered us amused smiles as they passed us by; some were deep in the exchange of sardonic remarks.

"Did you hear that rot? The Führer commanded," one spoke to the other mockingly. "Had he not commanded for Paulus to keep the position instead of retreating while he still could, the entire Army would still be fighting! And now he commands for us all to die in the name of the holy mission or some such?"

"Did you read the new orders from the Reichsmarschall though? We are to ram the Soviet aircraft if we are out of ammo, from this day on. Total war!" His friend rolled his eyes emphatically.

"I don't give a brass tack about that clubfoot's preaching or the fat man's orders. I'm not telling any men in my charge to ram anything," a decorated Hauptmann proclaimed much to everyone's approval.

"There, look," one of his younger adjutants pointed at Liza and me as he and two other servicemen leveled with us. We knew them from around; they always treated us to chocolate and tea whenever Liza mopped their room, or I brought the reports from Willy for them to distribute. We were good, old comrades by now. "Our most feared enemy stand there, according to *Herr Minister*. They started the entire affair, these two. They made us lose Stalingrad, too. The clubfoot is right then – dreadful enemy, unforgiving enemy, true savages; aren't they?" He picked up our hands ceremoniously and kissed them before giving each a thorough press. "Come along, dear enemy. We'll drink that he falls off the podium next time, that limping ass."

"Watch it, Guttmann. The Field Police will do you in for your big mouth," one of his comrades clapped him on his back even though his own eyes wrinkled with mischief.

"I waved that Field Police off just this morning as they were setting off in big tarpaulin-covered trucks; with a white handkerchief, I did! Waved them off straight to the front!"

"There's still too many of them around for my liking."

"Not enough to make us cheer their idiotic speeches anymore," Guttmann commented with a victorious grin. "Not one of them was in the hall today. Not a single one. All sent to the city outskirts to mind the partisans. I hope the forest brothers lay them all nicely there."

Liza gave me a meaningful look upon hearing those words. *Now, if only Lore's young fellow came through with the request, she'd put before him. We'd be free people then… how terrifying it was to dream of such a thing; how frightening to realize that our very fates depended on a boy from Poland.* Flanked by the Luftwaffe officers, we quickened our pace. Liza's hand was warm in mine. Despite all, we dreamed. We hoped.

Chapter 24

"Herr Hauptmann, allow me to report." As soon as Lore appeared in the office – blond braids and eyes shining with utter excitement – I rushed to lock the door. "The requested item has been procured on your orders." Immediately, she extracted a working permit blank from under her jacket; she lay it on Willy's desk with a triumphal look.

He pulled it toward himself at once and regarded it in amazement.

"The real one?" Disbelief was obvious in his voice after he inspected the blank and apparently found it faultless. "And the signatures? How did you obtain the signatures?"

"Not me." She beamed at him. "All the praise goes to Reuven – he's the mastermind of the entire operation."

When Lore had initially told me about that Reuven of hers, I was immediately suspicious. A young Polish Jew who managed to pass for a *mischling* and therefore enjoyed the benefits that the occupying forces offered the half-bloods, was a bit too cunning and shrewd not to cause suspicion. *How did he manage to get himself a position as a doorman who held the doors for the officers of the General-Kommissariat themselves? How did he manage to be on such good terms with the daughter of Hening, a civilian engineer and an assistant to Leutnant Shtamp – the head of the entire Labor Department in Minsk? How did he worm his way into that daughter's trust in the first place?*

To each of my questions, Lore had a nonchalant shrug and an answer. *He brings her little trinkets when she does odd favors for him; when one needs to have their work permit extended, for instance. She's often left in charge of the office when both Shtamp and Hening are gone and it's quite easy to persuade a girl to accept diamond earrings for a blank that her father wouldn't even miss. Conveniently enough, both of her superiors sign those blanks beforehand, so she only needs to type in the person's name, the description of the work, the name of the work supervisor, and the number of workers.*

"Reuven had to bring her a golden watch for this one and a few rings just so she'd leave it blank and didn't ask any questions," Lore explained. "She agreed very reluctantly and only after he swore to her on his parents' grave that she wouldn't find herself in any trouble for this. She said, if it has anything to do with partisans, she'll tell her father that he stole the permit. Reuven agreed to that."

"We'll need to type in his name with the rest then," Willy asserted at once. "Surely, he isn't staying behind."

Lore lowered her eyes. "He is, actually."

"But it's pure madness!" Willy regarded her in astonishment. "A suicide, no less! As soon as we don't make it back by the evening, they'll put two and two together at once and arrest him."

Lore only shrugged. "He said, if he doesn't present himself at his working place as usual, then they'll surely smell a rat and raise the alarm. Everything has to go as it usually does. Besides, he said he'll talk his way out of it. He always does…" she whispered, more to herself as though to persuade herself of her own words.

With both of them breathing heavily in excitement behind my back, I carefully typed the twenty-five names, including mine, into the working permit. However, I hesitated in spite of myself before typing Willy's name in, as our work supervisor. For an instant, some cold, alien fear clutched at my very heart and stole my breath away. I looked him gravely in the eyes. His face was alight with the glow of the setting sun. Before mine, the headline of the *Minsker Zeitung* suddenly stood. *"Captured squad of the Wehrmacht anti-partisan detachment summarily executed by Stalin's terrorist brigade near Nalibokskiy Forest."*

A chill crept further along my spine. It turned me cold with horror which I couldn't quite explain to myself. At that moment, just as my fingers hovered over the keys of the typewriter, had I realized that I wasn't really afraid of anything up until now; not of the SS man's boot on my back during the Purim pogrom and not even of Schönfeld's threats when he shoved his gun into my ribs. But now, I was gravely terrified of losing this man who stood before me, smiling softly and unsuspecting of the battle that was raging inside me, silent and still contained – by some miracle, no doubt.

"Are you sure about it?" At last, I asked him directly.

"Of course, I am! What kind of question is that?" He suspected nothing of my morbid and mortifying thoughts.

The kind that means if something doesn't go according to the plan, you'll get it much worse than we will, I was about to answer but didn't have the heart to put into words. *The kind that doesn't guarantee that the partisans won't take you for a spy once we're in their hands and won't order you shot, on the spot.*

"You're putting your life at great risk," I said carefully instead.

"I know," followed a simple reply.

I wanted to speak again but he only lowered his warm palm on my shoulder and kissed my temple with infinite affection. "Ilse, don't waste your time on empty talk. We live together, or we die together. That's how it is; that's how it was from the beginning. If I don't make it – for whatever reason – but you survive, that'll be enough for me to die in peace. I've lived a long life as it is—"

"What nonsense is this now?" I cried, my voice breaking with tears which threatened to spill over my cheeks. "You're forty-three only! A long life he says…"

"A long life," he repeated with stubborn determination. "And if I die, you'll find yourself someone of your own age and you'll live a very long life together and have many beautiful children—"

"That's it!" I pushed the typewriter angrily toward the wall. "I'm not putting your name there. We're not going anywhere! I'm not signing up for this!"

"Yes, we are." Willy calmly moved the typewriter back, put his arms over my shoulders and typed his own name into the blank. The paper swam in front of my eyes. The death sentence, at least for one of us. Willy extracted the blank from the typewriter and inspected it once again. "Come now, Ilse. We all have to hope for the best. The partisans will take me, you'll see. Even they need accountants."

In the corner, Lore snorted with laughter in spite of herself. When I looked at her, her face was just as wet as mine. She, too, didn't know if her beloved would survive the ordeal. She, too, had nothing else to do but believe him when he assured her that he would.

*

March 1, 1943

The morning dawned fresh and mother-of-pearl. Willy had been gone for the most part of the night and returned a mere hour ago, strangely agitated; muttered something on account of vehicle and weapons, smoked three cigarettes in a row, kept pawing at his breast pocket in which Otto's military Russian-German dictionary was and only relaxed after I took his hand in mine and led him to the bed.

"It's still early. Hold me, Willy, for the last time—"

"For the last time this morning. I'll be holding you tonight again before you know it."

Yes, that's a fine thing to believe in. Let's believe it then.

We dressed in silence. It took me longer than usual to put my woolen cardigan in order, as my fingers trembled so badly I could barely fasten the buttons. Having noticed that, Willy took my hands in his and kissed them, the usual soft smile playing on his face.

"Don't fret now, old comrade. Together, we'll get through."

I nodded stiffly and tried to smile back. He grinned wider and stroked my hair gently before placing a kiss on my forehead. "You're so brave, my Ilschen. So very brave."

No, I'm not. I'm terrified, and I can hardly breathe.

Downstairs, parked in front of the Government Building, a truck was waiting with the driver in it. The young Feldwebel jumped out as soon as he saw us approach and gave Willy a crisp salute. They chatted amicably on the way to the ghetto while I sat rigid as a statue, grateful that they didn't appear to bother with me in the slightest. I would hardly be able to reply anything intelligible if asked.

The main entrance. Bending over me, Willy presented the sentry with the working permit and a bright grin. "A beautiful morning, is it not?"

"It truly is, Herr Hauptman. Do you know the way to the Labor Exchange?"

A faint shadow of suspicion passed over the sentry's face. He knew all of the officers who picked up Jewish workers here on a regular basis yet he'd never seen Willy here before.

"Fräulein Stein does. She's our guide today. Her name is on the permit."

Another, barely noticeable, doubtful look from the sentry before he was back to studying the paper. Willy straightened slightly in his seat.

"I hate to rush you but we really should hurry. The damned partisans blew the train tracks and now it's a matter of hours before the entire Government Complex will be left without any heat. The morning may be beautiful but it's still blasted winter outside and I'd hate to get another dressing down from my superiors in addition to the one I'd already received this week."

The trick worked and the sentry even let out a hastily curbed chuckle. The kinship of orderlies triumphed over his diligence. He returned the work permit and brought his hand to his forehead in a salute.

"I won't hold you any longer, Herr Hauptmann. Heil Hitler."

"Heil Hitler."

The gates closed behind us.

"The partisans blew up the tracks?" the driver asked, risking breaking military protocol.

Willy's expression drew to a wry smile. "Nobody blew up anything. I just can't bear sitting in the cold while they pretend that they're earning their bread, the damned muttonheads!"

The driver laughed, along with him, at the SS sentry's expense. Without either one noticing, I released a sigh of immense relief.

At the Labor Exchange, groups of workers were already waiting. As soon as I spotted Liza and my sisters, I pressed myself against the window at once, signing to them. *They were all here. My girls.* Till the last moment, I was fearing that Lore would choose to stay.

"Those are our workers." Willy pointed the driver to the group before handing him the permit.

The Feldwebel jumped out of the truck, adjusted his overcoat and began calling out the names which I had typed into the permit – twelve women and thirteen men. Soon, they were huddling together in the back of the truck under the tarpaulin. Through a small window, I glimpsed Liza sitting next to Lily and Lore. She winked at me and demonstrated a freshly assembled rifle, her position hidden from the unsuspecting driver's eyes. How Willy managed to smuggle those into the wooden crate, with the tools, overnight, was anyone's guess but Liza's friend Sergei along with the few other members of the underground were surely very grateful.

Our destination was Rudinsk, a junction forty kilometers northeast of Minsk. With two officers and an official pass, we had no trouble getting through all the checkpoints. The truck rolled forward, leaving the heavily guarded city of Minsk behind. Willy opened the map and began giving the young Feldwebel directions. His stance tensed visibly when yet another check-point appeared on the road.

"They are sure fond of checking papers, the Field Police," Willy noted.

I carefully turned to the small window again, thinking about what sign to give to Liza and the others. If the Police decided to check the back of the truck, no weapons could have been visible, or we would all perish here; a machine-gun position, manned by two Feldgendarmes, came into view as we rolled to a stop. Liza winked at me again – *don't worry, we see them as well as you do. Everything's hidden.*

The heater worked inside the cabin, yet I couldn't stop trembling as one of the policemen approached our truck. After the usual exchange of salutes, he frowned at the destination marked on the paper.

"Rudinsk? That area is swarming with partisans, Hauptmann Schultz. Why would you want to go there?"

"We need to cut wood."

"Wood is all the same everywhere, last time I checked but there's a much lesser chance that you'll get a bullet between your eyes if you disembark your little brigade right here and chop our local trees."

Willy gave him a tight-lipped smile. I could see a sheen of sweat on his brow.

"With all due respect, my CO told me to go to Rudinsk."

"Does your CO want you dead for some reason?" The Feldgendarm chuckled jovially.

Willy only spread his arms in a mock-helpless gesture.

"Listen to what I tell you if you know what's good for you, Herr Hauptmann. Turn your truck around, park it a couple of kilometers from here and chop all the wood you like. You don't have to go to Rudinsk for some special wood."

"But what if a mobile SS squad appears with a check and we're here instead of Rudinsk even though the working permit is made out for Rudinsk?" Willy pressed, working what no German would ever denounce – the love of order. "How would I explain my decision then? That I was afraid of the partisans and disobeyed my superiors' orders because of that? And how would it make *you* look if I told them that you told me to cut the wood here instead of Rudinsk? I don't know about you but it's my most profound conviction that we'll both find ourselves in the same disciplinary battalion if that happens. For cowardice and disobeying the orders," he added emphatically.

The Feldgendarm pulled himself up at once, suddenly serious. He muttered something under his breath but returned the paper and motioned for the soldiers manning the bar to lift it. "Go ahead, Herr Hauptmann. I'll give you an armed escort though, to follow you at least for a few kilometers."

"It is not necessary—"

"No, no; I insist. It's only as much as I can do to provide you with a secure trip."

Despite his forced smile, I could tell Willy was cursing inwardly as the Feldgendarmerie patrol car began tailing us from the checkpoint on. In the back, I could see Liza's profile, strained with tension, watching it as well, unmasked hostility in her eyes.

As my gaze followed Willy's finger, tracing our progress on the map, I could feel him growing more and more anxious as we were getting nearer Rudinsk.

"Oh, for Christ's sake!" Apparently, he couldn't bear it any longer. "Wave him off." He turned to the driver. The latter looked at him uncomprehendingly. "Wave the escort off, I said! There are no partisans here."

"But—"

"Wave him off."

Whether it was the tone in which he said it or Willy's look, the young Feldwebel stuck his arm out of the window and waved the police escort off. The Field Police peeled off at once, apparently glad to be returning to the protection of their base.

We traveled the rest of the way in charged silence. The driver was growing uneasy now; I could see it in the shifting expression of his clean-shaven face. It turned outright frightened when Willy calmly said, "Don't slow down," when we approached the road sign that read, Rudinsk.

He kept the speed but made an uncertain motion, quickly countered by Willy's drawn gun. "Don't get any ideas now. Just keep driving and nobody gets hurt."

With his other hand, Willy promptly relieved the young man of his personal weapon and handed it to me. "You remember how to shoot it, right?"

"Yes."

"Good. Cock it and keep it that way."

The forest flew past us, white with snow. The ribbon of the road snaked and curled just like it did on the map. Willy's finger was stroking gently our final destination point – Rusakovichi, a small village near which the First Minsk Partisan Brigade operated. However, a sickening feeling of dread came over us as soon as the village came into view. It stood peaceful and quiet, just as it should have been, on the other side of the river Ptich. Only, the bridge that was on the map and which we were supposed to take to get to the other side, had been blown up. The driver stopped, looking anxiously at Willy.

Now what? His silent, imploring gaze said. *Let's turn back, and I'll pretend that it never happened...*

Willy motioned for him to get out. Soon, we all stood, eyes fixed with greedy fascination on the small houses on the other side – so close and so infinitely far.

"The bridge," Liza stammered, her hands still clasping the rifle. "It must be recent."

"It is," Sergei confirmed and spat on the ground. "When they gave us directions, it still stood, blast it all!"

"What now?" I voiced what was on everyone's mind.

In front of us, the dark waters ran deep and fast, framed by the ice which must have broken overnight.

"Nothing." One of the men from the brigade was already discarding his clothes. "Someone will have to swim to the other side, no? Or do you all prefer to stand here like muttons and wait for the first patrol to come and arrest you?"

Leaving his rhetorical question at that, he plunged into the water and reemerged within seconds, spitting and cursing in Russian and rather crudely at that. Huddled on the bank, we all watched his progress with wary eyes, hands clutched in silent prayers for the hero to make it safely to the other side. The steam was rising from the water; it would be a miracle if his muscles didn't freeze stiff in it. But the fates took mercy on us that day – after a few eternally long minutes, he was already on the other bank. He trotted toward one of the nearest houses, his body steaming much like the water from which he'd just emerged.

Next to me, someone began praying quietly in Yiddish. Willy pressed my hand tighter, still aiming his gun at the driver with the other one. The young Feldwebel looked like he was going to be sick any minute now. His face was taking on a green shade from the fear of what was coming his way and his superior's – *the fellow, who'd clearly lost his reason,* in the young German's eyes, that is. As soon as an elderly man came out as an escort to the now warmly dressed man from our brigade, the driver began trembling openly. A general commotion started in the village which had appeared to be deserted just moments ago. The elderly peasant was already aiding our comrade in pushing a rowboat into the water. As though in a dream I watched it glide toward us; Willy prompting me forward, my sisters took their places next to me and all of us rocking gently on the waves as the peasant worked the oars, demonstrating envious strength in spite of his advanced age. Catching my gaze, he smiled and said something reassuringly, out of which I only understood *horosho* – good. *Yes,* I smiled back, through tears. *Everything will be good.*

Soon, the partisans came, emerged right out of nowhere, from the invisible forest behind. Willy smiled at them and, in his halting Russian provided by Otto's dictionary, said, *"Zdravstvyite, tovarishy."* *Hello, comrades.*

We are finally home.

Epilogue

Byelorussian forest. Autumn 1943

On Commander Zorin's orders, the entire brigade gathered for a meeting. I had a feeling it had something to do with Boris's return from Minsk; however, this time instead of bringing people with him as was his habit, he returned alone, his face grim and forbidding and positively refused to answer any questions before he could talk to his comrade Brigadier.

The wind caressed bare treetops above our heads. The forest had long become home for many of us. Where I perceived alien and threatening wilderness before, fir trees now promised shelter and freedom. The mist had invaded our parts once again and now its cold, glittering drops that had accumulated on the trees overnight, were falling on our anxious faces – premature tears we didn't bother to wipe.

Boris and Zorin emerged from Zorin's dugout, at last, hats with red ribbons – partisans' insignia – in their hands, gazes riveted to the ground, words failing them for a few interminable moments. We waited patiently; the old, the children, the men, and the women, most coats still bearing faint outlines of the hateful yellow patches; faces were drawn and lined with memories of wasted lives and far too many deaths. Zorin was about to say something but then signed to Boris instead – *you brought the news, you announce it. I have not the heart…*

The wind was growing stronger, chasing torn clouds along the leaden sky. I turned my collar up. Boris released a tremendous breath and stepped forward.

"Comrades. More than two years ago, in August 1941, we appealed from our underground to the Jews in the Minsk ghetto with the warning, 'ghetto means death! By every means possible, break down the fence around the ghetto!' By the end of the first year of occupation, we had opened a way to the partisan forest. Now we must bring you the dreadful news – the ghetto no longer exists."

A collective groan rolled around the campsite. We had all sensed that it was what he was about to say; we had awaited the dreadful news long enough but were still unprepared to hear the truth.

"There are no more Jews in that city where entire generations of Jews shaped its Jewish look, its Jewish character, and molded its way of life with their blood and their sweat," Boris continued meanwhile. "They no longer exist, the Jews of Minsk, who contributed so much to our national and cultural advancement. In the streets of Minsk, you can no longer hear the sound of our Yiddish speech. It no longer exists, the city which witnessed the flowering of Yiddish art and literature. And there is no longer any hope of saving it. We are all orphans, we, the last Jews of the ghetto…"

Boris's voice broke after those last words. He couldn't speak any longer. All around, the weeping grew louder. And then, in the middle of collective mourning, came a sudden, "If there are no more Jews, then we shall be the Jewish people."

I looked up at Willy. A soft grin playing on his face, he circled my waist with his arm. As though sensing his touch, our child stirred inside – *a future partisan,* as Zorin himself announced with a wink one day in summer, when it became impossible to hide my pregnancy from the rest of the brigade any longer. In Willy's uniform cap, on top of torn German insignia, the same red ribbon of a partisan now gleamed with pride.

"We shall be the Jewish people," I whispered after him.

"We shall be the Jewish people," next to me, Liza asserted.

"We shall be the Jewish people," my sisters repeated in German.

"We shall be the Jewish people," came the stubborn oath of the partisans.

The desperate, tear-stained faces around us brightened; the eyes now shone with fearless determination; hands linked, chained us one to another – forest brother to forest sister, forest mother to forest child, a German to a Byelorussian, a Russian to a Pole and our voices rose in a unanimous kaddish which soon transcended into something fearsome and awe-inspiring – we sang the partisan song.

A Note on History

Thank you so much for reading *The Girl Who Survived*. Even though it's a work of fiction, most of it is based on a true story. Ilse Stein and Willy Schultz (the names weren't changed) indeed met in Minsk in 1942 after Schultz's brigade was killed by the SS during the Purim massacre the day before that. Their meeting itself and the following development of their relationship are also true to fact. I tried to stick to reality as much as I could while working on this novel and used any information available concerning Ilse or Willy to paint as accurate of a portrait of both as I could. Ilse's family history, including their move from Nidda to Frankfurt and her further employment at the parachute factory and eventual deportation, are all based on fact, same as Willy's family history and the history of his employment and war service.

The history of the organization of the ghetto, its structure, etc., I also tried to keep as close to reality as possible. I preserved all the names of the streets, including "exits" used by different resistance members (unlike many other ghettos, the Minsk one wasn't surrounded by a brick wall but only by a fence of barbed wire which wasn't electrified and therefore, due to this fact and lax patrolling of the perimeter, the members of the ghetto underground and also children who begged for food on the "Russian side" almost daily, could more or less freely crawl through it when the occasion presented itself). The Labor Exchange, the Orphanage, the Hospital, the Jewish Cemetery, the Market set up on Krymskaya Street, Jubilee Square – everything was transferred into the narration as described by the ghetto survivors.

Most of the characters, including secondary ones, are also based on real people, such as Oberscharführer Scheidel, who "welcomed" Ilse and her family upon their arrival to Minsk; his boasting about "freeing the space" for the German Jews by killing thirty-five thousand Soviet ones is also based on truth; his words I tried to change as little as possible while preserving the message. General-Kommissar Kube was also a real senior official in Nazi-Occupied Byelorussia, who was later assassinated by the Byelorussian partisans in 1943. Known to be a vicious anti-Semite, he nevertheless treated German Jews (called "Hamburgs" by the locals since the first transport from Germany arrived from Hamburg) differently from their Soviet counterparts; the occasion where he protested against the treatment of former decorated war veterans is real (at the end of the note I'll provide an actual letter to the Reich Commissioner of Ostland, H. Lohse), just like his idea to provide them with "skilled worker's" cards to protect them from selections by installing a wagon workshop in their Sonderghetto.

Police Superintendent Richter, his brutal treatment of the ghetto inhabitants, including setting his dog on them and his infamous "Sunday concerts" are also based on the facts provided by the survivors of the ghetto (you can read in more detail about him in H. Smolar's memoir *The Minsk Ghetto* or a collection of memoirs of the ghetto survivors, "We Remember Lest the World Forget").

Ghetto Elders Dr. Frank (the Sonderghetto) and Ilya Mushkin (the Ostjuden ghetto) are also based on real people. Mushkin was indeed captured by the Gestapo and executed for aiding a German officer who wished to defect; what happened to the officer himself is not known but most likely he was court-martialed as well.

The members of the ghetto underground and their activities are also based on real people and true events. The character of Boris Makarsky is a fictionalized version of Hersh Smolar, who was considered a leader of the ghetto underground. The underground printing press was indeed in use in the ghetto and many of the printers were captured and publically hanged in May of 1942, just as described in the novel. However, this didn't stop the production of the underground leaflets after new people took over the positions of the executed members of the resistance. Many other instances of the underground sabotage activities are also based on historical fact, such as Jewish workers smuggling gun parts and bullets out of German factories in their boots and mess tins, the attack directed on the SS barracks (mentioned by Ilse in her conversation with the pilots quartered with Willy), smuggling children out of the ghetto and setting them up with Gentile families or orphanages for the Gentile population (as was supposed to have happened with Ilse's sister, Lore); the case with the Jewish sculptor and his spying on the Wehrmacht officers while drawing their portraits; Reuven's dealings with Hening's daughter and his "buying" permit blanks from her (Reuven, Lore's boyfriend, is based on a real young Polish boy Reuven Liond, who indeed worked as a doorman in the *Kommissariat* headquarters and helped many people by getting permits for them. You can read more about him in B. Epstein's book, *The Minsk Ghetto 1941-1943. Jewish Resistance and Soviet Internationalism.*).

Liza Gutkovich (the name was unchanged) was indeed Ilse Stein's best friend. It was her who approached Ilse on the day when Ilse first met Willy Schultz and asked how Ilse knew him and why he was so friendly with her. Liza was indeed appointed by Schultz as Ilse's substitute and later treated as Willy's own confidante. The instances, where he asked Liza what could be done to help Ilse are described by Liza herself both in B. Epstein's book and the documentary, "The Jewess and the Capitan," which tells a detailed story of Willy's and Ilse's relationship. Liza's risky enterprise with listening to the Soviet radio in Schultz's office is also based on Liza's recollections. The events surrounding the surrender of the 6th Army in Stalingrad and the German command's reaction to it are all based on historical facts. There weren't any announcements acknowledging the surrender until Goebbels's infamous "Total War" speech in Berlin's *Sportpalast* (its parts were used in the novel, unchanged).

Willy indeed had a friend who was willing to take the risk and fly the couple – Willy and Ilse – across enemy lines and who was later transferred to the front. Since his name was lost to history, I took the liberty of naming him, Otto Weizmann. His further destiny is, unfortunately, also unknown.

All of the pogroms (or *Aktionen* – SS-conducted massacres) mentioned in the novel were also described based on recollections of the ghetto survivors. Adolf Eichmann indeed supervised the Purim massacre during which over five thousand people were killed and eventually buried in what was later known as the Pit (or *Yama*). It was said that General-Kommissar Kube, who was present during the pogrom and had a fondness for children, was indeed throwing candy into the pit where children from the Jewish orphanage were being thrown alive to be later shot or buried alive.

The July pogrom, which lasted four days and during which Willy Schultz hid his brigade in the cellar of the Government building, is also based on the survivors' recollections. According to their memoirs and the historians' accounts, not only Schultz but several other officers in charge of the brigades hid "their Jews" during the pogrom to save their lives, even though such actions were usually severely punished by the SS. However, it was said that Schultz was well-connected and most likely that was the reason why he could get away with such risky arrangements.

The daring escape itself is based on true historical fact. After getting notice of his imminent transfer, after the SS got wind of his relationship with Ilse Stein, he secured the permit for the wood-cutting brigade and also a truck with carefully concealed weapons. After gathering the brigade, they managed to get through all of the checkpoints without any trouble and eventually got to their destination in the partisan zone, Willy holding the driver at gunpoint. The bridge was indeed blown up and one of the brigade members did take the risk of jumping into the freezing cold water to get to the other side. The partisans arrived soon after and, after interrogating Schultz for the entire day and realizing that he wished to defect to stay with his beloved, accepted him into the brigade. The driver was offered to stay as well. Ilse and Willy later had a son together.

If you'd like to know what happened to Ilse and Willy after the war, feel free to contact the author. I'd like to finish their story on this happy note, which proves once again that even in the darkest of times love will always be stronger than hate. Let their story be an inspiration for us all.

A Letter from Ellie

Dear Reader,

I want to say a huge thank you for choosing to read *The Girl Who Survived*. If you did enjoy it, and want to keep up to date with all my latest releases, just sign up at the following link. Your email address will never be shared and you can unsubscribe at any time.

www.bookouture.com/ellie-midwood

Thank you for reading the story of this truly wonderful couple. I hope you loved *The Girl Who Survived* and, if you did, I would be very grateful if you could write a review. I'd love to hear what you think, and it makes such a difference helping new readers to discover one of my books for the first time.

I love hearing from my readers – you can get in touch on my Facebook page, through Goodreads or my website.

Thanks,
Ellie

EllieMidwood
elliemidwood.com

Acknowledgments

First and foremost, I want to thank the wonderful Bookouture family for helping me bring Ilse and Willy's story to light. It wouldn't be possible without the help and guidance of my incredible editor, Christina Demosthenous, whose insights truly bring my characters to life and whose support and encouragement make me strive to work even harder on my novels and become a better writer. Thank you Kim Nash, Noelle Holten, Ruth Tross, and Peta Nightingale for all your help and for making me feel welcome and at home with your amazing publishing team. It's been a true pleasure working with all of you and I already can't wait to create more projects under your guidance.

Mom, granny – thank you for always asking how my novel is doing and for cheering me up at every step. Your support and faith in me make this writing journey so much easier, knowing that you always have my back and will always be my biggest fans. Thank you for all your love. Love you both to death.

Ronnie, my love – all of this wouldn't be possible without you. Every time you meet a new person, the first thing you say about me is "my fiancée is a great novelist, you simply must check out her books!" I always grumble that you're embarrassing me with all that attention, but inwardly I'm so very grateful for you being so very proud of me. Thank you for all your support and for putting up with my deadlines and all that research information I keep dumping on you. You are my rock star.

A special thanks to my two besties, Vladlena and Anastasia, for their love and support; to all of my fellow authors whom I got to know through Facebook and who became my very close friends—you all are such an inspiration! I consider you all a family.

And, of course, huge thanks to my readers for patiently waiting for new releases, for celebrating cover reveals together with me, for reading ARCs, and sending me those absolutely amazing I-stayed-up-till-3 a.m.-last-night-because-I-just-had-to-finish-your-wonderful-book messages, for your reviews that always make my day, and for falling in love with my characters just as much as I do. You are the reason why I write. Thank you so much for reading my stories.

And, finally, I owe my biggest thanks to all the brave people who continue to inspire my novels. Some of you survived the Holocaust, some of you perished, but it's your incredible courage, resilience, and self-sacrifice that will live on in our hearts. Your example will always inspire us to be better people, to stand up for what is right, to give a voice to the ones who have been silenced, to protect the ones who cannot protect themselves. You all are true heroes. Thank you.

Made in the USA
Monee, IL
04 April 2023

31326962R00156